"I need your hands on me," Gil said and dropped his mouth to hers.

Finally.

He kissed her deeply, earnestly, stealing her breath along with coherent thought. He tasted like malt and smelled like early morning on the lake and every last one of her nerve endings writhed with need.

And warning.

Kerry ripped her mouth away from his and took deep, gulping inhales. "Are we really doing this?"

Gil shuddered as he fought to catch his own breath. He swallowed then rested his chin on the crown of her head.

"Yes?" he said hopefully.

Her nerves jangled with anticipation. "I don't think this is a good idea."

He ran a hand through his hair and it gave her pause. He looked younger without his glasses. Or maybe she was feeling older. Having a sense of adventure used to be so much more appealing.

A year ago she'd learned how terrifying the consequences could be.

Dear Reader,

I'm thrilled to welcome you back to Castle Creek! At long last I give hardware store owner Gil Cooper his happy-ever-after, but of course I make him work for it. When Gil meets enigmatic bartender Kerry Endicott, who's only in town long enough to make things right with her estranged father, they instantly hit it off. Then Gil discovers Kerry is a former felon, and he has a hard time seeing the good-hearted person behind the mistakes. There's nothing I enjoy more than showing a hero how wrong he is, and I've always had a soft spot for stubborn heroines. I hope you find something in Kerry and Gil's story that resonates with you, too!

I have to say, this was a tough book to finish. It's the final book in my Castle Creek series, and it's also my final Superromance, since the line will be discontinued in June 2018. I'll miss Superromance like mad, not only because of all the amazing books I've enjoyed over the years, but because of the brilliant editing team who dedicated their whole hearts to the line. They're incredibly clever and creative, and so very generous with their story savvy. On top of that, they're truly lovely people. I wish Victoria Curran, Megan Long, Karen Reid, Piya Campana and Birgit Davis-Todd the absolute, very best. Writing romance will not be the same without them.

Here's to Happy-Ever-Afters.

Hugs,

Kathy

KATHY ALTMAN

Making It Right

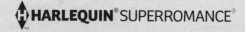

Recycling programs
for this product may
not exist in your area.

ISBN-13: 978-0-373-64055-3

Making It Right

Copyright © 2017 by Kathy Altman

All rights reserved. Except for use in any review, the reproduction or
utilization of this work in whole or in part in any form by any electronic,
mechanical or other means, now known or hereinafter invented, including
xerography, photocopying and recording, or in any information storage
or retrieval system, is forbidden without the written permission of the
publisher, Harlequin Enterprises Limited, 225 Duncan Mill Road,
Don Mills, Ontario M3B 3K9, Canada.

This is a work of fiction. Names, characters, places and incidents are
either the product of the author's imagination or are used fictitiously,
and any resemblance to actual persons, living or dead, business
establishments, events or locales is entirely coincidental.

This edition published by arrangement with Harlequin Books S.A.

For questions and comments about the quality of this book,
please contact us at CustomerService@Harlequin.com.

® and TM are trademarks of Harlequin Enterprises Limited or its
corporate affiliates. Trademarks indicated with ® are registered in the
United States Patent and Trademark Office, the Canadian Intellectual
Property Office and in other countries.

Printed in U.S.A.

Kathy Altman writes contemporary romance, romantic suspense and the occasional ode to chocolate. She's also a regular contributor to USATODAY.com's *Happy Ever After* blog. Kathy prefers her chocolate with nuts, her Friday afternoons with wine and her love stories with happy-ever-afters. Find Kathy online at www.kathyaltman.com. She'd enjoy hearing from you!

Books by Kathy Altman

HARLEQUIN SUPERROMANCE

A Castle Creek Romance

Tempting the Sheriff
A Family After All
Staying at Joe's
The Other Soldier

To Suzanne Cox, Barbara Kopsic and Dolores Minter, a super-sweet, super-supportive trio of reader friends. Many thanks, you gorgeous girls, for all the trips you've taken to Castle Creek!

Acknowledgments

Heartfelt thanks go to critique partners Toni Anderson and Robin Allen, whom I cherish for many reasons but mostly because they inspire me to do better; to my editor Claire Caldwell, who is staggeringly clever and gracious; to the treasured readers who value happy-ever-afters as much as I do; and to my family, who couldn't be more supportive if they tried. (Well, my mother could— how about letting me win a Scrabble game every now and then, Mom, hmm?)

Much love to you all!

CHAPTER ONE

"THAT'S FAR ENOUGH."

Kerry Endicott lifted her gaze from the graveled path and stared into the scowling face of the man she'd traveled five hundred miles to see.

"You need to leave," he continued, his tone curt. "Now."

The man who obviously had no interest in seeing *her*.

Even after all this time.

After all she'd been through.

A cold, quiet curl of hurt lodged in her chest. But what did she expect, after what she'd done?

Kerry drew in a slow breath and gazed mutely over his shoulder, at a trio of Quonset huts. Shadowed rows of hanging baskets inside each plastic-wrapped structure accounted for the rich odor of damp earth delivered by a teasing April breeze. Weathered outbuildings and shrubs with spindly arms bowed by the weight of sunshine-yellow blooms dotted the property around the huts. To the right of the driveway, at the crest of a long, gentle slope, sat a two-story farmhouse, its plain white exterior brightened by apricot shutters. To the left, the backdrop of feathery pines gave way to vivid green Pennsylvania farmland and a horizontal strip of blue that had to be Lake Erie.

This place—Castle Creek Growers—was much nicer than he'd described. Then again, that last mention had been more than two years ago. They'd talked only once after that, when she'd begged him to visit her. He hadn't even hemmed and hawed. Just offered a naked no.

"It's beautiful here," she said.

He took a hesitant step forward. Kerry held her breath. Then a woman called his name from inside one of the huts and he pushed out his chin and widened his stance, as if prepping to protect the owner of the voice.

From Kerry.

She tightened her grip on the keys in her right hand and a sudden staccato blare made her jump. Her heart flung itself into a slam dance. *Car alarm. Chill.* Stones skittered as she whirled toward the driveway and fumbled to press the panic button again on her fob.

Finally, silence. An echo pulsed in her ears, but it wasn't the rhythmic shriek of the alarm.

"You need to leave," he'd said.

Slowly she turned back to face him. "Dad," she croaked, half greeting, half protest. "Aren't you going to say hello?" No response. Her cheeks heated and her eyes burned. "I've been driving all day," she said thickly.

His gray-blue eyes had gone hard. "No one asked you to."

God. She'd known this would be tough. She just hadn't expected it to be this tough.

A door slammed. A girl in jeans and a pink sweatshirt clomped down the porch steps. His boss's daughter? Nicole? No. Natalie. As she jogged around the side of the house, she aimed a curious glance at Kerry.

"You're late" came the gruff words from Kerry's father.

The girl's gaze moved to the older man. "Can't help it. Mom made muffins. Growing bones and all that. Banana chocolate chip. Too bad I didn't save you any." With a smart-alecky grin and one last glance at Kerry, she took off across the yard, toward the nearest Quonset hut, brown hair bouncing on her shoulders.

Harris Briggs's snort bore more affection than pique. "If she thinks she's going to eat all the muffins and get out of snail duty, too, she has another think coming."

"What's snail duty?"

The indulgence on his face dimmed and his gaze dipped to Kerry's ankles. He wouldn't be able to see anything, since the hem of her dark gray pants reached nearly to the toes of her high-heeled boots.

"Been six months already?" he asked, almost idly.

"All things considered, time went a little slower for me."

He grunted. "I have to get back to work. Anyways, the answer is no."

She stuffed her hands into the pockets of her light wool jacket to keep from yanking at her hair. "I haven't asked a question."

"You didn't come all this way just to show off your bare ankle. You should have saved your gas money. I'm done opening my wallet for you."

"I didn't come to borrow money. I came to return it."

Her father, a former marine with more hair in his eyebrows than on his head, folded his brawny arms across his chest and waited. Good grief, he looked even more intimidating than she remembered. But she wasn't a little girl anymore.

She felt like one, though.

Kerry licked her lips. "I mean, I don't have the money now. But as soon as I get a job, I'll be able to pay you back."

"And you think I can help with that." His thick brows lowered. "If you're countin' on me getting you a job here with the Macfarlands, you'll be sorely disappointed. Reid's been through enough, and his wife, Parker? Don't know what I would do without her. She's like the—" He stopped.

"The daughter you never had?" Kerry swallowed. This was worse, so much worse than she'd expected. But at least he was talking to her.

Heat swept her cheeks, but she had to ask. "Would it be possible to stay with you? Just until I find my own place."

"If you're bent on stayin', there's a motel down the road a ways."

She bit back a sigh. A motel it would be, though she couldn't afford more than a couple of nights. She'd better find a job quick, or she'd be sleeping in her car.

"But it'd be a hell of a lot easier on everyone concerned," he continued, "if you just headed on back home and forgot about writin' a check I won't ever be able to cash."

She tipped up her chin. "Easy got me into this mess. I'm not going anywhere."

Approval was too much to hope for, but anything other than the stark disbelief on his face would have been welcome.

"*You* got you into this mess. Anyways, what kind of job you thinkin' you can get in Castle Creek that'd pay enough to get you out of debt?"

She was tempted to tell him she'd be dealing drugs, but he'd probably believe her. "Any job that's available."

His face said that yeah, he'd believe her. "Dad."

He flinched yet again. She'd have to find something else to call him. "I'm not the same person I was. That's why I'm here. To prove that to you."

"I'm not interested in your money, and I'm sure as hell not interested in your promises."

"Eugenia, too. I want you to know she'll get every penny back."

He paled, and his thick arms dropped to his sides.

Oh, no. "You two aren't together?"

"Not anymore."

So it was more than the return of the prodigal daughter that had him looking so miserable. "May I ask what happened?"

His expression soured. "She wanted to invite you to the wedding."

Kerry sucked in a breath. This wasn't going to work. Why had she thought this would work? She stumbled in a half circle and started back to the driveway. She'd managed two steps when the voice she'd heard calling her father stopped her.

"You're not leaving, are you?"

Kerry hesitated, then turned slowly back around as the woman added, "Harris? Aren't you going to introduce us?"

A tall, striking redhead in overalls and a long-sleeved plaid shirt almost identical to the one Harris was wearing stood sandwiched between him and the girl who'd run out of the house earlier.

"I'm Parker Macfarland and this is my daugh-

ter, Natalie. When Harris here isn't home practicing his grump face, he's pretending to help my
husband and me run this place. And you are?"

She already knew. Kerry could tell by the chirp
in her voice.

"No need to be pokin' your nose in the pepper
patch," Harris said stiffly.

Parker offered him a lofty eyebrow. "If you'd
followed that same advice, I wouldn't be about to
celebrate my second wedding anniversary, now,
would I?"

"And I wouldn't be getting a little brother," Natalie added.

Kerry's gaze dropped to Parker's stomach, but
there was no telling what she was hiding behind
those baggy overalls.

Parker laughed. "I'm about four months along.
Overalls aren't the most flattering thing to wear,
I know, but they're comfortable. Practical, too.
The other night I walked out of the house with a
roast beef sub and a dozen chocolate chip cookies
stashed behind this bib, and no one had a clue."

"We knew," said Natalie smugly.

"You did?"

Her daughter rolled her eyes. "You were looking a little lumpy, Mom. I dared Dad to go up
and give you a big, squeezy hug, but he said we
shouldn't keep you from your picnic with The
Munchkin."

Her mother's eyes went soft. "I see." She smiled

at Kerry and patted her belly. "That's what we're calling this little guy until we can agree on something more permanent." Her gaze sharpened. "And speaking of names…"

Kerry forced her lips into a curve. "I'm Kerry." She couldn't manage any more than that. Couldn't bear to see her father flinch again. "I'm glad to meet you. Congratulations on the baby. And on your home. It's lovely here."

"Thank you," Parker said. "It's about time you introduced us to your daughter, Harris Briggs."

"Wait, what?" Natalie swept her bangs out of her eyes and passed a frown from the older man to Kerry and back again. Parker made a sound that was half warning, half distress, but the oblivious teen shook her head in confusion. "You never said anything about a daughter."

STARING DOWN THE invoice for sixty seconds straight hadn't scared it into dropping any zeroes, so Gil Cooper slammed it on top of the stack in the accounts payable tray, also known as IOU oblivion. His elbow jostled his coffee cup and tepid black liquid sloshed onto the arm of his shirt, his open package of peanut butter crackers and the fresh stack of bills he hadn't had the balls to open yet.

Damn it, he'd already rolled his sleeves up as far as they would go to hide the orange juice stain he'd created that morning. Good thing denim could disguise a lot. Since he took his coffee black, at least he wouldn't be smelling like French vanilla or butter pecan all damned day. Still, maybe he should consider giving up coffee, like he'd given up his beloved sports channels and his Friday night sirloin. He could avoid stains and save a few more bucks at the grocery store.

Screw that. He picked up his Cap'n Crunch mug and tossed back the rest of the not-so-fresh brew inside. If he gave up coffee he wouldn't be able to concentrate on scrambling an egg, let alone finding a way to keep Cooper's Hardware open.

His jaw started to ache and he unlocked his molars.

Besides, he'd only find something else to spill.

Gil picked up the carton he'd just signed for, carried it out front and set it on the counter between items that hadn't changed since his grandfather opened the shop eighty years ago. Aside from the cash register, which Gil had replaced with a digital version, praise God, it was all the same. Friendly Village china creamer with a chipped handle that did a damned fine job as a pen holder. Wicker basket of fresh apples and walnuts still in the shell, complete with nutcracker. Glass jar of stick candies that for some unnatural reason saw less action than the fruit basket.

The smell of the place hadn't changed, either— at least, not since Gil was a kid. Still a mingling of machine oil, fresh sap, paint thinner and rubber. What would he do if he couldn't breathe it in anymore?

He swallowed a hot, useless surge of anger and methodically emptied the carton. Smaller boxes of screws, nails, wing nuts, washers. He tossed the outer box aside, picked up a container of nails and headed for the galvanized metal bins against the back wall.

Five steps away from the counter, he tripped over an uneven joint in the aged hardwood floor and lost his grip on the container. A jangling thud as three thousand plastic cap roofing nails hit the floor. Bits of bright orange skittered under the counter and beneath the shelving, like prisoners eager to escape their cage.

He could relate.

He could also see a lot of time on his hands and knees in the near future.

With a sweep of his foot, Gil shoved the nearest band of fugitives aside and assumed the position. An unseen nail bit into his kneecap and he swore.

And got smacked upside the head.

"What the—?" He twisted around.

Seventy-something Audrey Tweedy stood over him, legs braced, eyes righteous, her puke-green monstrosity of a purse cradled in both hands. He jumped to his feet before she could strike again.

"Audrey." He dusted off his hands and pushed his glasses up his nose. "What can I do for you?"

"Besides watch your language?" Her high-pitched, pixie-like voice matched her short, tousled hair but not her lumberjack physique. A plastic strip of bacon as long as his pinkie dangled from each earlobe.

"I didn't know you were there," he muttered. He kicked more nails under the counter and rubbed his head. "I apologize."

"You can make it up to me by helping me find a wedding present."

"Who's getting married?"

Audrey shifted her grip on her purse. Luckily, the thing jogged his memory without making contact.

"You and Snoozy," he said. "Next weekend. Justice of the peace, right?"

She beamed. Wisecracking, protein-pushing, tougher-than-toenails Audrey Tweedy goddamn *beamed*, and Gil felt a burn in his throat that had nothing to do with stale coffee.

"Less than two weeks," she said reverently. "I can't wait to be a bride."

"Audrey, that's—"

An exasperated glance and a beefy elbow to his gut turned the rest of his words to a wheeze. So much for sentiment.

"I need a gift for my bridegroom," she said. "I seem to have caught you at a bad time, though." Hands on hips, she surveyed the orange-dotted floor, then pointed at his knee. "You might want to get that."

He looked down. Oh. Right. He freed the nail protruding from his knee. Luckily the thing had grabbed more denim than skin.

"A broom would work better." She rummaged in her purse, gave a satisfied cluck and held out a squat tin can.

Gil squinted at the label. "You have to be joking."

"If you ate more protein, you'd have probably been reaching for a broom before that box even hit the floor." She lifted an eyebrow, as if expecting him to start slurping the contents of the can right then and there. Yeah, not going to happen.

When he slid it onto the counter, she sighed and nudged a roofing nail with the toe of her tennis shoe. "These are pretty, dear. What are they for?"

"Roofing felt. And house wrap."

"Do they come in other colors?"

"You cannot be considering these for a wedding present. How would you feel if Snoozy got you a box of thumbtacks?"

"You have a point." Audrey snorted. "See what I did there?"

The cowbell over the door did its thing and Gil braced himself for the Hazel and June show. Wherever Audrey Tweedy was, her cohorts, the Catletts, weren't far behind.

Ever since the sisters had been elected co-mayors of Castle Creek, their appearance made people especially nervous: they never walked away from a conversation without first having talked someone into donating their time or their money in support of the Catletts' longtime pet project, the community center.

At the moment Gil was short on both, which meant only one thing. He'd have to throw Audrey under the bus.

When feed store owner Seth Walker strolled into the store instead, Gil relaxed. Until he got a load of the look in his trail buddy's eyes.

Crap. Saturday night.

Gil backed toward the counter and reached out, blindly searching for a distraction. His fingers closed around the gift from Audrey. Meanwhile Seth smoothly greeted the older lady while laser-beaming his disapproval at Gil.

"Fish balls," Gil said.

"Yeah, you should be worried." Seth threaded his fingers together and made a show of cracking his knuckles. "How about after you finish up with Audrey here you meet me out front?"

Gil shook the can at Seth, thinking its easy-open lid probably tasted better than what was inside. "I'm trying to be polite here by offering you a snack."

Seth squinted at the label. "Glad you finally got yourself some balls, man. A little big for you, aren't they?"

Audrey tut-tutted at Seth. "That's not very nice."

"Neither is standing up a date. One who was

so excited about your dinner plans that she went out and got herself a new dress."

Gil winced.

Audrey gasped. "Gilbert Wayne Cooper." She snatched the can of fish balls out of his hands and shoved it back into her purse.

"I didn't stand her up," he protested. "I canceled in plenty of time."

Seth crossed his arms. "She got a text while Mama Leoni was leading her to your table."

"She hadn't ordered yet. It's not like she was out the price of a meal."

"Seriously?" Seth's disgust was a lot harder to take than his hard-ass bit.

Audrey's bacon strip earrings swayed as she wagged her head. "You owe that young woman an apology."

Yeah, he knew it. What he didn't know was why he'd allowed Seth to set him up in the first place. Gil liked his privacy. Sure, he liked sex too—a lot—but nine times out of ten, everything that came along with it wasn't worth the effort.

The one time it had been, she'd waited until the day they returned from her birthday gift— a long weekend in Cancún he'd had no business springing for—to tell him she'd decided to give her ex another shot. Was it any wonder his ego had issues?

Seth was staring daggers at him. If Gil didn't make things right, and fast, he risked losing the best friend he ever had. Plus Seth would probably want his weight bench back. Then again, the guy seemed to be doing just fine without it.

"It was easier for you," Gil said. "You never dropped your date's house keys down an elevator shaft, or leaned in for a kiss and chipped her front tooth, or took her to the diner when she was wearing white and knocked her into a server carrying five orders of blueberry cobbler."

Seth grinned. "I remember that. They never did get the purple splotches out of the ceiling."

Audrey was shaking her head. "Just because you're a klutz doesn't mean you get to be an asshat."

The only sound in the store was the chiding hum of the cash register. There was something very wrong about that word coming out of those straight-laced lips.

Gil coughed. "I'll call Olivia and apologize. Meanwhile, Aud, mind if I get back to you on Snoozy's gift?"

"Not at all, dear." She headed for the door, then swiveled back to Seth. "Just out of curiosity, what did Ivy give you when you two got married?"

Seth shifted his weight as blood hauled ass into his cheeks. "A, uh, part for my truck. J-jumper cables," he stuttered, and it was so obviously a lie, Gil hooted and Audrey's expression graduated from curious to determined.

"It's personal," Seth growled.

Audrey nodded. "Uh-huh. Where is your wife now? Is she at home?"

Seth's eyes went wide. "She won't tell you."

The old woman patted her purse. "Never underestimate the power of a summer sausage."

Gil let loose a strangled laugh while Seth pulled out his phone and started texting.

"Discuss the subject of my wedding gift amongst yourselves, boys," Audrey said. "And make sure you come up with something good, because this prime piece of meat is looking forward to a whole lot of tenderizing the weekend after next."

Once the door shut behind her, Gil and Seth groaned in concert.

"If only we could unhear that." Seth banged his palms against his ears. "Guess I should have listened when you said you weren't into Olivia."

"She's not into me, either. She only agreed to the date as a favor to you."

Red flashed back into Seth's cheeks. "Maybe," he muttered. "Okay. Fine. I'll stay out of it. But you owe me one. Hubbard Ridge this weekend?"

Gil and his mountain bike both needed the workout, but he couldn't pull an economic miracle out of his ass if he was sitting on it.

"Sorry, man. I need to be here. Rain check?"

"You're not getting enough exercise, Coop. Last time we rode, you puked. Twice. You're not careful, you're gonna lose that manly figure."

Gil wanted to ask what the hell that mattered, since no one would be seeing him naked, but that sounded too pathetic, even for him.

When he didn't respond, Seth shrugged. "But Joe's tomorrow night, right?" He read the answer on Gil's face and sagged back against the counter. "Are you serious right now? You're blowing off poker night, too?"

"Duty calls."

"C'mon, bro. We're already one man down. Harris didn't say what he's got going on, but it must be serious if the old man's willing to miss meatball night. Can't your shit wait?"

The truth about Gil's "shit" was that he couldn't afford to play because he couldn't afford to lose. And he always lost. But if he fessed up, Seth would insist on staking him.

"Do me a solid, Walker, and let it go."

Seth pushed upright. "Maybe that's what you need to be thinking about doing."

"Don't even."

Seth waved an arm at the paint cans and power tools, croquet sets and fishing rods surrounding them. "You're killing yourself here. And for what?"

"Like you weren't putting in eighteen-hour days when you were running the feed store and working at Ivy's farm at the same time."

"That was love, jackass. What's your excuse?

We both know you'd rather be anywhere else than here."

"We both know that's you, not me."

Seth jerked his head back. "I don't have anything against the store. It's what you're letting the place do to you, for no reason."

"No reason?" Gil grabbed a straw broom off the rack behind him. He gave the floor a vicious sweep, enjoying the rattle as roofing nails scattered. He shot Seth a warning glance. "We're not going there."

"Apparently we're not going anywhere." Seth stalked out of the store, and moments later Castle Creek's sole real estate agent sauntered in.

Gil clutched the broom tighter, momentarily tempted to brush her right back out again. This was shaping up to be one hell of a day and he hadn't even knocked over his second cup of coffee yet.

Valerie Flick tossed her jet-black, corkscrew ponytail over her shoulder and glanced out the front window at Seth, who was slamming into his ancient pickup truck.

"Looks like you two might need couple's counseling," she said drily. She turned away from the window and scanned the store. With a delighted "Ooh," she click-clacked over to the display of paperwhite growing kits. "One of these would look great on my desk." She glanced over her shoulder. "Know what else would look great on my desk? A contract with your signature on it. Changed your mind about selling yet?"

Gil concentrated on long, steady strokes of the broom. "Go away, Val."

"I came to sweeten the deal."

"Yeah?" He didn't look up. "How?"

"I'm trying to show you," she said, voice edged with impatience.

He raised his head. She was leaning back against the counter, the spread of her elbows pulling her suit jacket open to reveal the lacy, dark pink cups of a barely-there bra. Damn, he hadn't even realized she wasn't wearing a shirt under there. She'd kicked off one high heel and was running the ball of her foot up and down the smooth expanse of her other leg.

He couldn't deny she was a hot-looking woman. Yet his dick didn't so much as wiggle.

Gil stacked his hands on the end of the broom and averted his gaze. When he didn't speak, Val rolled one shoulder. "Nothing to say?"

"Only that it's ridiculous to pretend you're attracted to someone for the sake of a sale."

"It's more about the commission," she said, and gave the hem of her jacket a yank. "Anyway, give me a break. Cooper's has been circling the drain for years. Let me have the building. You won't recognize it when I'm done."

"Therein lies the problem."

She huffed hard enough to blow her bangs out

of alignment. "At least let me tell you what I have planned for the space."

"This is not a *space*. It's a piece of history, and I wouldn't sell it to you if you planned to turn it into a free clinic for kids." He hesitated. "You're not planning to turn it into a free clinic for kids, are you?"

She laughed, genuinely amused. "In Castle Creek? It would be empty half the time." She tipped her head. "Kind of like your hardware store."

Gil propped the broom against the nearest shelf, walked to the door and held it open. "Cooper's is not for sale."

Val advanced slowly, trailing a polished fingernail along the length of the counter. When she reached the cash register, she gave it a pat. "That's not what Ferrell said."

Gil released the door and strode back inside. "When did you talk to him?"

"Last week. He said he'd reason with you. Help you understand it's time to negotiate."

Gil's laugh was ugly, even to his own ears. "I haven't had a conversation with my brother in six years and I don't intend to start now. I suggest you break the habit yourself. He's gotten all he's going to get out of this place. Unless you plan to select something from one of these shelves and lay down money for it, you have, too."

He marched back to the door and shoved it open again. He had to raise his voice above the clatter of the yardsticks he knocked over in the process. "Cooper's is here to stay. Unlike you, Val."

She plucked an apple from the basket on the counter and joined him at the door. "You'd better start practicing your social skills, Gilbert. You won't be able to finance this hideout of yours forever."

She tossed the apple up in the air, caught it and sidled out the door.

Her laugh drifted back down the sidewalk, and for the first time in a long time, Gil let himself wonder what the hell he'd do if he didn't have Cooper's Hardware in his life.

KERRY SAT IN the corner booth by the restroom, hands wrapped around her second cup of coffee. She should eat, but swallowing coffee presented enough of a challenge, thanks to the regret clogging her throat.

It had been two days since she'd met Parker and her daughter, but the girl's shocked comment to Kerry's father lingered like the smell of fish reheated in a microwave.

"You never said anything about a daughter."

As much as the words stung, they made sense. Harris Briggs didn't have a daughter. Not really. Not one he deserved. Not someone like Parker Macfarland, who ran a successful business and a loving household and never took advantage of anyone.

And had the respect of others.

Kerry hunched deeper into the roomy, navy knit of her favorite sweater. *You have to earn it first, chickie.*

Unfortunately, that was proving more difficult than she'd anticipated. She'd applied for admin work at the courthouse, the grocery store, the animal hospital and Castle Creek's sole real estate office, each time bracing herself for the inevitable questions about her background. She'd never gotten that far. No one was hiring.

Not even here at Cal's Diner, and the fact that she'd checked testified to the strength of her desperation. She'd sworn after waitressing and tending bar in college for infinitesimal tips that often ended up in the bottom of half-full plastic tumblers that she'd never be a server again.

Famous last words.

She'd have to spread her net wider. Chances were good she could find something in Erie. That would be counterproductive, though. Kerry wanted to stay close. Show her father she was in earnest. Let his friends see she was making amends.

At least, that had been her intention. Now it seemed that if she stayed in town her father would avoid her like...well, like he'd been doing since she'd borrowed money from his girlfriend two years ago.

Prickles of heat swept across her chest. Correction. His *ex*-girlfriend.

A metallic crash in the kitchen brought her head up. The diner wasn't busy, probably because it was a weekday morning, and for that she was grateful. Kerry had fielded a few curious glances, though no one but the server had approached her. Once she'd learned there were no openings, she'd ordered a coffee and claimed a table. Now no one paid her any attention at all.

She relaxed her shoulders and let her gaze skim the gray Formica L-shaped counter, the alternating mustard- and ketchup-colored stools, the desserts under glass and the old-fashioned, stainless steel milkshake machine that any other day would have been too much to resist. Same for the friendly smell of sausage, bacon and pancakes. It all seemed so...cozy. Welcoming.

Homey.

Why had she never visited? For years her father had made Castle Creek his home and not once had Kerry driven up to see him. Could she blame him for not making the trip to see her?

"Kerry?"

She blinked. A middle-aged woman with blond hair and kind eyes hovered near the table, a white takeout bag in one hand and a designer clutch in the other.

"Kerry Endicott, right?" Her smile was tentative, but at least it was a smile.

Here we go. Kerry entwined her fingers in her lap and squeezed. "I really want to say no."

The other woman chuckled, though the sound held more strain than humor. "You look too much like your father for that to work. Before he lost all his hair, anyway." She stretched out a hand. "I'm Eugenia Blue."

Her father's ex. Kerry nodded. "I recognized your voice."

Her blush deepened. The one and only time she'd spoken to Eugenia, she'd begged her over the phone for a loan. Kerry released Eugenia's hand. "Do you have some time? I'd appreciate the chance to talk." She caught the other woman's flinch and rushed to add, "About paying you back."

Eugenia averted her gaze. "I'd like to talk with you, too."

Kerry exhaled. Progress. She might not look thrilled about it, but at least Eugenia hadn't followed Harris's example and refused to speak with her.

Eugenia bit her lower lip as she glanced around the diner, then down at Kerry's table, bare of all but condiments and a coffee cup. "Are you waiting for an order?" When Kerry shook her head, Eugenia motioned toward the door. "Then why don't you come back with me to my shop?" She gave the bag a gentle shake. "I just happen to have two of Cal's famous cinnamon rolls in here. I had every intention of eating them both, so please say you'll come save me from myself. Besides, you need more than coffee for breakfast."

CHAPTER TWO

WONDERING WHAT EXACTLY she was letting herself in for, Kerry followed Eugenia out of the diner and down State Street. Flowering cherry trees shaded the sidewalks and shed pale pink petals that clung like glitter to wrought iron benches, lampposts, trash cans. Old-fashioned storefronts competed for attention with boldly painted doors, brightly striped awnings and outdoor lights hung in half moons.

"I can see why my father likes it here." Kerry scooted out of the way of a man setting up a sidewalk sign advertising tiger butter fudge.

"'Dark chocolate, white chocolate, peanuts and peanut butter,'" Eugenia read. She smacked her lips and tugged Kerry away from the sign. "Sounds amazing but trust me, after eating one of Cal's cinnamon rolls, you won't have room for even a whiff of fudge."

Fifteen minutes later, they sat on either side of a café table in the back room of Eugenia's chic but playful dress shop, walled in by unpacked boxes and racks of clothes. Eugenia had given Kerry a whirlwind tour—conservative silk blouses paired with bright sequined scarves, and a crocheted sheath dress on a model wearing purple high-tops. That had been an instant mood lifter, and Eugenia seemed gratified when Kerry said so. Between them rested a freshly brewed pot of Constant Comment and a china plate that seemed far too fragile for the pair of dinosaur-egg-sized cinnamon rolls Eugenia had lovingly arranged on it.

"How long have you been in town?" Eugenia forked a roll like it was a porterhouse steak, plopped it onto another plate and handed it to Kerry.

Kerry watched Eugenia do the same with the second roll and felt her eyes stretch wide. No way her slim-hipped hostess could polish off one of these things, let alone two.

"Kerry?"

"Oh. Yes. Sorry." She accepted a fork and a linen napkin, which she smoothed over the knees of her gray pants. "I've been here a couple of days now."

"So you have seen your father."

"Briefly." Kerry took her time with the cup and saucer Eugenia handed her next. "He…wasn't feeling it. Not that I can blame him." China trembled against china. She tipped forward and set her tea on the table before looking up. "But this is about you. I don't even know how to apologize for what I've done, let alone make it right."

"That's not necessary," Eugenia began.

"Of course it is. Please don't be any kinder than you already have been. I don't deserve it. I borrowed money from you, a stranger, knowing full well I couldn't pay it back. In fact, we both know *borrow* isn't the right word." She shoved her hands into the pockets of her sweater. "Besides. I'm the reason you and my father broke up."

Eugenia bristled. "He told you that?"

"I took advantage of you, and that must have humiliated him. He has a lot of pride." Unlike his daughter.

Eugenia made a sound of half frustration, half affection. "Too much pride. He's also a stubborn ass."

Kerry surprised them both with a smile. "Do you still love him?"

Eugenia snatched up her plate, forked up a generous bite of pastry and took her time chewing. Finally she pointed the fork at Kerry. "You know what? You're right. You do owe me. But the debt is between you and me. Please don't entertain any misguided notion about getting Harris and me back together. That won't square us."

"I understand."

"Good. So. When you said Harris wasn't 'feeling' your reunion…"

"He's not ready to talk yet."

"Yet?" Eugenia set down her fork. "Does that mean you're going to stick around until he does? I admire your determination, but that could take a while. If you do manage to find a job, the cost of a motel room will gobble up your paycheck."

"I'd hoped to stay with Dad." The word already felt too intimate to use. "But that request was a bit premature. Anyway, my plan is to get a job and start paying down my debts. You and Dad are the top two people on my list."

It all came down to money, didn't it? Her abuse of it had landed her in this situation. Her lack of it meant she wouldn't be getting out of said situation anytime soon.

She needed a job.

Eugenia seemed to read her mind. "What kind of work are you looking for?"

"Anything, really." Kerry had enjoyed her position as a database administrator for a government contractor, but the felony conviction had meant the loss of her security clearance. Her probation officer had found her a data entry position at a telemarketing firm. She'd almost rather wait tables. Not that she could afford to be selective. "I haven't had any luck yet, but there are several places I haven't checked."

Eugenia hesitated.

Despite the tea warming her cup, Kerry's fingers felt stiff with cold. "Did you bring me here to tell me I should just head back to North Carolina?"

"Goodness, no." The pitch of Eugenia's voice made it clear her surprise was unfeigned. "I think it's brave of you to be here, and the right thing to do. Your father will come around."

"I don't know if he will. I don't know if he should. But I have to try." Eugenia crossed and uncrossed her legs for the second time. Dread kicked up the chaos again in Kerry's belly and she pushed away her untouched roll. "Is there something you need to tell me?"

Eugenia opened her mouth, closed it, jerked forward. Tea sloshed over the rim of her cup onto her saucer. "There's an apartment upstairs," she blurted. "It's been sitting vacant since I bought a house a few months ago. It's yours if you want it. You can work for me, here at the shop." She motioned with her chin at the cartons stacked to her right. "I have twenty boxes of summer inventory waiting to be unpacked, with more on the way."

Slowly Kerry collapsed against the back of her chair. "That's incredibly kind of you. Especially considering what I put you through. But Eugenia, if I do either of those things, my father will never speak to me again."

"It's not his business. This is between you and me."

"He won't see it that way."

"At least think about it. The sooner you get settled, the sooner you can start paying him back. And you'd be doing me a favor, keeping an eye on the place. Plus, you'll be saving me the trouble of looking for an employee."

"Do you really need help?" In all the time they'd been sitting there, not once had the bell over the door announced a customer.

"Not full-time, no, but having you here would free me up to take care of things at my new house. Like cleaning. Unpacking. Figuring out a way to disinvite the raccoons living over my garage."

A lightness expanded behind Kerry's breastbone. A job and a place to stay, just like that. Seemed she'd gotten her first break since that peremptory knock on her front door, almost a year ago now.

The offer was as tempting as that second cinnamon roll seemed to be to Eugenia—lust gleamed in the dress shop owner's eyes as she considered Kerry's plate. And yet…

With shaking fingers, Kerry folded and refolded the napkin on her knee. She'd opted for the easy route far too many times. That kind of cowardice had earned her a divorce, a handful of victims she'd never be able to make things right with, six months of house arrest and a lifetime supply of shame and regret.

Besides, it had been obvious from the moment she'd approached Kerry at the diner that Eugenia had struggled with whether or not to extend this offer.

An offer that could so easily put Eugenia right back into victim mode.

If Kerry's father found out, it would damage

whatever chance he and Eugenia had of reconciling. And if Kerry stayed in Castle Creek and didn't find a job, Eugenia would repeat the offer. Harris would find out one way or another. If Kerry landed another job, eventually the news about her conviction would spread, and her father would be humiliated all over again.

She placed her napkin on the table and straightened her shoulders. "Thank you, Eugenia. You don't know how much your generosity means to me. But I can't take advantage of you again. That's why I'm here, to stop the cycle." She slapped her thighs. "I'll try to talk to my father one more time. Then I'm going home."

"You can't quit now."

"I'll be in touch. I promise. As soon as I find a job, I'll start making payments." Maybe the telemarketing firm would take her back.

"Kerry. There's something you should know." Eugenia reached out, adjusted the teapot and flashed a trembling smile. "Your father has a heart condition. And it's starting to get the better of him."

THIRTY MINUTES LATER, Kerry pulled in a breath and followed Eugenia into Snoozy's Bar and Grill, the local hotspot, according to Eugenia. She must have meant it literally, because someone had set the thermostat to stifling. Kerry shrugged off her sweater and gazed longingly toward a tidy but well-used wooden bar.

Tossing one back wouldn't make the best impression. And one drink wouldn't be anywhere near enough to help her forget that two years earlier, her father had been diagnosed with something called viral cardiomyopathy and hadn't cared enough to let her know.

Eugenia tugged her deeper into the bar. No surprise the place was deserted—according to the sign on the door, it didn't open until eleven.

It wasn't as dimly lit as she'd expected. Sunshine streamed through a wide front window bracketed by dusty brown shutters, revealing what looked like a fancy hutch beneath, chest high, made of wood and acrylic. Strategically placed rocks and leaf-heavy branches decorated the emerald-colored outdoor carpet that lined the bottom of the pen.

Like a terrarium.

For reptiles.

Big ones.

Kerry stumbled back a step, wondering if she was staring at the reason the owner hadn't managed to find a fill-in bartender. What the hell was in there?

"There he is," chirped Eugenia.

Kerry jumped, and craned her neck. "Where?"

"Here." Eugenia clutched her elbow and swung

her around. "Kerry, meet Snoozy. Snoozy, this is my friend Kerry."

Kerry felt a squeeze in her chest. Eugenia had used the word *friend* so very casually.

"Nice to meet you, Kerry." A lanky, mournful-looking man with a handlebar moustache and shadows under his eyes dried his palms on a towel and slung it over his shoulder. He thrust out a hand. "Didn't catch your last name."

She stuffed her left hand in the back pocket of her jeans to hide the tremble. Would he recognize the name?

Here we go.

But before she could say anything, Snoozy dropped her hand and yanked the towel from his shoulder. He bent toward the glass.

"Smudges," he muttered, and made a few swipes with the towel. "I hate smudges."

She released a shaky breath. *How about ex-cons? Do you hate those, too?*

Eugenia made an *ahem* noise.

Snoozy straightened. "You ladies hungry? I just put together a big pot of chili you're welcome to try. New recipe," he said, and winked.

That's what she'd been smelling. Oregano and cumin. Her stomach rumbled.

Eugenia reached out and grabbed a handful of Kerry's long-sleeved top, as if in warning. Surely she couldn't mean…

Kerry shuddered and gestured awkwardly at

the pen. "Please tell me you didn't cook anything that lived in there."

Snoozy's mouth dropped open and he staggered back a step. "Mitzi? I'd never *think* of—" His eyes narrowed. "You been talking to Audrey?"

"His bride-to-be," Eugenia explained to Kerry, and gave her arm a let-me-handle-this pat. To Snoozy, she said, "I understand you're still looking for someone to fill in while you're on your honeymoon. Kerry here is interested in the job."

His face cleared. He stroked his moustache and regarded Kerry with fresh interest. "Got any experience?"

"I tended bar in college. It was a long time ago, but I still make a mean margarita." Maybe he'd ask her to demonstrate. A jigger of tequila would come in handy right about now.

"I'd need you to do more than tend bar. I have a server for lunch and dinner. While she runs the front, I run the grill in the back."

Oh. Damn. Disappointment tugged at Kerry's shoulders. She was a capable cook, but not much more than that. She glanced away from the encouragement in Eugenia's eyes. "I can mix drinks under pressure. Cooking, not so much."

"We could probably talk Ruthie into trading places when necessary." He didn't give her a chance to gush her thanks. "Got any questions for me?"

She burst out with "Who's Mitzi?" *What's* Mitzi?

Eugenia hid a smile behind her hand.

"You didn't see my sign out front?" Snoozy scratched his chin with long, thin fingers. "Maybe I should get a bigger one."

She'd seen the sign. Python Petting Zoo. "I thought that was some kind of dirty joke."

"Mitzi is no joke," Snoozy huffed. "I'd be pleased to introduce you."

Kerry glanced uneasily at Eugenia. The other woman lifted an eyebrow and Kerry got the message, loud and clear. *How badly do you want this job?*

She tipped up her chin and sidled over to join Snoozy beside the pen. He scanned the interior, then pointed to the far left corner. Kerry followed his finger, and froze.

Something slithered.

Something big.

"Beautiful, isn't she?" Snoozy spoke in hushed tones.

Teeth digging into her lower lip, Kerry watched as a thick, round body, brown with gold markings, coiled around a horizontal tree trunk. The sinister motion seemed endless, and Kerry didn't know whether to be impressed or terrified that there was no sign of the snake's head. She looked around for Eugenia. Her "friend" was standing on the other side of the bar, pretending to have a fervent interest in a grouping of neon signs announcing You've Been Drafted, Beer Yourself and Someone Get the Lites.

Kerry swung back around and willed her gaze to return to the snake. There was some comfort, anyway, in knowing where the thing was. "How big is she?"

"Ten feet. She weighs sixty, maybe seventy pounds."

"Um…would that be part of the job? Taking care of…Mitzi?"

Snoozy sagged. Even his moustache seemed to wilt. "This is why I'm not crazy about going away. No one appreciates Mitzi like I do. But Audrey has her heart set on a honeymoon."

Eugenia crossed the room again, giving Mitzi a wide berth. "The good news is, you won't come home and find out she's been barbecued, since the person who suggested eating her is the same person sharing your honeymoon."

Snoozy brightened. Kerry hugged her sweater closer, no longer enjoying the smell of that chili.

Eugenia clapped her hands. "Let's get this show on the road. I need to get back to my shop."

The door swung open, letting in the sounds of traffic. A heavyset man with a bushy gray beard stood blinking at them.

Snoozy waved him away. "Not open yet."

"C'mon, Snooze, I'm hungry."

"And it'll be my pleasure to feed you, Dale. At eleven-oh-one."

The man stomped back outside.

Kerry aimed a tentative smile at Snoozy. "So. Not being a big fan of snakes is strike one against hiring me."

He shook out the towel and folded it in half. "There a strike two?"

She nodded. "Harris Briggs is my father."

Snoozy went still, and scrunched his forehead. "That means…"

"Yes. I was convicted of a felony and spent six months under house arrest."

He cast a furtive glance at Eugenia. "Had something to do with money, I heard."

Kerry managed a nod. "Receiving stolen property and conspiracy to commit fraud."

Eugenia opened her mouth, then closed it. A familiar flush of shame heated Kerry's cheeks. There were no extenuating circumstances. No defense for what she'd done.

"When do you leave on your honeymoon?" she asked the bar owner quietly.

"Ten days." There was no mistaking his reluctance, and Kerry's heart sank. "We'll be out of the area for three weeks," he continued.

"What if I work the first week for meals only?" When the sides of his mouth curved downward, she pushed her shoulders back. "I'm desperate for this job. I hurt a lot of people, financially and emotionally. I have amends to make, and I intend to make them. But I can't do it without a job."

"A lot of folks would say you should have thought of that before spending money you didn't have."

"A lot of folks would be right. There's nothing about this situation that doesn't shame me, except for my resolve to fix it."

"This place is all I have," he said gruffly.

"I understand." Kerry forced a smile. "Thank you for even considering it."

"Well." Eugenia sighed the word as she adjusted the buckle on her purse. "At least Harris will be relieved."

Snoozy's gaze sharpened. "What's that supposed to mean?"

"The man is being his usual pigheaded self. Not only did he dismiss Kerry's plan to pay back her debts, he refused to let her stay with him. He sent her to Joe's instead. She's been there since Monday."

Snoozy regarded Kerry with a combination of disgust and speculation. "Harris sent you to Joe's motel?"

"To be fair, he had no idea I was coming to town."

"Your own father sent you to a motel." Snoozy's mouth tightened. "You know, he mocked my Mitzi."

"No." Eugenia gave the word enough lingering, horrified glee to make a daytime soap star green with envy, and it was all Kerry could do not to roll her eyes.

Snoozy nodded emphatically. "He asked if Audrey would be making her own wedding dress. Out of *snakeskin*."

"He didn't."

Snoozy pressed a fist to his mouth, made a gurgling sound and nodded again. Eventually he held up a hand and cleared his throat. "Tried to patch things up by offering to put together Aud's bouquet using Parker's specialty tulips, but the bottom line is, doing that man a favor ain't exactly my priority." His somber gaze settled on Eugenia. "You'll vouch for her?" When Eugenia answered with an unequivocal yes, Snoozy slid the towel from his shoulder and dabbed his forehead. "Then I suppose it won't hurt to give this a try, Kerry Briggs."

The embarrassingly loud sound of Kerry's thankful gasp was smothered by Eugenia's delighted clap. "Thank you so much," Kerry said. "I won't let you down. It's not Briggs, though. It's Endicott."

"Okay, Kerry Endicott. You're in for some long hours. I'll expect you to do things my way and not question why. The sheriff's a good friend of mine. I'll be asking him to check in regularly. No telling when he'll stop by."

"I understand."

"Good. You can start tonight."

Kerry blinked. "Tonight?"

"I need time to find someone else if you don't work out."

Relief warred with panic. "Fair enough."

"Just who else do you think you're going to get?" Eugenia demanded.

"Liz, maybe." Snoozy hesitated. "Or Hazel. She offered to help out for free."

"Liz is far too busy working with Parker at the greenhouses and raising that baby boy of hers," Eugenia said. "And Mayor Hazel doesn't have time for anything but that community center she and her sister are determined to finally make a reality. Besides, give her any control here and the first thing she'll do is install a condom machine in each of the bathrooms."

Snoozy's face glowed red and Kerry fought *not* to smile.

Eugenia crossed her arms. "The second thing she'll do is organize a wet T-shirt contest. Only male contestants need apply."

The extra color faded from Snoozy's cheeks. "Might bring more ladies in," he said thoughtfully. "Which in turn would bring in more men."

"Oh, for heaven's sake." Eugenia dropped her arms and bopped Snoozy with her clutch. "Hazel Catlett doesn't know a Woo Woo from a Snake-bite."

Snoozy tugged at his moustache. "Don't get

much call for Woo Woos here. Beer, whiskey and wine. Even old Mr. Katz can handle that."

This time Eugenia thumped Kerry with her clutch. "What's in a Woo Woo?"

"Vodka, peach schnapps and cranberry juice."

"There you go," Eugenia said smugly. "Anyway, can old Mr. Katz or even Hazel handle drink deliveries, or cleaning up this place the morning after payday? Think of the business Kerry will bring in. Once people find out the new bartender is Harris's daughter, you'll be in danger of violating the fire code."

Okay, that was a cheerful thought. Not.

"Guess I'll see you tonight, then." Snoozy sighed. "Don't worry. I'll find someone else to look after Mitzi."

"Thank you," Kerry said.

"Glad we got that settled." Eugenia nodded crisply. "Now we should have plenty of time to get you moved out of the motel and into my apartment before you have to report back here."

Kerry glanced uneasily from Snoozy to Eugenia. "That's kind of you, but—"

"I'm not being kind, I'm being practical. How are you supposed to pay anyone back if you're spending all your money at the motel? Besides, the sooner you settle your debts, the sooner we can gloat to your father about how wrong he was."

"Sounds good to me." Snoozy's grin took ten years off his face. "Can't have you working for free, now, can we?" He nudged Kerry with a bony elbow. "I'll start you off low, though. Even with tips, you won't be making much."

"Any amount will help. I promise I won't let you down." Kerry shook his hand. "By the way, congratulations on your upcoming wedding."

She hid a belated flinch. How long ago had Eugenia canceled her own ceremony?

Before she could issue an apology, the door opened behind them. Snoozy paled, and Kerry and Eugenia turned to see who had come in.

A rigid Harris Briggs stood in the doorway, in worn jeans and a maroon thermal shirt. His color was high, his eyebrows low. His disbelieving gaze traveled from Eugenia to Kerry to Snoozy. His massive chest swelled as he inhaled.

"Traitors," he growled.

Slam.

Eugenia stared at the door, Snoozy at the ceiling and Kerry at Mitzi's pen. An elongated, V-shaped head with obsidian eyes stared back at her through the plexiglass, and Kerry could almost hear the snake wondering what a North Carolina girl might taste like.

Panic baked the inside of her mouth. No way she could stay in Castle Creek. Her plan had always been to pay her literal dues, then return to blessed urban anonymity, not become part of a community where everyone would know not only her name, but every one of her failings, too.

It took her two tries to get the words out. "Sure you don't need me to demonstrate my cocktail skills?"

"Good idea," Snoozy said hoarsely. "I'll take one of those margaritas."

"Count me in," Eugenia said, and marched toward the nearest wooden stool.

Kerry hoped Snoozy carried a decent cider, because she was opting for a Snakebite.

Might as well get it over with.

HER FIRST SHIFT at Snoozy's, and Kerry started out doing everything right. She exchanged her usual heels for comfortable, nonslip shoes and wore a sleeveless top with her black jeans, in deference to the bar's subtropical temp. She showed up early and immediately checked her stock. The bar was astonishingly low on pineapple juice and mint, but when she mentioned it to Snoozy, he snickered and said they'd be in good shape until the order arrived the following week.

She made the sour mix, refilled the ice well and wiped everything down while familiarizing herself with the setup. She gave the bathrooms a once-over and verified drink prices with Snoozy.

But she couldn't help feeling she was doing it all wrong. With every lime she sliced, cabinet she explored and pour spout she inserted, shame nagged. Slowed her thought processes, and made her fingers clumsy. She couldn't stop seeing the wounded look on her father's face when he'd walked into the bar that morning.

Traitors.

She was doing it again. Dragging the innocent down with her.

"Easy there, barkeep." Snoozy put a finger on the tip of the stainless-steel spoon she was using to stir a Brass Monkey. "You're mixing a drink, not calling in the ranch hands for dinner."

With a feeble chuckle, Kerry surrendered the bar spoon. She garnished the drink with an extra cherry, set it on a cocktail napkin and slid it across the bar to a woman who, fortunately, was paying too much attention to a man at the corner table to care how much time the bartender had taken with her drink. Or how much of a racket she'd made.

"Enjoy," Kerry told her.

The woman nodded distractedly and turned away.

Kerry offered her boss a rueful smile. "Good thing it's not as busy as you thought it might be." Especially since Ruthie had called in sick. Kerry couldn't help wondering if the server was staging some kind of protest, but Snoozy didn't seem worried.

The bar had been empty when she'd arrived, and still smelling of chili, with the biggest noise-maker the lazy, rattling hum of the overhead fans. Ninety minutes later, a mere half-dozen customers were enjoying *The Very Best of Neil Diamond* crooning through Snoozy's surprisingly advanced Bluetooth speakers. Still, a french fries and grilled onions haze had overtaken the smell of oregano, and Snoozy kept Kerry sufficiently busy to prevent her from scoping out the lock on Mitzi's pen every ten minutes.

A glance at the Yuengling clock over the bar showed it had been closer to thirty. Her chin jerked toward the pen. Yep. Padlock in place. She turned back to Snoozy, who rolled red-rimmed eyes.

"We're only slow because no one knew you'd be here tonight," he said. "Tomorrow night it'll be a different story."

Kerry's stomach dropped. Which of her customers would stare, or shake their heads in disgust, or even walk out if they knew she was an ex-con? All of them? None of them? Did they know her father? Would it make a difference?

Or would they slide onto one of the scuffed wooden bar stools, lean in and ask if she'd ever met Piper Kerman of *Orange Is the New Black* fame and did she get any tattoos and not that they wanted to be nosy, but did she really go without sex the entire time she was behind bars?

Nobody wanted to hear about boring ol' home detention.

She pulled in a breath. She had no business thinking of Snoozy's patrons as *her* customers, anyway.

"I'm sorry," she finally said. "For causing trouble between you and my father."

"Don't be sorry. Be dependable."

She suppressed the urge to protest. If there was one thing she'd learned from her dealings with the court system, it was when to keep her mouth shut.

A pang of regret darted through her chest. The best way to fight it? Motion. She opened the refrigerator and peered in, took stock again, made sure the pour spout on the half-and-half was closed. Then she faced her new employer, a question about whether he allowed customers to run tabs hovering on her tongue.

But instead of keeping an eye on her, Snoozy was tossing lingering glances around the bar, as if filing away memories to call on during his time away. Or maybe he was gauging how much damage she could do. Kerry used the bar spoon to straighten the orange wedges in her garnish tray. Either way, it was clear he was having second thoughts.

Who could blame him? She was, too.

Her gaze followed the path Snoozy's had taken, from the giggly girl smoking two guys at pool, to the middle-aged couple sitting side by side in a booth, nursing their drinks and staring more at each other than the menu, to the nerdy-looking dude in the corner, who appeared more interested in his laptop than the beer Snoozy had set him up with an hour ago.

Or maybe he was trying to make it last so he wouldn't have to get his refill from Kerry. They'd made eye contact once, and he hadn't looked impressed. Not that she'd expected him to. Or wanted him to.

Just as well. No guy would be interested in a woman with a past like hers. Anyway, she needed to focus her energy on one thing.

Atonement.

The door opened, and the bar quieted as all eyes landed on a thin teenage boy with pale skin and shoulder-length red hair. He wore faded yellow high-tops and a long-sleeved tee over shiny black basketball shorts. Just as Kerry was wondering with a sinking feeling if he was chasing down a missing parent, Snoozy gestured for her to follow him to the end of the bar, where he waved the boy over.

"Kerry, I want you to meet Dylan. He'll be looking after Mitzi for me."

"You will?" She grabbed the teen's hand with both of hers and laid a fervent shake/squeeze combo on him. "My hero," she said.

He blushed so hard, his freckles disappeared. "No big deal," he muttered. "Mitzi's cool."

"Heroic *and* humble." Kerry smiled, leaned in.

"Truth is, Mitzi freaks me out a little, so I'm glad you'll be around."

She was laying it on a little thick, but the purple shadows under the teen's eyes made her heart hurt.

Dylan's blush deepened. "I can take out the trash. Do other stuff you need."

"That would be great. I can see you're going to be a huge help."

He dipped his head. When his phone pinged, he hustled off into a corner and started typing with his thumbs, stopping every now and then to shoot a glance back at the bar.

Snoozy gave Kerry a considering look. "That kid's standing a foot taller."

"There's something about him…"

"He's had it rough." His face tightened. "He lives four blocks away, so he doesn't have far to walk. He'll be in every day after school to change Mitzi's water and clean her bedding. A few odd jobs on top of that won't hurt, but don't keep him long. He'll have homework and chores of his own at home. I'm putting him to work right away so he can get used to the routine. He'll be starting tonight."

"He'll feed Mitzi, too?"

"On Tuesdays. She only needs to be fed once a week. I'll make sure someone's around to help, though Dylan knows better than to handle her on his own."

"She only eats once a week?"

Snoozy nodded. "Obesity's a problem for pythons in captivity."

"Interesting. Although," Kerry said, drawing out the word, "the fatter she is, the slower she'll move."

"Pythons don't chase their prey. They're ambush hunters."

"Is that supposed to make me feel better?" She scrambled for a change of subject. "It's okay to let a minor in the bar?"

"As long as he's supervised. Don't let him wander off or we could get in trouble. If the bar's busy, keep him with you, or ask him to come back later. I'm going in the back to make some phone calls. Any other questions?"

"Would you happen to have a sweater I could borrow? It was pretty warm in here this morning and now I'm wishing I'd worn something with a little more fabric." Though they both knew her goose bumps had little to do with the cool air.

"Yeah, the AC's temperamental. Kind of like my bride-to-be." He grinned, and some of the tension in Kerry's shoulders eased.

"Let me see what I can find in the back," he said.

"You can borrow mine."

Kerry swung around. A smiling blonde flanked by two other women held out a purple cardigan. She gave it a shake when Kerry hesitated.

"It's okay," the blonde said. "I don't need it."

"That's so nice of you, Allison." Still Kerry hesitated. "But I might spill something on it."

"You remembered my name." The other woman beamed. Kerry didn't deserve her delight, though. She couldn't help but remember, considering she'd run into Allison probably two or three times a day for the past couple of days. Allison Gallahan and her husband, Joe, owned Sleep at Joe's, the motel where Kerry had stayed before moving into Eugenia's apartment that afternoon.

"It's washable." Allison tugged at Kerry's hand and draped the sweater over her forearm. "It has to be. I have a kid. You've met Parker, right?"

Kerry managed a smile for Parker Macfarland, who stood on Allison's right. The redhead wore jeans, an emerald top and an expression free of censure.

"It's nice to see you again," Kerry said.

Snoozy held up Allison's sweater so Kerry could poke her arms into the sleeves. "This third one here, she's trouble." He winked at the woman on the other side of Allison, the youngest of the three—and the least friendly looking.

"I'm Liz," she said. She flicked a mass of pale blond corkscrew curls over one shoulder and thrust a hand across the bar. "Liz Watts. I used to work here."

"Liz left us to work full-time with Parker. Place just isn't the same. Say…" Snoozy directed the word to his feet. "Mind if Kerry gets your number? Case something comes up while I'm gone?"

"Good idea." Liz stared, unsmiling, at Kerry. "Because you never know."

Parker tossed a quick side-eye in Liz's direction. "Though I'm sure you'll be fine."

"And if you're not, we'll help," Allison added firmly. "After all, Eugenia sent us to offer moral support for your inaugural shift. Didn't she, Liz?"

Liz grunted, sounding eerily like Snoozy.

"That's kind of you," Kerry said. She seemed to be saying that a lot these days. She really was grateful, but she couldn't help feeling uneasy, too. She was racking up a lot of favors.

Allison waved away her compliment. "We're not kind, we're curious. Plus, Liz and I are in dire need of a little baby-free time."

Kerry nodded in faux understanding. These three had each other's backs. What would that be like?

Stop taking advantage of people and maybe someday you'll find out.

Snoozy rapped his knuckles on the bar. "Glad we got that that settled. I'll let you ladies talk."

His sound system started playing "Hotel California" and he whistled as he headed toward the kitchen, quicker than Kerry had seen him move all night.

"So what can I get you three to drink?" she asked.

"A mocktail for me." Parker patted her baby

bump. "Bet you all didn't think I knew that word. Here's another. I'll have a no-jito. Get it? That's a mojito with no alcohol." Her bravado slipped as she eyed Kerry. "Can you do that?"

"I can definitely do that." Though that would probably use up the last of the mint. Next round she'd have to talk Parker into something else. Kerry turned to Liz and Allison. "And for you two?"

"We'd each like to try a Blue Hawaiian," Liz said.

"We would?"

Liz elbowed Allison without looking her way. "Have you heard of it?"

"I haven't, but I can look it up." Kerry retrieved her tablet from under the bar and pressed a few keys. When she located the recipe, she couldn't help a chuckle.

"Rule number one." Liz glared. "Don't make fun of a customer's drink choice."

"I'm so sorry. I promise I wasn't laughing at your order. Earlier I told Snoozy we were low on pineapple juice, and he looked at me like I'd grown a second head. I should have enough for two of these, though." Kerry scrounged for the professionalism that had once made her a passable barkeep. "Did you know the Blue Hawaiian is also called the swimming pool cocktail?"

Liz's expression cleared. "Snoozy always was surprised when we ran out of fruit juice and peach schnapps. You might want to go ahead and pick some up, and reimburse yourself from petty cash. That is…" She cocked her head. "Is he even trusting you with the petty cash?"

CHAPTER THREE

PARKER SUCKED IN a breath.

"What the hell?" Allison whispered harshly.

Even Liz looked startled by what she'd said.

"He is trusting me with the petty cash," Kerry said evenly. No need to point out Snoozy was trusting her with the whole damned bar. "I don't intend to let him down. Excuse me while I find the curaçao."

She turned away and scanned the mirrored shelves. She knew exactly where Snoozy kept the blue curaçao, but she needed a moment to remember how to breathe. Liz's words may have been unkind, but they weren't unfair.

She walked away from the furious whispers behind her, rolling her shoulders in a futile attempt to shake off her distress. Gratitude was what she should be feeling. For freedom. For second chances. For this job.

She caught sight of Nerdy-Looking Dude's reflection in the mirror as he stood and stretched. The hem of his short-sleeved shirt rose, and Kerry stilled. *Holy Hannah.* Absently she added manly stomach muscles to her mental gratitude journal.

She barely stopped herself from turning to get an eyeful of the real thing.

That was a surprise. Sitting behind his laptop, with his black-rimmed glasses and striped button-down shirt, he hadn't looked quite so...toned.

He chugged the remains of his beer. Good. She was glad he was leaving, because she'd wasted way too much time and brain power wondering what the heck he was up to over there in the corner.

The woman with the Brass Monkey had been wondering, too. She sat two tables away, hunched over her drink, chin in hand as she watched Nerdy-Looking Dude's every move. He hadn't glanced her way once. Probably because she had a good ten years on him. He looked to be around thirty. Kerry's age.

The longing on the woman's face made Kerry want to give her a hug.

She grabbed the bottle of curaçao and turned back to her customers. While Parker, Allison and Liz stood in a huddle, continuing their confab while watching Kerry's every move, Kerry grabbed a highball glass and two hurricanes and set them on the bar mat. As she reached for the shaker, she tipped over one of the hurricane glasses. Luckily she caught it before it rolled off the mat, but her rhythm was off. She'd never manage to mix these drinks without breaking something.

She dumped crushed ice into the shaker and

added blue curaçao, coconut cream, pineapple juice and white rum. Liquor dripped all over her hand and down the side of the bottle. The pourer was loose on the rum. With a slow inhale and exhale, she reseated it.

The whispering intensified. She wiped her hands on her jeans, reached for the shaker lid and promptly dropped it. It thumped onto the floor and she wanted to drop down beside it.

A distraction. She needed one. Desperately.

Snoozy, where are you?

A cheer erupted at the pool table, but it wasn't enough to pull the trio's focus from Kerry and the mess she was making of their drinks. For God's sake, where was a fire when you needed one?

Thunk. An empty beer mug appeared before her. She looked up and met the brown-eyed gaze of Nerdy-Looking Dude.

"Maybe you ladies could wait for your drinks over there." He nodded at the booth farthest from the bar, pulled a handful of coins from his pocket and let them clatter onto the counter. "I have some negotiating to do. I'd rather you not add to my humiliation by watching."

Kerry swallowed a sigh of relief as Allison led Parker and Liz over to the booth. She nodded her thanks, and wiped her hands on a towel. "Another beer?"

"Boston lager," he said, and settled on a stool as she fetched a mug. "Better make it half." He gestured at the change on the bar and flashed a sweet pair of dimples. "Not enough coin, and all."

"And make myself look too cheap to spot you?" She set a full mug in front of him and went back to mixing cocktails. "Besides, I owe you. You probably saved me having to replace a good twenty dollars in glassware."

He shrugged. "All I know is I had a drink emergency."

"Your last drink sat in front of you for an hour before you finished it."

"Hence the emergency. I need something to wash away the taste of warm brew."

If only he'd stayed in the corner. The abs and the gallantry had been intriguing enough. Now she was getting an up-close-and-personal view of attractively rumpled blond hair and a strong, stubble-covered chin. The regret she'd brought into the bar was extending beyond money matters.

Damn it.

She finished up her orders as quickly as she could, the sound of the shaker precluding further conversation. As nice as the guy had been, the last thing she needed was to encourage anyone to take an interest in her. When she'd tended bar in college, she'd been instructed to develop a following. A bartender with fans meant higher sales numbers and bigger tips. Win-win.

Only she didn't want fans. Not now. Not here. Didn't need them, either. What she needed was to keep her head down and do a good job and hopefully secure a solid reference for the next gig, whatever that might be.

Eugenia had shown her a lot of undeserved faith. No way Kerry would let her down.

She went overboard on the garnishes for all three cocktails. With a cheerful smile, she delivered the drinks, made recommendations for round two that involved neither mint nor pineapple juice, checked on her other customers and returned to the bar well to clean up.

Nerdy-Looking Dude sat silently sipping his beer while she washed and dried her implements and wiped down the bar. Now she needed a distraction from her distraction.

Said distraction was stacking up the coins he'd tossed on the bar. "You need a tip jar."

"I think that's a little premature."

He gave her a half smile that could charm the stripes off a tiger. "I'm Gil. Gil Cooper." He extended his hand across the bar.

"Kerry." His hand was hard and warm around hers. She refused to let it give her ideas.

"I take it, Bartender Kerry, that this is your first night on the job?"

"Hopefully not my last."

"So that—" he made an almost imperceptible motion with his head toward the newly occupied booth "—was just first-night jitters? Or did they say something to you?"

"Jitters," she said easily. He knew the three friends. She could tell. Even if their suspicions weren't justified, she had no intention of stirring up trouble.

He reached for the bowl of pretzels she'd set out and knocked over the stacks of coins. His hand jerked in a belated attempt to keep the towers intact, and pretzels scattered across the bar. Seemed they were two of a kind. He muttered under his breath and cleaned up after himself.

She forced her gaze away from his hands. "Can I ask you a question?"

"No," he said, brightening. "I'm not married."

She fought a smile by pursing her lips. "I was going to ask if you're a regular."

"I'm thinking we don't know each other well enough to discuss my bathroom habits."

"Not *irr*egular. *A* regular." His sense of silliness sparked a wistfulness inside that she had no business feeling. "Do you come here often? To—" she used both hands to gesture from him to the laptop he'd abandoned at the corner table "—do whatever it is you do?"

"I am a regular." He dusted the salt from his hands. "Starting tonight. Is that your question?"

No way she was responding to that, though in an absurd way, his declaration made her feel less lonely.

"My question is, does she bother you?" She

jerked her chin toward the pen. "Mitzi? Everyone seems to take her in stride."

"She bothers you."

"I don't count." When he raised an eyebrow, she added, "I mean, I won't be here long. I'm only filling in while Snoozy's on his honeymoon."

"He'll be gone a couple of weeks, right?"

"Three."

"Long time to be looking over your shoulder. You're going to have to find a way to lighten up about the apple of Snoozy's eye."

Kerry set a bowl of popcorn on the bar, eyed Gil's elbow and moved the bowl farther away. "I'm open to suggestions," she said. She caught the mischief on his face and added, "About getting used to Mitzi."

"How about a joke?" He narrowed his eyes, then snapped his fingers. "What was Mitzi's favorite subject in school?"

Kerry raised the other eyebrow.

"*Hiss*tory."

She groaned and started to move away.

He held up a finger. "One more. 'Cause everyone deserves a second chance. What's Mitzi's favorite TV show?"

"I don't know." Glass clinked as Kerry rearranged her speed well, the thigh-high rack for a bartender's most commonly used bottles. *"When Animals Attack?"*

Gil chuckled, then made a sound like a buzzer. "Wrong. *Monty Python.*"

She laughed, and looked up, and intercepted an appreciative glance. Did a decent job of ignoring it. "Your jokes are almost as bad as my dad's."

The moment she said it, she regretted it.

"His must be terrible, then." Gil tossed a piece of pretzel into his mouth. "Give me an example."

Kerry caught the eye of Brass Monkey Woman and realized she was doing a rotten job of looking after her customers.

"Yeah, well, it's all fun and games until a reptile gets out of her pen," she said. "Excuse me. I need to check on someone."

"You don't need to worry," Gil said to her back. "She got away from Snoozy once. No way he'll let it happen again."

Kerry whirled around. "She got out? When was this?" When Gil lowered his head and pushed his glasses higher up his nose, hiding a smile, she slapped the bar. "Now that was mean."

Brass Monkey Woman came up beside Gil, carrying her empty glass. Kerry swallowed a sigh. *Be dependable.* That's all Snoozy had asked and already she was sucking at it.

She apologized to the woman and asked if she'd like another of the same. When the woman nodded, Kerry retrieved a fresh glass and gestured at Gil. "Don't you think that was mean?"

The woman nodded again, this time with a

conspiratorial smile curving her lips. She never looked away from Gil's face.

"It's the truth," he said. "This was quite a few years back, before Snoozy set Mitzi up here in the bar. He was going through a divorce and his wife deliberately let Mitzi out of the house. Half a dozen years later, Allison found her coiled up in a wall at the motel. Mitzi, not Snoozy's ex."

Kerry paused in the act of unscrewing the lid on the orange juice. "Wait, Allison found Mitzi? At the *motel*? I was just *there*." Thank God for Eugenia and her dress shop apartment.

Gil helped himself to a handful of popcorn. "I'm sure if she'd had any roommates, they'd have found them by now."

Brass Monkey Woman made a small noise of distress and shifted on the stool.

Kerry sent her an empathetic glance and turned a glower on Gil. "You're a real hoot."

"Relax. They had an exterminator out there and everything. Besides, it was a good thing. Mitzi brought Joe and Allison together."

Kerry stirred the cocktail, added two cherries and slid it across the bar. "I'm not big on reptiles."

"I can see that."

Brass Monkey Woman handed Kerry a credit card and reached for the bowl of popcorn. Gil offered her the pretzels, as well, and she beamed.

"So, you're staying at Joe's," Gil said casually. He didn't notice Brass Monkey Woman's sharp glance.

"I was."

"You don't have friends or family in Castle Creek?"

"There wasn't room for me."

"What happens when Snoozy gets back from his honeymoon? You plan to hang around?"

Brass Monkey Woman sniffed, picked up her drink and made her way back to her table.

Kerry winced. Gil seemed oblivious, his attention trained directly on Kerry. She had to admit, it made for a nice change.

"I haven't decided yet," she said. "Snoozy won't need me here, so I'd have to find another job." Which would not be easy. She started to swipe her palms down the front of her shirt, remembered Allison's sweater and swiped them on her hips instead. "I'd also forgotten how sticky I get by the end of the day." She lifted first her left, then her right shoe, wincing at the sound her soles made as they separated from the tacky rubber mat. "Me and the floor."

She wouldn't miss much about bartending, that was for sure. So far she was managing, but ever since her arrest, she'd longed to do something that would allow her to spend more time in the sun.

Allison appeared beside Gil, waving Kerry off when she apologized for not making it back to their table. "Two margaritas and a Shirley Temple, please." She poked Gil in the shoulder. "We're over there talking about you. Still running that online forum?"

Gil hesitated, and Kerry could practically hear him turning red. He mumbled something about collaborative math projects, whatever those were.

Allison watched Kerry mixing drinks. "Parker says Nat's having a hard time with algebra. Maybe you could give her a call, see about signing the kid up for some tutoring?"

"Sure," Gil said.

Aha.

He *was* a nerd.

Albeit a hot one.

She followed Allison to her table to deliver the girls' drinks and turned to find Gil had returned to his laptop. Ignoring a twinge of disappointment, she checked in with the pool table crowd and the couple too into each other to eat, then moved back behind the bar and got busy washing glasses. A hoot of masculine laughter sounded outside the door right before two men walked in. Kerry registered a cop's uniform and dropped one of the hurricane glasses.

Glass shattered, and the bar went silent.

THE CHILLY NIGHT air plucked at Eugenia's skin, raising gooseflesh. Still, her temper burned hotter than the habaneros in Snoozy's chili, which she'd done her darnedest to warn Kerry away from. As she glared at Harris's front door, shrouded in shadow, a butter-colored moon peered through gauzy strips of clouds, casting enough light to reveal the small potted tree to her left. The two leaves that elevated it from stick status were brown. A sudden sadness gathered in her throat, and it hurt to swallow.

This time when she pressed the doorbell she didn't let go.

"I know you're in there, old man," she called. "You might as well open up because I'm not going away."

The door swung wide. "Sure you will," he said, his voice all gravel. "You did before."

Eugenia put her hands behind her back and gripped her own wrist. Otherwise she might find herself trying to smack the stubborn right out of the man. He must have recognized her urge to do violence because he eased back a step. She took the opportunity to trespass.

"That thing is dying." She jabbed a finger toward the sickly tree. "You should be ashamed of yourself."

"Talk about the pot callin' the kettle black." He hesitated, then closed the door, shutting them both inside. He heaved a gusty sigh and with a hand to her back, guided her away from the foyer and into the living room. "I know why you're here."

She pulled away and walked to the far end of the sofa, long faded from sitting beneath a front window with curtains Harris never bothered to draw.

"Do you," she said.

"I do, and I'm too damned tired to deal with it. I appreciate the thought, but you best go on home now, Genie."

Eugenia ignored the traitorous tingle at the nickname he hadn't called her in forever and focused instead on his jackass-ery. "Don't you shoo me away, old man. What on earth is going on in that thick, naked noodle of yours?"

"You were the one doin' the shooin'." He pounded his fist once on the back of his recliner, sending it rocking. "Damn it, I'm not an old man and I *like* my naked noodle." His words lingered in the dusty plaid of his living room. When he realized what he'd said, he flushed.

"Happy to hear it," she said. She'd grown rather fond of it herself, until the weight of Harris's stubbornness had pressed his personality flat.

He grumbled under his breath. "You're not here to tell me my daughter's lookin' to borrow money again?"

"She told you why she's here."

"She's told me a lot of things over the years. I've learned to close one ear and stick my finger in the other. I know damned well she's back for another handout." He rubbed a palm over his head. "I, uh, apologize for callin' you a traitor."

She lifted her chin, and the stiff wool collar of

her pea-green jacket scuffed the nape of her neck. Now she remembered why she rarely wore the thing. "Harris Briggs, you're a jackass."

He set his jaw. "That's what you came to tell me?"

"It is."

"I'm a jackass. 'Cause I'm smart enough not to let my ex-con daughter take advantage of me?"

"'Cause you're dumb enough to let your only child believe you don't love her anymore."

"Well, that…that's not true," he blustered. He moved deeper into the living room and stared down at a half-empty bottle of beer on the coffee table. Which he'd protected with a ceramic coaster, she was gratified to see.

He gave a harrumph, and crossed his arms. "I never said that."

"You didn't have to. You've showed her, over and over again." She braced a hand on the back of the sofa. Damn the man for his ability to sap the starch right out of her knees.

"And she sent you to tell me this?" His breathing roughened. "So you are working against me."

Slowly Eugenia pushed upright. Coming here had been a mistake. She was only making Harris more suspicious of his daughter.

"You know what?" Absently she twisted a button on her jacket. "I did it again. Inserted myself where I don't belong. This is between you and

Kerry. But think, Harris. Please think about the message you're sending by refusing to see her."

He snatched up his beer, took a swig and shook his head. "She's here for another charitable contribution, not a reconciliation. I know my daughter, Genie."

No, he didn't. Not anymore. Now all Eugenia could do was keep her fingers crossed that he would give himself the chance to.

"All righty, then," she said stiffly.

He tipped his bottle in silent invitation and she shook her head. She missed him, God help her. His strength, his solidity, even the stupid cinnamon smell of his chewing gum. If she didn't get out of here soon, she'd find herself bawling into that horrible flannel shirt. She marched back to the door. "I won't bother you again."

"Genie?"

She stilled, her hand on the doorknob.

"There's a difference between dead and dormant. That tree on my porch. It'll come back. You think I killed it, but I didn't."

Eugenia squeezed her eyes shut. Harris Briggs was far from the beat-around-the-bush type. The last time they'd talked…the things she'd said… She'd made him tentative.

"I knew you loved me, Harris," she said. She touched her palm to the smooth coolness of the door. "Just not enough to compromise. On pretty much anything."

"That was all up to me, was it?"

Wearily she faced him. "I didn't come here about you and me. I came about you and your daughter. But it was a mistake and I apologize."

Harris gave a strained chuckle. "This is payback. That's what this is."

"What are you talking about?"

"You asked me to marry you. I said no. That's when our troubles began."

"Our troubles began when you refused to include your daughter in our lives."

"She made that choice, not me."

"Bull crap," Eugenia said crisply.

Amusement flashed across his face. "You never did give me a chance to explain why I turned you down."

"This isn't about that." The remembered pain of his rejection knifed into her lungs. "This is about your daughter and how much she needs you."

His nostrils flared and he turned a disturbing shade of red. "What about how much I needed you? How do you think I felt when I walked into Snoozy's today?"

"Harris."

"You know what?" He pressed a palm to his chest. "I'm not feeling up to this tonight."

"Harris," she repeated, unable to keep the alarm out of her voice.

"I'm fine," he muttered. "Don't go gettin' your dress over your head."

"You're not the one I'm worried about." Abruptly she dropped a hip onto the little table beside the door. Something was wrong. She couldn't breathe. Her heart beat too fast as she tugged at the neckline of her sweater. Did he have the AC on? She really needed some AC. "I think you'd better call 911."

CHAPTER FOUR

ON THE WAY up to his apartment over the store—a big selling feature, Valerie Flick kept insisting, if only he'd call it a "loft"—Gil tripped on one of the narrow steps of the wrought iron staircase. In an ungainly attempt to avoid hitting his head, he twisted his body. His solar plexus connected with the railing and punched the air from his lungs. Son of a *bitch*.

Hand pressed to his chest, and with one long, drawn-out wheeze, he jerked sideways and slid onto his ass. The cold metal chilled his spine.

He dropped his head back and sucked air, finally opened his eyes and stared up into the thick black sky, awash with twinkles. The stars seemed friendly. Gil could use friendly. In fact, if it weren't already fifty degrees and falling, he'd be just as happy staying on these steps all night. And if he'd tossed back as many beers as he'd wanted to, he wouldn't have cared about the temperature at all. But it wouldn't have been worth the hangover, especially since in the morning he'd get right back to worrying about what his asshole brother might be up to, and whether Cooper's Hardware would survive another quarter. That second mort-gage he'd taken out six years ago to cover the shortfall his brother's scheming had created was taking a toll on the store's bottom line.

He'd be in better shape if he hadn't had to shell out for a new roof last year. And yeah, okay, if he hadn't let a few people slide on their tutoring tabs. But those students had recruited others who had managed to cough up the fees, so Gil had chalked that up to clever marketing.

His knee started to pulse. He didn't remember banging it, but no surprise that he had. He rubbed absently at the ache. Damn, he was tired.

A breeze pushed past, dropping off a tiny yel-low bloom and the scent of grilled hamburger. His stomach heaved a wistful sigh and he hoped to hell he had something edible in the fridge. He hadn't lingered at the bar long after Kerry had dropped that glass. He'd jumped up to help, then realized how asinine that would look. Anyway, she seemed to have it under control. He didn't know what the hell had happened, but as soon as Sheriff Suazo had walked in, *crash*.

"Damn it," Gil muttered. It had taken him long enough to get over his last girlfriend. Why would he consider angling for another? Especially one so obviously out of his league?

When his stomach rumbled, he smacked a hand down on the step digging into his ribs. Turkey. He had deli turkey in the fridge. Swiss cheese, too, and the soft rye he liked because the crusts weren't too dry.

And beer. He had plenty of beer.

But what he was really hungry for had long, thick brown hair gathered into a ponytail and big, green, wary eyes. The wariness intrigued him and though he didn't know her, it concerned him, too. Her curves were generous, and ridiculously tempting, and despite seeming more nervous than a novice driver during rush hour, she carried herself with a mesmerizing grace.

Unlike you, asshole. Stop daydreaming and get moving.

He pushed himself up and continued climbing. Let himself in and tossed his keys at the table just inside the door. They missed the basket, rattled across the polished wood and landed on the floor. "Nice shot," he muttered.

No need to turn on the light—the floods on the outside of the store provided plenty. He rounded the table and bent to scoop up his keys, and spotted the mobile alarm clock he hadn't been in the mood to chase that morning. With the two oversize rubber wheels on either side of a small white plastic body, and two buttons positioned like eyes, the thing reminded him of Princess Leia. It chirped and beeped like an overcaffeinated R2-D2.

"There you are, clock-bot." He reached under

the table and snatched it up. "Why are you hiding? Tell me you didn't eat my turkey."

His cell rang, and he frowned at the unfamiliar number on the screen. "Hello?

"How's it hanging, G?"

Gil swallowed an oath. He lurched at the wall and slapped around until he found the light switch. The inside floods did their thing and he blinked in the sudden brilliance.

"I understand you've been talking with Valerie Flick," Gil said tightly.

"She's been trying to negotiate a deal with me since she got her real estate license. You know what kind of commission she'd get for handling the sale of Cooper's?"

"No surprise the bottom line is all about your bottom line."

Gil stalked into the kitchen and opened the fridge. Damn it. Something reeked and he hoped to hell it wasn't his turkey. He grabbed a beer, popped the top and settled on a stool at the butcher block island that served double duty as his dining room table. "Even if I had the money," he ground out, "you wouldn't get it. You know as well as I do you already got your hands on more than your fair share of the business."

"You just can't let it go, can you, G?"

"I can forgive, but I'm sure as hell not going to forget. Not if it means setting myself up to get fleeced again."

"If you can say that, it means you haven't forgiven me at all."

Gil banged an elbow onto the island, shoved his fingers through his hair and rested his forehead on the heel of his hand. "I'm not singing this refrain with you, Ferrell. Not anymore."

"You're a hard man, bro. What's the matter, no luck with your Millenium Falcon prize problems?"

Gil let loose a bitter chuckle. His brother had mashed together a *Star Wars* reference with the Millenium Prize, which offered one million dollars for the correct solution to any of seven unresolved math problems.

He wished he had time to concentrate on something like that. For years, he'd been fascinated by the mass gap. But he barely had time to do the books for the hardware store at night while honoring his online tutoring commitments. What he earned from tutoring kept him in groceries. And the occasional poker game.

"No," Gil said. "No luck." But it was Bartender Kerry's face that floated across his brain.

He wondered where she was living now. Had her friends made room for her?

"I'm not giving up on this," Ferrell said. "You don't want to be there at the store any more than I like being poor."

"So everyone says."

"You'll never make a go of it."

Gil sat up and swigged his beer. "I hear that a lot, too."

When his brother progressed to threats, Gil disconnected the call and set his phone aside.

Ferrell hadn't sounded high, but that didn't mean he wasn't still on drugs. Asking wouldn't have accomplished anything.

Finally, tiredness gave way to exhaustion. Gil banged his empty bottle on the island and turned toward his bed. His sheetless bed. He'd dumped the linens in the washer before opening the store that morning and forgot all about them.

Hell. He wanted to sleep, not make the damn bed. But no way he'd catch any Zs without a sheet over his bare feet.

He yanked off his jacket, let it drop to the floor and went over to the bed. Grabbed a fresh set of sheets from underneath and tossed them onto the mattress.

With one hand, he snagged a pillowcase. With the other, he picked up a pillow with a little too much force and it ended up sailing over his shoulder. It caught the blinds beside the bed and with a rattling protest, the vertical slats popped out of alignment.

Gil bit out an oath and swung around to fix it. Through the opening he caught a glimpse of the opposite side of the street and froze.

What the—?

He pulled at the blinds, widening the gap, and pressed his nose to the glass.

In the dress shop parking lot across the street, Kerry paced behind the bumper of an older Honda. Her arms were folded across her chest as her hands rubbed fiercely at her bare arms.

What was she doing over there? And where the hell was her sweater?

She sagged against the bumper. Pushed one hand into her hair.

The blinds clattered back into place as Gil lunged for his jacket.

WITH A FRUSTRATED MOAN, Kerry dug in the side pocket of her purse for her cell phone. *Way to go, chickie.* Not even twenty-four hours in the apartment and already she was calling Eugenia for help. At eleven thirty at night.

Her brand-spanking-new landlady would not be impressed.

She dropped her purse on the trunk, sagged down onto the bumper and reluctantly thumbed through her contacts. It could have been worse. She could have been making this call at two in the morning. Though the reason Snoozy had sent her home early was hardly something to celebrate.

She had to do better.

A scuffing sound had her jerking to her feet. With liquid knees, she squinted through the late-night gloom.

Gil Cooper loped toward her, blond hair flopping, glasses glinting as he passed under a street lamp. The lean, muscled ease of his movements was a clear contrast to the gracelessness he'd shown at the bar. The disparity intrigued her, while his undemanding smile provided an instant balm to her frustration.

Despite the heavy pull of a plaintiveness she was damned tired of feeling, she straightened her spine.

"Hey," she said.

He stopped a few paces away and gave his head a shake when he had to catch his breath. "Now you know I'm out of shape."

An exaggeration if she'd ever heard one. Still, she rested her free hand on one well-padded hip. "Who am I to judge?"

His gaze dropped, and even in the anemic glow of the dress shop's outdoor lights she could see the smolder. She couldn't help a rush of gratification, even as she acknowledged he wouldn't look at her that way if he knew what she'd done.

He held out the jacket he carried. "I'm wondering if I should call the sheriff. You look like you're casing the joint."

Her lungs seized and she fell back a step. God. Maybe he did know. And he was still talking to her?

"What?" she croaked.

The amusement leaked from his expression. "Bad joke."

She pulled in a breath. "I'm staying in Eugenia Blue's apartment."

"I figured that." He pushed the jacket into her hands. "Either she didn't warn you about the cool spring nights in Castle Creek or you forgot your sweater at the bar."

She took her time tucking her phone into her back pocket, then accepted his jacket with a lofty air. "Or maybe I'm conducting an experiment."

His eyes lit up. "What kind of experiment?"

"The kind that involves postdusk lake proximal air and…and the exposed skin of a—" she floundered "—Southern urban-type female."

His lips twitched. "Your conclusion?"

"Goose bumps are a natural phenomenon that cannot be considered region-dependent."

"You speak geek."

"I used to work for a software development firm." *Why did you go there?*

"I don't have my keys," she added quickly. "I was about to break the news to Eugenia."

"No need." He dangled a braided plastic key ring. "Eugenia and I exchanged keys when she first opened her store. I'm sure she wouldn't mind if you hung on to this until you find yours."

"Thank you," Kerry breathed, and offered an apologetic nod as she took the key ring. "That's twice you've rescued me tonight."

"I don't think you were in any danger of freezing to death."

"I meant back at the bar, when you saved me from demolishing Snoozy's entire supply of hurricane glasses." She grimaced. "Three martini glasses and a brandy snifter weren't quite so lucky. That's why he sent me home early. I think he was afraid if I stayed, I'd start working my way through the liquor bottles."

"He didn't fire you, did he?"

The alarm in his voice touched her. "No," she said. "But he probably should have."

When she shuddered, he mistook it for cold. "You should go in."

Yes. She should. She didn't want to, but she should. She forced herself to take a step away from the car, then another, until finally she turned and started toward the metal staircase that led up to the second-story apartment.

He followed. "Sorry you had such a rough day." Something about the way he said it...

She paused at the bottom of the stairs. "You, too?"

"Let's just say that ten minutes ago, I was seriously considering heading back to the bar. For another beer, I mean," he added hastily.

She snorted. "You'd have probably had to drink it out of a to-go cup."

When she made to shrug out of his jacket, he stopped her with a quick squeeze of her forearm.

"Why don't you wait till we get to the top? Sometimes the key sticks."

Kerry managed a nod and led the way up, her palms going slick as she grew overly aware of the brush of his jacket's sleeves across the bare skin of her arms, the chill of the night air soothing her blush, his solidness at her back.

Would he kiss her?

When they reached the top of the stairs, she unlocked the door and turned to face him. "Thank you for looking out for me," she said huskily.

"Don't even. It was my pleasure." He lifted an arm, but by the time she realized he was only gesturing her over the threshold, she was already stepping in for a hug.

She slid her arms around his waist and pressed her forehead to his chest. A telltale cylindrical bump revealed the presence of a pen in his shirt pocket and she almost laughed out loud. Or maybe that was from the pleasure of touching him.

Not that she should be touching him. But God, it felt good. His back was warm and hard beneath her palms, his chest a tantalizing sanctuary of firm muscle over bone. He smelled like sunshine and maple syrup, and it kicked off a hunger that had nothing to do with pancakes.

For long seconds his arms hung awkwardly. Then he raised his hands to her shoulder blades. She fought the need to free one of her own hands and press it to her heart, where an actual ache had set in. Instead she lifted her head and nestled against his throat. His skin was cool from the night air, and the almost irresistible urge to taste him left her trembling. The ache had spread, traveling east and west to her nipples, which were smashed enticingly against his chest, and south to her belly. The ache was seriously considering venturing even lower, where a dangerous heat had already started to build. The attraction was one part physical, one part remedial and two parts situational.

Free. She was *free*.

Free to find herself unable to let go of him.

"Thank you," she murmured. "This feels good."

Good? This was pure bliss.

"You can say that again," he rumbled, and this time the cylindrical shape pressing against her was *not* an inanimate object.

A thrill shot through her. At the same time she shoved back a step and ran a self-conscious hand through her hair. "Pathetic, I know, but I don't remember the last time someone hugged me."

"So what you're saying is, nothing personal?"

"How can it be?" she said lightly. She hunched her shoulders under his jacket, suddenly wishing she could keep it. A flash of brass gleamed as the zipper caught the light. "We just met."

"I'm glad we did."

The conviction in his voice pushed her back another step. "I won't be in Castle Creek for long."

She reached behind her and swept a hand up the wall. Light from inside the apartment illumined the stark need on his face and she went still. An answering need surged into her chest, like the foam of a poorly poured Guinness, and she pushed the words out before she could second-guess them. "But I'll be here long enough to share a drink with you before you go back across the street. You know, to toast the end of what has been a sucky day for us both."

"That's not much of a trade." His words were all grumble, but the low-pressure kind.

"It could be," she said archly. "I mean, it depends on what's in the fridge."

He laughed out loud, then shot her a curious glance. "Wait, you don't know what's in your own fridge?"

"I just moved in today. I never had the chance to look."

"Knowing Eugenia, there's probably enough provisions in there to last a month. She likes to be prepared."

"We could check it out together," she said, not quite managing a casual tone. "Or if you need to go now, I'll make sure the next time you're here I can tell you exactly what's on offer."

He lifted an eyebrow.

"To drink," she added. She was too distracted to be embarrassed because, of course, there wouldn't be a next time. Living in an everyone-knows-your-name location like Castle Creek guaranteed it wouldn't be long before he'd heard every last detail of her sordid story. Was she so wrong to want to savor each moment before he did?

"I could definitely use something wet," he said.

It was Kerry's turn to laugh out loud. "Then follow me." She winked. "To the kitchen."

"That's as good a place as any."

With a shake of her head, Kerry led him through the living room and dining room to the kitchen, which overlooked both the side parking lot and the street. Their teasing had diffused the tension. She would offer the man a drink, share a few more laughs with him and send him on his way. Yes, being in his arms had helped ease the relentless ache of her father's rejection, but using him to temporarily forget her problems was not the way to go about rehabilitating herself.

"This is great," he said behind her. "My space seems bigger, but maybe that's because—" He stopped.

Kerry turned and leaned back against the refrigerator, the immaculate white enamel cold and unyielding against her spine. She tipped her head as he hesitated in the kitchen doorway. "Because you're lonely?"

They stared at each other across the small space. Gil's jaw had gone tight, his narrowed gaze focused on Kerry's face. Her breathing got desperate and his gaze dropped to her chest. Color invaded his cheeks and a shimmering warmth flooded her belly.

Something shifted in the sink—the spoon she'd used for coffee, maybe—and the sudden metallic clatter had the effect of a starter pistol on Gil. He was across the room in two strides and shoving his own jacket off Kerry's shoulders. His hands followed the sleeves down her arms until he reached her hips.

Meanwhile his mouth... Holy Hannah, his mouth. He used it to get acquainted with her neck, then her jaw, alternately kissing and rubbing, using the occasional scrape of teeth and touch of tongue to build a frenzy of anticipation. She wanted that mouth on hers. *Now.*

She moaned with impatience and he chuckled against her skin. But he didn't move on to her lips. His fingers, on the other hand—on *both* hands—never hesitated to get up close and personal. They roved and squeezed, roved and squeezed, from her butt to her hips to her ribs. He had her shoulder blades pinned to the refrigerator and her pelvis pressed to his.

She couldn't help swiveling against him. He hissed in a breath, yanked his glasses from his face and set them on top of the fridge.

"I need your hands on me," he gritted. He bent his knees and whipped the jacket from her wrists, then straightened and dropped his mouth to hers. *Finally.*

He kissed her deeply, earnestly, stealing her breath along with coherent thought as hot ripples of pleasure hijacked every muscle. He tasted like malt and smelled like early morning on the lake and every last one of her nerve endings writhed with need.

And warning.

The warning part she chose to ignore. The need part she embraced wholeheartedly. She dug her fingers into his back and dragged them all the way up to his neck. He gave his blessing with a groan, tightening his hold on her hips. She gripped his shoulders, reveling in the feel of solid muscle as he plundered her mouth.

When his hands slid over her ribs and cupped the sides of her breasts, she bucked against him. His grip faltered momentarily, and a sliver of common sense wormed its way between them.

She ripped her mouth away from his and took deep, gulping inhalations. She clutched his wrists. "Are we really doing this?"

He shuddered as he fought to catch his own breath. He swallowed then rested his chin on the crown of her head.

"Yes?" he answered hopefully.

Her nerves jangled with anticipation.

"But if you're having second thoughts, we should have that drink you offered and talk about it."

She laughed unsteadily. "Because alcohol will clear our heads?"

Slowly Gil pulled his arms away and moved back. "Juice, then."

She shivered and wrapped her arms around her waist. *Why* had she opened her mouth?

"I don't make a habit of this," she said.

"Neither do I. Which explains why we're feeling awkward."

"Let's revisit the drinks idea, then." She pushed away from the fridge and opened the door. A jug of tea, a half gallon of milk and five bottles of beer.

Her father's brand.

Bottles rattled as she swung the door shut again. "I don't think this is a good idea."

He ran a hand through his hair and it gave her pause. He looked younger without his glasses. Or maybe she was feeling older. Having a sense of adventure used to be so much more appealing.

A year ago she'd learned how terrifying the consequences of that could be.

Gil continued to back to the far side of the kitchen until he leaned against the counter. He curled his fingers over the edge. "Adding milk to my coffee without checking the expiration date this morning was not a good idea. Climbing a ladder with a stack of weed whacker spools in one hand and a hot cup of coffee in the other was nowhere near a good idea. This right here, with you and me…this is the best damned idea I've had in months."

"It's been a while for me, too," she said softly.

"The hug pretty much gave that away." He gave a graceless sort of one-shoulder shrug. "I'm happy to help you brush up. You know, so next time you don't embarrass yourself."

"Yes, please," she said.

He blinked and pushed upright.

This time she met him halfway. He folded her against him, swung her around and laid her carefully on the kitchen table. She begged him not to be gentle with her again, and he wasn't. Not on the table, or against the dining room wall, or even when he had her bent over the back of the living room sofa.

If she'd been looking for punishment, she hadn't found it. Never had she climaxed so hard, or so loudly. Never had she laughed so often, or given so much pleasure.

The punishment came when he finally left the bed, and she knew he wouldn't be back.

WITH A GROAN, Gil sat up and scrubbed his hands over his face. He recognized that ringtone and was tempted to ignore it. Especially since he'd managed maybe two hours of sleep the night before.

Images of *why* he hadn't managed much sleep flickered through his mind, like someone thumbing through a deck of X-rated playing cards. Damn, he'd had fun. Kerry had been sweet and giving, and once they'd gotten that first furious coupling behind them, she'd relaxed, and revealed a ready, husky laugh that had charmed him, and a relentless hunger that had flattered him.

That hunger had also challenged the hell out of him. He was still exhausted. He should tell Seth to go work out by his own damned self.

But Gil could use the distraction. As much as Kerry had seemed to enjoy herself, she'd lost her smile when he'd asked for her number. Getting her to agree to an actual date seemed unlikely.

His excitement faded at the same time his cell quieted.

Knowing Seth, the quiet wouldn't last two minutes.

Gil rolled out of bed.

Kerry had reminded him more than once that she wouldn't be in town for long, but he'd charm her number out of Eugenia and call her anyway. He didn't want last night to be the end of it.

Maybe he'd try to seduce her with his glasses again, of all things. Every time he'd taken them off she'd started to squirm.

As expected, his cell resumed the chirping. He scooped up his jeans with his foot and scrabbled at the back pocket.

"Yeah?"

"Wakey, wakey, Coop. You got fifteen minutes."

"Screw that," Gil said. He hung up and headed for the kitchen. Never had he needed coffee more.

They played the same game twice more. The fourth time Gil answered the phone, Seth warned him he was down to ten minutes.

"Before you show up with breakfast?" Gil asked hopefully.

"Before I show up and haul your ass out of bed. I know where you keep the key."

"Remind me again why we're friends?"

"Just get your gear on. What do you say to Hubbard Ridge? I'll have you back in time to open the store."

Gil retrieved his coffee mug from the sink and frowned at the muck in the bottom. Time for a fresh cup, though none of his others held heat as well as the Cap'n. "Don't you have cows to milk or something?"

"Dude, you know that's crack-of-dawn shit. See you in a few."

He made it down the stairs just as Seth pulled up in Bertha, his ancient pickup. Gil stumbled around the front of the truck and buckled himself in, and with a jaw-cracking yawn slapped away Seth's attempt at a fist bump. "You should have let me sleep."

Seth grinned and put the truck in gear. "You can catch a nap later, old man."

Gil leaned back against the seat and closed his eyes. The moment he was thinking clearly again, he was going to kick Seth's ass. "Why are you doing this to me?"

"Ivy won't be around for evening chores, so she advised me to get my break in now."

"And you're spending it with me? I'm touched."

Seth scoffed. "Just sit back, smartass, and enjoy the ride. You're going to have to work a little harder during the next one."

They followed the road toward the small purple-rimmed ridge of mountains east of the lake. Gil raised his window to lessen the chilly slap of morning air, still damp and smelling of fresh mulch. They whipped past fields so thick with grass they resembled shag carpets. The fields gave way to clusters of barns and produce stands with striped awnings, and those gave way to rows and rows of wooden posts supporting thick, ropy grapevines, curved and twisted like stick figures caught mid-shimmy. On their left, farmhouses gilded by the rising sun fronted the lake, which lay placid and lazy.

The infinite blue soothed Gil and his eyelids drooped.

Seth poked him. "You need more coffee."

"I need sleep," he grumbled, and yawned. "How about we go fishing instead?"

"So you can scare all the fish with your snoring? Dream on."

"I would be, if you hadn't gotten me out of bed."

Seth signaled his lack of sympathy with a single finger.

Half an hour later, while Seth freed their bikes from the rack on the back of the truck, Gil stood at the foot of Hubbard Ridge and eyed the trail, favored for its varied terrain. Rocks, ravines, steep rises, moss-covered stretches as carnivorous as quicksand, exposed roots as thick as a man's thigh.

Eight miles to the summit. How would he manage it?

With an evil grin, Seth wheeled Gil's bike over. "Scared?"

"Skeptical."

Seth grabbed his own wheels and they walked their bikes to the mouth of the trail. Gil's stomach rolled. This climb was going to be a bitch.

They took a few minutes to fasten their helmets. As Seth pulled on his gloves, he gave Gil the side-eye.

"So, who is she?"

"Who's who?"

"C'mon, Coop. It's not a hangover that has you looking all wrung out and dazed. You either stayed up all night watching *Star Wars* or you got laid."

"Maybe I did both."

"Pretty sure those two are mutually exclusive."

"As Harris would say, don't get your dress over your head." Gil threw his leg over his bike and gripped the handlebars. "It was a one-time thing. So let's drop it, okay?"

Seth pedaled a few feet, adjusting his gears. He stopped, twisted and looked back. "But you'd like it to be more."

"Are we here to ride, or exchange heartfelt confessions?"

Seth tossed him a water bottle and a baggie crammed with homemade protein bars. "Let's see what you can do."

He did just fine, thank you very much, until he tried to bunny hop a pair of basketball-sized rocks smack dab in the middle of the trail. He might have been able to make it, too, if he'd been going any faster. Instead he ended up over the handlebars and flat on his back.

As he gasped for breath and stared up at the tops of the pine trees and the orange-yellow morning light seeping through the needles, Seth's face came into view. The jerkwad was fighting a smile.

"You okay?"

"My bike?" Gil wheezed.

"Is intact." Seth dropped to the ground beside him. "You really like this girl, don't you? How long have you known her?"

When Gil grunted, Seth pointed his water bottle at him. Water splashed across Gil's face and he sputtered.

"All right, all right." He swiped a glove over his face and sat up. "I just met her. Last night."

"Seriously?" Seth gave his beard a doubtful scratch. "What'd she do, come in for some caulk?"

Gil gave his head a disgusted shake. "I will never know what Ivy sees in you."

Seth grinned. "She likes how handy I am with caulk."

Gil gave him the finger, pushed to his feet and walked stiffly over to his bike. Thank God he hadn't damaged the thing since he couldn't afford to pay for repairs.

"Okay, I'll behave," Seth said. "Where'd you meet, Snoozy's?"

"Yeah." Gil plopped down onto the rocks he hadn't managed to clear with his bike. "He hired her to run the bar while he's on his honeymoon."

"What's she like?"

Sexy. Sweet. Smart. And a bit of a nerd herself. On the table next to the bed, he'd discovered her reading glasses on top of a copy of *The Hitchhiker's Guide to the Galaxy.*

When she did as he asked and put her readers on, she'd instantly become every man's fantasy librarian. She was all curves and swells and mock stern expression. When she'd pulled her gloriously messy hair into a makeshift bun, he'd dropped into a straight-back chair and she'd accepted his invitation without hesitation, settling onto his lap, shedding her guardedness as she'd shed her clothes.

Until he'd asked to see her again. Then it was shields up.

Fingers snapped in front of his face. "Earth to Cooper."

Gil blinked, and scowled. "I don't know what you want me to say. She's pretty. I like her. Her name's Kerry."

"Kerry," Seth repeated slowly, an odd expression on his face. "That's all you know?"

"She lives in North Carolina."

"Shit." Seth lowered himself to the rock next to Gil's. "Listen, Coop. I need to know if we're good."

"Why?"

"'Cause I'm about to break your heart."

Seth stretched out his legs and stared at a bruise on his shin. "I found out what was bugging Harris the other night. It's his daughter. She's back in town. Says she wants to make amends."

Gil snorted. "Good luck with that."

"Right? She messed him up. Bad. You remember how she did that?"

Gil frowned. "You want to tell me what this is all about?"

"Just humor me, okay?"

Gil took an impatient swig of his water. "He told us at poker one night. Said he didn't want us to hear it from anyone else that his daughter's a convicted felon."

"Right. She may look all cute and innocent on the outside, but on the inside? Nothing but bad news."

"Wait, so you've met her?"

"No. But you have."

It took a second for the penny to drop. When it did, Gil's water bottle followed suit, hitting the ground with a sloshing thud.

He shot to his feet. "Son of a bitch." Bartender Kerry was Harris's crooked daughter?

"Sorry, man." Seth stood, as well. He walked to his bike and took his time sliding his water bottle back into the holder. Giving Gil a chance to process the bad news.

"Son of a bitch," Gil repeated. A sense of betrayal sliced through him like a hot knife.

Yeah, they'd used each other. For comfort, had been the idea. But apparently, she'd had more on her agenda—like using him to get on her dad's good side.

He slapped the dirt off his ass and huffed a sour chuckle. She'd made it clear. One night only. Now he knew why. It was his own frickin' fault he hadn't been able to stop himself from hoping for more. Hell, he'd started hungering for another night in her bed way before the first one had ended.

No more. He'd just lost his appetite.

KERRY HUGGED THE velvet bolster to her chest and blinked against the heavy lure of sleep dragging at her eyelids. She should give in to it. She needed the rest. In three hours, she had to report back to the bar for a marathon eleven-to-one-a.m. shift.

But her mind refused to give in to the exhaustion pinning her body to the mattress.

The moment Gil's mouth had bumped against hers and that searing, aching need had rocketed from her lips to the soles of her feet, she'd known she would take him inside her. She'd *needed* him inside her. Not just to ease the loneliness but to feel his breath on her face, his fingertips on her skin, his hands tangled with hers.

Touch. Not something she'd take for granted, ever again.

But even as they'd yanked furiously at their clothes, guilt had slithered in. He deserved to know who she was. What she was. He had to know her father—Cooper's Hardware sat right across the street from Eugenia's dress shop, for God's sake. One-night stands were supposed to be anonymous, or at least I-barely-know-you-ous, but how long could she fly under the radar in a place like Castle Creek?

She hadn't been able to keep herself from wondering…how much would he despise her when he found out she'd kept a little something like a felony conviction to herself?

Or maybe he wouldn't care. Maybe he'd be all kinds of grateful she'd provided him with an easy out.

"Stop thinking," he'd said. Then his mouth had

closed over her nipple and she had. Until hours later when he'd been preparing to leave and asked for her number.

An electronic trill had her pushing away the bolster and rolling onto her left side. She grabbed her phone off the nightstand and squinted at the screen. Not a number she recognized.

Her stomach bobbed up and down. Could it be her father?

"Hello?" she said, and winced at the hope that made the word flutter.

"Kerry? This is Parker Macfarland. I thought you'd want to know. Eugenia's in the hospital."

CHAPTER FIVE

EUGENIA WAS EXHAUSTED. Long hours at the dress shop, moving into her new house, struggling with the sadness that still haunted her after her breakup with Harris and knowing she'd contributed to the rift with his daughter—it was all so draining. Melancholy lay heavy and stubborn on her chest, as if Joe Gallahan's twenty-pound ginger tabby had curled up for a nap. The pressure forced her to take shallow breaths.

Harris, bless his obstinate heart, had taken charge like the marine corps master sergeant he'd once been. From the moment she'd collapsed he'd snapped orders, demanded updates, and delegated ice chip and warm blanket retrieval missions. Eugenia had been beyond charmed.

The nurses, not so much.

Eugenia shifted position and winced at the tug of the IV. How she'd missed having someone look after her. Care for her. Want her. She almost missed it enough to give in to the jackass former marine.

But that wouldn't do anyone any good. Least of all Kerry.

"Eugenia." The object of her thoughts appeared at the foot of her bed, hair in a lopsided ponytail, face as colorless as the fluid trickling its way through Eugenia's IV tube. "How are you feeling?"

"Better than you look, I must say." She soothed the sting of her words with a smile, and held out her hand. "Did something happen?"

"Yes, something happened. You ended up in here." Kerry came around the bed and squeezed her hand, then perched on the edge of the padded guest chair. "Parker called. I wanted to come see you before my shift at the bar."

"You didn't have to, but I'm glad you did."

Kerry eyed the flowers on the table by the bed. A basket of plump lavender hydrangeas squatted beside a clear glass vase of pink and white tulips. "How very lovely. I should have brought you something."

"Yes, you should. I could use one of your margaritas right about now. Though I guess a Bloody Mary would be more appropriate, considering I just finished breakfast." When Kerry smiled, Eugenia relaxed back against her pillows. "Sutton brought the hydrangeas in."

"Sutton?"

"A very nice man I've been dating."

"Oh." The word was one long, drawn-out sigh of disappointment.

Eugenia could relate. She'd felt the exact same way the first time she and Sutton had kissed.

"The tulips came from Parker. She specializes in geraniums, but she's trying to branch out." Eugenia folded her hands on her stomach. "She told me how Liz acted at the bar last night."

"Liz used to work for Snoozy. She was just being protective."

"Well, don't let her discourage you. I need you to stay here in Castle Creek. How else am I going to get you and that pigheaded father of yours back together?"

Kerry shot Eugenia a pointed glance. "You first," she said.

"Don't you go getting any ideas, Kerry Mae. What's done is done."

"How did you know my middle name?"

"Sweetie. Not everything your father says about you is disapproving."

"Just most of it?" Kerry glanced again at the hydrangeas and her mouth drooped. "It's my fault you're in here, isn't it?"

"Oh, for Pete's sake. Of course not." Eugenia made a face. "I had what turned out to be a hot flash. The first of many, I suppose."

Kerry pressed a hand to her chest. "You didn't have a heart attack?"

Eugenia shook her head. "Not even a little. Too much coffee on top of my crazy hormone levels put my poor heart into overdrive. And of course

I panicked, which only made things worse. I'm scheduled for another EKG, but I'm sure they'll send me home this afternoon." She reached out, smiling when Kerry squeezed her hand. "Rest assured that none of this is on you."

"That's a bunch of baloney and you know it." Harris stood in the doorway, jaw set, head thrust so far forward, Eugenia feared he might topple over.

Then again, a solid whack on the head might do him some good.

"Shut up, old man," she said. "This is no one's fault but my own."

Abruptly, Kerry got to her feet and moved away from the bed. "I'll get out of your way. If it's all right, I'll call and check on you later."

"Of course it's all right. And you are not in the way."

"Speak for yourself," Harris grumbled.

"That's enough." Eugenia slapped her IV-free hand down on her bed. The blanket muffled the sound, so she snatched up the plastic water pitcher and banged that on the bedside table instead. "What are you, five years old? Wise up. You're a full-grown military man. Start acting like one."

"This military man is goin' AWOL."

Harris swung toward the door then hesitated. "I'm really just goin' for a cookie," he said to the hallway. "I will be back." He stomped out of the room.

Blessed silence descended.

Kerry's overbright gaze rested on Eugenia. "I'm so glad you're okay. I can't thank you enough for all you've done, but I need to leave Castle Creek. My dad refused to talk to me before you ended up here, and now that he blames me…" She tried and failed a smile. "This just isn't going to work."

"He doesn't blame you, kiddo. He blames himself."

"That's not what he said."

"Of course not. He's angry. He lost your mother, he lost you, and he thought he was about to lose me."

"He did lose you. Thanks to me."

"He knows better, even if you don't."

"My mom and me, he didn't lose. He pushed us away."

"I don't know about your mother, but with you there was pushing on both sides." With a weary flap of her hand, Eugenia settled back into a recline. "Give it a couple of days. Your dad needs a chance to calm down. I can't help feeling you'll regret it if you give up now."

"By the way," she continued, "I suspect you'd probably like to make some more money, since Snoozy isn't paying you anything near what you're worth. I have a suggestion. Cooper's Hardware."

"A-as in, Gil Cooper?"

Eugenia busied herself smoothing the wrinkles out of her blanket. Those last two words had been pitched so high, it was a wonder dogs weren't storming her hospital room. "Does that mean you've met him?"

"I… Yes. I served him a beer last night. And later he had to let me into the apartment." She winced. "I borrowed Allison Gallahan's sweater and put my key in the pocket, then ended up leaving both at the bar. But don't worry. I know right where the key is. I'll get it back today. I'll get them both back. Here I am trying to convince everyone I've gone straight and already I've stolen a sweater."

Eugenia frowned. That wasn't funny.

Kerry dropped her chin and fiddled with her ponytail. "Anyway, I don't think taking on a second job is a good idea. Not right now. I need to stay available for Snoozy. I gave my word I'd help him any way I could."

"But you're only managing the bar until he gets back from his honeymoon. If you already have something else lined up, at least you won't be completely out of work. Besides, Harris thinks a lot of Gil. He's one of his poker buddies."

Kerry blanched. "Buddies?"

"Impress Gil and that will go a long way toward convincing Harris he needs to keep an open mind."

Kerry tried to smile, but the result was more of a spasm.

Oh, Lord. Eugenia gave herself a mental slap

upside the head. She should have realized. Chances were Gil already knew Kerry's story. Then again, from what Parker had said about Kerry and Gil hitting it off at the bar, it sounded like he didn't know yet that Kerry the bartender and Kerry the daughter of Harris were one and the same.

"Think about it," Eugenia said.

Kerry mumbled something and Eugenia sighed. How was Kerry supposed to fall in love with Castle Creek if she spent all her time in a dark and dingy bar?

She closed her eyes the moment Kerry left. What seemed like almost immediately after that, an annoying sound startled her awake. Was that... crunching? She opened her eyes to see Harris staring at her from the foot of her bed, a half-eaten cookie in one hand and a waxed bag in the other.

He tossed the bag into her lap. "I heard Sutton Vincent was in to see you."

"He's handsome and charming, and he's a wonderful cook."

Harris jammed the rest of the cookie into his mouth.

"He's not grouchy, he doesn't lecture me about money when I buy him a gift, and he doesn't tease me about my baking."

"Catch of a lifetime. Good for you."

"Actually, he's boring as hell." She opened the bag and peered inside. "But he pays attention to me, so I'm not sure I want to throw him back."

Harris swiped at the crumbs on his mouth. "I called 911 like you asked me to last night. Dumped the ice out of that pitcher there 'cause I know you don't like it, asked that lady wearin' the pink pajamas to change your breakfast sausage to bacon, and left you here alone with my daughter like you wanted even though she has nowhere near earned the privilege of spendin' time with you. Now if that's not payin' attention, I don't what the hell is."

"The privilege of spendin' time with you." Why couldn't he have said things like that when they were a couple? And when he wasn't in the middle of a rant?

He watched her closely, his massive chest heaving, and her fingers itched to glide over the sexy, springy hairs she knew were hidden beneath his customary plaid flannel shirt. Lest her own chest start to heave, she dropped her gaze and with her index finger traced the logo on the bakery bag.

"Sutton pays attention every day," she said. "Not just in a medical emergency. And they're not pajamas, they're scrubs."

"You know he's only after your money, right?"

"In the first place, Harris Briggs, screw you for thinking no one but you could be interested in me romantically. I'm kind, I'm a decent conversationalist, and I have a snappy sense of humor. My body may be on the downhill slide to sixty, but it can still wrap around a hot, hunky male, thank you very much."

He snorted, and she was gratified to hear the sound carried as much uneasiness as disgust. "Now, don't go greasin' both sides of your bread."

"What is that supposed to mean?" When he didn't answer, she tossed back her hair. Since she wore her hair short the toss probably looked more like a seizure, but whatever. "You're right, Sutton is after my money, but only so he can invest it. He wants me to be able to afford nice things, like that trip to Austria you kept promising you'd consider."

"Why do you want to go to Austria? What's wrong with stayin' on this continent? You ever even been to Colorado? Or Wyoming, or Montana? Accordin' to Audrey Tweedy, the prime rib is lovely this time of year."

Eugenia sighed. She was tired of arguing. More important, she couldn't think of a clever comeback.

Harris pulled a stick of gum from his shirt pocket and took his time unwrapping it. "I hope you're not thinkin' of sharing any investment dividends with my daughter."

Eugenia shot upright. "You don't get to bully me anymore, Harris Briggs. Especially about Kerry."

His eyebrows rushed at each other like lovesick caterpillars. "So you're settin' conditions now? I make nice with her and I can get back into your bed?"

A fortysomething nurse with a scowl as dark as the jet-black, close-cropped hair on her head marched into the room. She wagged a finger at them.

"We can hear you two all the way down at the nurse's station." She turned her scowl on Harris. "Keep it down or keep out."

"We're sorry, Nadine," Eugenia said meekly. An aide had already given Eugenia the heads-up—patients who stayed on the head nurse's good side got ice cream between meals. Lord knew Eugenia had earned it.

Nadine clicked her tongue. "I wasn't talking to you, sweet baby."

"I'm leavin'," Harris said, his voice as rough as tree bark. When Nadine didn't move, he lifted a wheedling eyebrow. "One minute to say good-bye?"

"As long as you say it and don't yell it." With another click of her tongue, she left the room.

Harris rubbed a palm over his head. "I never meant to bully you, Genie."

"I think you did. And you didn't like that I pushed back."

"It's a self-defense mechanism."

"It's a deal-breaker."

Red rushed his cheeks. "I'm glad you're okay, Eugenia Blue. You rest up." He turned, stopped and jabbed his chin at Sutton's hydrangeas. "Nice flowers," he muttered, and disappeared behind the curtain.

Eugenia watched him go, pressure building behind her eyes. "I prefer cookies," she whispered to the empty room. She dug into the bag, pulled out a snickerdoodle and slotted it into her mouth like a DVD into a player.

FOR THE LAST few hours of her second shift at Snoozy's, Kerry dreamed of a hot shower and cool sheets. By the time she was headed home her feet throbbed, her back ached, and she was desperate for something to eat that didn't involve grease.

She forgot all of that when she pushed out of her car and spotted Gil leaning against the outside stairs.

Her pulse thickened and her head spun, as if she'd tossed back one too many tequila shots. Her fingers tightened around her key ring, which now sported the recovered key to Eugenia's apartment. She shifted the strap of her shoulder bag, pulled in a breath that made her lungs protest and started across the parking lot.

It had rained earlier. Her footsteps were damp, splattering smacks on the pavement. Moonlight mingled with the glow of the security lights, puddling and shifting on the damp black ironwork of the staircase. But she didn't need daylight to detect Gil's anger.

His arms were crossed, his face as rigid as the metal at his back. Her fantasies of an encore of last night died a fast and furious death.

She blinked vainly against the moist ache of regret and stuffed her hands into the pockets of her light wool jacket. First chance she got, she was making a break for the door. She didn't care how ridiculous she looked scrambling up the stairs— she'd look a lot worse crying her heart out in the parking lot.

"I'm guessing this is about more than asking for your key back," she said. She'd tried for blithe but managed miserable instead.

"Last night," he said tightly. "That was about your father, wasn't it?"

"Excuse me?"

"I heard you came to Castle Creek to patch things up with your father. But he doesn't want you here, does he? When we met at the bar you said you were staying at the motel because your family didn't have room for you. That was a lie."

Somehow Kerry managed not to flinch. She raised her chin. "You're right. He doesn't want me here. I plan to change his mind, but that doesn't have anything to do with last night."

"Yeah, it does, because now you two have something in common. Me."

It took a moment for the penny to drop. Then her jaw followed suit. "You think I pretended I didn't have my key so you'd have to let me in? How on earth was I supposed to know you had a spare?"

"Don't even," he bit out. "You didn't have to know. I own a hardware store. Of course I can open a damned lock."

"It was almost midnight. I wouldn't have knocked on your door at midnight. And anyway, I couldn't know for sure you even knew my dad."

"But you thought about it."

That she couldn't deny. "Last night was not about my father," she said through gritted teeth.

"Maybe not. But it wasn't about me, either, was it? You just needed to get laid."

"Apparently you did, too." Kerry grimaced. Since Gil was one of her father's buds, his resentment made perfect sense. Unlike this cold, sharp loss she felt, as if ice cubes were stacked in her stomach. "None of this matters," she said tersely. "I don't care what you think of me. We were never going to see each other again, anyway."

"Except at the grocery store or the bank or the frickin' diner."

"You know what? I lied. I do care what you think about me. I do care that people look at me like I'm a host for some deadly, disfiguring plague. And yes, I realize that's my own fault."

"Good for you. Listen. I came to tell you

your little plan is a bust. I will not defend you to your father."

"Do you plan to tell him you had sex with me?"

"Son of a bitch," he whispered. "So that's what this is. A shakedown." The sound that scraped from his throat was probably supposed to be a laugh. "I'm seriously considering canceling my satellite TV so I can afford insurance for my pickup and you want to blackmail me? You'll be lucky to get enough to buy a cup of coffee."

Hurt swelled her throat and she could barely squeeze out a response. "I have no intention of telling my father anything. Go home, Gil Cooper. I don't know you and you don't know me. It's better if we leave it that way."

He hesitated, then with a curt nod swung away. She couldn't watch him go. Instead she kept her eyes down as she trudged up the stairs, marveling at how just a few minutes ago she'd intended to run them. Now if it weren't for the banister and the siren call of hot water and ice cream, she'd still be frozen at the bottom.

She stepped onto the landing, reached into her pocket and froze. *Damn* it.

She still had his key.

GIL'S BRAIN HAD refused to shut off, so it was no wonder he hadn't managed much sleep. He'd rolled out of bed before sunrise, descended the outside stairs at a sedate pace (because, just in case) and hit the pavement for a run.

And he hated running almost as much as he hated knowing Seth was right. He did need the exercise. He hadn't hurled, but he'd struggled like a maniac to breathe without gagging. He shouldn't have let his increasing concern for the hardware store throw him off his game. He knew better. The more stress you were under, the higher the benefit of exercise.

No more slacking. Now that Seth had finally gotten him off his ass again, he'd get back into his routine and stay there.

He paid no attention to the little voice inside that wondered slyly if it wasn't someone a hell of a lot prettier than Seth who deserved the credit.

His run blessedly over, Gil showered away the sweat. His legs trembled the entire time. He'd seriously considered hosing himself off out back so he wouldn't have to climb the stairs back up to the second floor.

Maybe instead of working out more, what he needed was an elevator.

Ten minutes later he zipped up his jeans and grabbed a shirt. Barefoot, he strode to the kitchen. The shower had felt good, but it hadn't done a thing to dispel the fog in his brain. His trouble-making neurotransmitters were playing keep-away with his nerve impulses—how the hell was he supposed to get anything done when his post-synaptic potential was being held hostage?

What he needed was coffee.

But when he pulled the shiny red bag from the freezer, he couldn't help remembering the fridge in Eugenia's apartment, and all that he and Kerry had done against it.

Damn it, she didn't look like a felon. She didn't even look capable of telling a lie. Had she really done what she'd been convicted of?

Hell. He drummed his fingers on the counter as the rich smell of his favorite brew started to kick neurotransmitter ass. He had no idea who she was or what she'd done, yet here he was, trying to find excuses for her. And based on what, an hour's conversation across a bar top? They certainly hadn't talked much in bed.

So what if she had a sweet smile with one adorable off-kilter tooth? And a killer body and a fun sense of humor?

So what if she'd gotten his Monty Python joke?

Get a grip.

So he'd had a moment with a girl in a bar, only to find out she wasn't a nice person. Nice people didn't swindle. Harris had never gone into detail about what had landed his daughter behind bars, but he'd dropped enough hints for the poker posse to know it involved other people's money.

Gil already had enough money drama in his life, thank you very much.

What the hell was Snoozy thinking, trusting her with the bar? Yeah, it was only for three weeks, but it didn't take long to build a nice bottom line skimming cash. Gil should know.

Maybe that's why the sheriff had stopped by. To make sure she knew someone would be keeping an eye on her.

Not that Gil cared one way or another. Harris trusted his daughter as much as Gil trusted his brother. 'Nuff said.

He grabbed his Cap'n Crunch mug from the sink and filled it with brew. Thank God he hadn't talked himself into giving up coffee. He'd never manage without it.

It took him a whole two sips to register that the thumping sound he thought was his kick-started heart was actually someone at the door to the hardware store.

"They know we don't open for another hour," he said idly to the Cap'n.

Bang, bang, bang.

Gil exhaled. Well, he could use a distraction. Some breakfast, too. Maybe he could shame whoever was at the door into picking him up some pancakes from the diner.

But when he got downstairs he realized he was out of luck. Audrey Tweedy stood on the other side of the glass, nose pressed to the pane. If he asked her to pick up pancakes, she'd only lecture him on the superiority of protein and bring him back a couple dozen sausage links instead.

He grabbed an apple from the bowl by the register, just to be ornery.

When Gil turned the lock, Audrey bustled into the store and tugged at the hem of her long-sleeved top, which matched the avocado halves hanging from her ears. "Mighty nice of you to open up early for me."

"No problem," he said drily.

Audrey slapped her hands on her hips and watched Gil take a bite of apple. "You and I need to talk." When her cell started blaring the theme to *Rawhide*, she plucked it out of her big green purse and held up a finger. "Hold that thought." She strode down the nearest aisle to answer her call.

Gil scrubbed a hand over his face and turned toward the staircase. Coffee. He needed his coffee. The cowbell over the door clanged again. Damn. Maybe all he needed to do to improve his bottom line was change his hours.

He turned to greet another early bird customer and froze.

The woman responsible for his lack of sleep two nights in a row walked toward him, her smile tentative. With her light blue dress and prim sweater, her hair a shiny tumble past her shoulders, she looked more like a kindergarten teacher than a bartender.

Or a thief.

CHAPTER SIX

GIL RESENTED THE hell out of Harris's daughter being in his store. And he wasn't in the mood to hide it.

He pointed with the hand that held the apple. "What are you doing here?"

She faltered over his flinty tone. "I was hoping we could talk."

"Not interested."

As he turned away, he bit into the apple. It took him a second to realize the specks he was seeing were bits of apple juice on his glasses. He tugged a cleaning cloth free of his back pocket.

Kerry appeared before him. "I made a bad decision."

"By trying to blackmail me? Yeah, you did."

"By spending the night with you. I shouldn't have put you in that position."

Briskly he cleaned his glasses. "Which position in particular? We tried so many."

She rolled her eyes. "Can we call a truce? I don't want any of this to affect Snoozy's business."

"You mean you don't want to lose your job."

"No, I don't, and can you blame me? Not only do I need the money, but Eugenia got that job for me. I can't let her down."

He slid his glasses back into place. "Maybe you should have thought of that two nights ago."

Even as her cheeks paled, she lifted her chin. "You're right. I should have."

Damn it. "Okay, that wasn't fair. I knew you were having second thoughts and I talked you out of them. Yeah, I'm pissed, but the blame's as much mine as it is yours."

Her gaze remained steady. "And you won't hold any of this against Eugenia?"

"Why should I?"

Her shoulders relaxed a bit. "Good."

"That doesn't mean I'm interested in a truce." He turned away with every intention of taking the stairs two at a time to get to his coffee.

She blocked him. "You don't believe in second chances?"

"Harris said he gave you several."

"He did." She looked down, then turned her attention to her purse and poked around at the contents. When she looked up again, her eyes were overly bright.

Nice try, lady.

She held out a familiar length of braided plastic. "I forgot to give you your key last night."

Gil accepted the key. He refused to feel bad about it. He exhaled.

Okay, so he felt bad about it.

She backed toward the door. "Just FYI, if I'm behind the bar the next time you're there, I won't make it weird for you. No garlic powder in your beer, or anything like that."

"Good to know." But he wouldn't be back. Not while there was any chance she'd be there.

She'd almost reached the door when Audrey bustled out of the fasteners aisle. Gil exhaled. Fabulous. Frickin' fabulous.

"I'm ready," Audrey announced, her half avocados swinging wildly.

"What for?" Out of the corner of his eye he noticed Kerry lingering at the door, no doubt fascinated by the older lady's taste in jewelry.

"To hear your idea." Audrey snapped her fingers in his face. "Pay attention, young Cooper. You and Seth promised you'd come up with the ultimate gift for my man."

He blanched. "We never used the word *ultimate*."

Her defeated expression shamed him. "Do you have any ideas at all? Or am I going to have to go with those roofing nails?"

"I'm sorry, Aud. I know it's no excuse, but I forgot."

Kerry approached, wearing the professional smile that had been such a turn-on for Gil two nights earlier. "I know this is none of my business," she said, "but are you talking about a bride-groom gift for Snoozy?"

Audrey perked up. "Yes. And you are?"

"Snoozy hired me to look after the bar while you two are on your honeymoon. I'm Kerry Endicott."

Gil frowned. Endicott instead of Briggs? Hadn't Harris told them she was divorced?

Does it matter, asshole?

"A pleasure to meet you. I'm Audrey Tweedy. Thank you for helping us out." Audrey thrust a Slim Jim into Kerry's hands. "I'm more of a Guinness gal myself, but Snoozy talked up your margarita so much, I'm determined to try one. Now, what were you saying about a gift idea?"

Expression dazed, Kerry tucked the Slim Jim into her purse. "I don't know Snoozy well, but he does talk about you all the time. He gets this little half smile, like he has a lovely secret."

"He does," Gil said. "He's getting ready to raise his prices."

Audrey elbowed his ribs with enough force to push him off balance. He stumbled two steps sideways into a rack of paint chips, and an entire row hit the floor with a muted slap.

"You should talk," Audrey said. "Last week your topsoil was fifty cents cheaper."

Gil righted himself, removed his glasses and pinched the bridge of his nose. "I have things to do. You two can handle this gift thing without me."

KERRY'S STOMACH WAS a churning mass of acid. She'd intended to apologize, ask for a cease-fire and make herself scarce. Now she'd managed to insert herself in Gil's personal business and he'd resent her even more.

It was official. His interest in her had crumbled under the weight of her mistakes.

"You stay right where you are," Audrey said to Gil. "We might need your input." Her school-teacher scowl relaxed as she turned back to Kerry. "Let's get back on track. Tell us your idea, dear."

Kerry inhaled. "It's a little unorthodox," she began.

Eyes trained on the fruits the size of golf balls hanging from Audrey's ears, Gil snorted. The old woman jabbed him again and the next sound he made was more of a wheeze.

Kerry barely resisted the urge to offer Audrey a high five. "Snoozy doesn't strike me as the kind of man who'd be happy with the standard engraved watch, or a power tool he already owns, or even a personalized bobblehead."

Gil perked up. "Might want to rethink the bob-blehead."

Kerry ignored him. "So I got to wonder-ing about what he values most. Next to you, of course."

"The bar." Audrey nodded faster but her gelled hair stayed in firm, spiky place. "Which is why I was considering getting him new stools. With leather seats." When Kerry hesitated, she plucked at her lower lip. "A foosball table?"

Gil opened his mouth but Kerry stepped in front of him before he could utter the "hell, yeah" she figured was coming.

"I was thinking more along the lines of something for Mitzi," she said.

"You know my intended better than you think you do," Audrey said drily.

"The other night he was complaining about a backache. Apparently he's been carting Mitzi up and down the stairs so she can soak in the tub?"

"She does love a bubble bath."

Kerry smiled hesitantly. "What do you think about installing a tub in her pen? Then she could soak whenever she wanted to."

Audrey clapped her hands. "I love it! And my beloved could spend more time carrying *me* to the bath."

"TMI, Aud." Gil scratched the back of his shoulder. "Joe and I could manage that. We'd have to punch a few holes in the wall, run some pipe, but yeah. Totally doable."

Audrey scrunched her forehead. "Think you could do it before the wedding?"

"Uh…how about before you get back from your honeymoon?"

"That's better, anyway. Otherwise Snoozy would be watching every move you make. He's that protective of *you know who*." Audrey gave

Kerry's arm a grateful shake. "What a wonderful idea. He'll be so touched. Which means I will be, too. In fact, the next time I get lucky, young lady, I'll be thinking of you."

Kerry blinked, and glanced over at Gil. Big mistake, since the half horror, half fascination on his face almost had her laughing out loud. Until he caught her eye and shut down.

Right. Because she was *persona non grata*.

Audrey pawed through her big green purse and handed each of them a can of Vienna sausages. "Be well," she said, and bustled toward the exit. The clang of the cowbell signaled her departure. In the silence that followed, Kerry and Gil looked everywhere but at each other.

Kerry was the first to crack. "That purse, um… sure would be a handy thing to take to a picnic."

"Her purse is the picnic. Bet she even has a blanket stashed in there." With a frown, Gil retrieved his half-eaten apple from a shelf that held a colorful array of flowerpots. "Aud and her crew are known for being prepared. At least we didn't have Mayor Hazel in here handing out her special brand of treats."

"What does she hand out?"

"Never mind."

Kerry huffed a puny laugh. "Since your neck is turning as red as that fire extinguisher over there, I'm guessing it has something to do with sex or menstruation. So which is it? Condoms, or tampons?"

"Condoms," he muttered.

"Wait. Mayor Hazel. I have heard of her. Snoozy mentioned she volunteered to run the bar for him."

"If he'd taken her up on it, the place would be a strip joint by now."

"That's basically what Eugenia said."

Another awkward silence descended.

Kerry stuffed the can of sausages in her purse.

The cowbell jangled. Holy Hannah, how could Gil put up with that racket all day? Two older women entered the store, one with a phone to her ear, the other wearing a dust-covered sweatshirt and protective goggles around her neck, as if she'd stopped mid-DIY.

"Damn it," Gil muttered. "Why does everyone have to touch the glass?"

"Hinges?" the woman with goggles asked.

"Yes, ma'am." Gil pointed. "Aisle two."

Phone Lady gawked at Kerry. She lowered her cell and leaned to her right to whisper to her friend, realized she'd already disappeared and scurried after her.

Kerry gave Gil a nod. "I'll let you take care of your customers."

As he bent to pick up the paint strips he'd knocked to the floor, Kerry made her slow way back to the entrance, suddenly nostalgic for the old-fashioned vibe and the metal and sawdust smell of the store.

And yes, idiot that she was, for its sexy-turned-hostile owner, too.

The sense of loss for the brief closeness they'd shared was ridiculous in its intensity, and almost as strong as the stinging ache in her chest that represented all she couldn't share with her father.

She was unfolding her sunglasses before pushing through the glass door when a female voice said her name. She turned, but spotted no one other than Gil as he restored order to his paint sample rack. Since he had his back to her, she indulged in a good old-fashioned ogle, feeling the stuttered rush of her pulse as she eyed the tempting spread of his shoulders and the muscled curve of his butt.

Her palms itched.

He's not for you, chickie. He deserved better than a needy woman with daddy issues.

As she lifted her shades to her face, the sound of her name drifted her way again, from the far end of an aisle to her left.

"Endicott," the woman said. "He obviously didn't want her going back to the family name. Can you believe her nerve, showing up after all this time?" The cigarette rasp of her voice gave her away as the woman with the goggles around her neck.

"Well, he is her father." That must be Phone Lady. Somehow she'd recognized Kerry.

"He'd rather not be, from everything I've heard," said Goggle Lady.

Kerry's chest tightened. She didn't dare look over her shoulder to see if Gil was hearing this, too.

Go. *Go.*

But she couldn't push herself out of her horrified inertia.

She had earned every spiteful, disbelieving comment. Might as well learn what she was up against, and what her father had been forced to contend with.

"She's probably just here to hit him up for more money," Goggle Lady continued.

"We don't know that."

"We know he's sick. Surely she realizes that having to deal with her issues on top of everything else can only make matters worse."

"Maybe that's her plan." Phone Lady's tone was sly.

"What, you mean to give the man a heart attack?"

"Can't get an inheritance till someone dies."

Kerry pressed a hand to her mouth. Yes, she was an idiot and a thief. Ex-thief. The idiot part still applied. But dear God, that didn't make her a murderer.

Her throat stung with gathering tears and her

muscles quaked with the urge to set these ladies straight. But their words carried enough truth to give her pause.

And Gil would not thank her for causing a disturbance in his store.

God. What if he shared their suspicions?

He appeared at her elbow, and she jumped.

"Ladies," he called out. He ignored Kerry when she shot him a glance. "Can I help you find something?"

They came bustling to the end of the aisle, Goggle Lady in the lead. When she spotted Kerry she stopped. Phone Lady walked right into her and the resulting *oof* eased the ache in Kerry's throat.

"I think she heard you," Goggle Lady whispered.

"Me?" Phone Lady squeaked back.

"Just curious." Kerry tugged off her sunglasses. "Did either of you happen to come across any rat poison back there?" She gave them a conspiratorial wink. "Never hurts to have a plan B."

As the pair murmured to each other in shocked tones, Gil stepped in front of Kerry and gestured at the packages in Goggle Lady's hands. "Let me ring you up." In an aside to Kerry, he said, "You. Stay."

"Sure," she managed, though her instinct was to run. Why should she hang around? He was going to either read her the riot act or call the sheriff.

Or maybe both.

But there was always the off chance that he'd reconsidered the truce thing.

While Gil worked the register and his customers took turns casting Kerry wary glances, she spun a slow circle, cataloging the store's layout. Prior to her career as a database administrator, she'd worked in retail management. She might be able to make some recommendations for improving Gil's business. Assuming, of course, he could bring himself to care about anything she had to say.

The sound of the cowbell followed Goggle Lady and Phone Lady out of the store. Kerry turned to apologize to Gil at the same moment he rounded on her.

"Good for you, for wanting to make up for whatever mistakes you've made." His brown eyes were fierce behind his glasses. "Congratulations on seeing the light. That doesn't mean everyone else has to stand back and watch you make things worse while you play at undoing the damage you've already done."

Whoa. "I'm not playing at anything."

"What was that about the rat poison?"

She bit the inside of her lip. Maybe pretending to plan a murder wasn't the smartest thing she'd ever done.

"I apologize. I shouldn't have let them get to me." She straightened. "Will you be calling the sheriff?"

"What? No."

Oh. Then…yay. "I have to ask. What's wrong with trying to make amends? You make it sound as though that's worse than anything I could have done in the first place."

"What's wrong is that you get to feel good twice about what you've done. Once when you're doing it, and again when people get all misty-eyed and hug-happy because you're apologizing for it. Meanwhile the people you've wronged are forced to either forgive you or look like assholes."

"You're saying I'm entitled." When he lifted an eyebrow, her face went hot. "You don't know me."

His silence made it clear he didn't want to, either. Ridiculously, that hurt more than the entitlement thing.

"Something I said upset you, and for that I apologize. I have no idea what happened to you—"

"Apology accepted," Gil said curtly. "Now I have work to do."

Not wanting to push her luck, she made a beeline for the exit. The door was halfway open when she paused, stopping the cowbell midclang. Ignoring Gil's thunderous expression, she gestured with her sunglasses at the tower of paint cans in the center of the store.

"You might want to consider moving that whole display to the perimeter. It's hiding those shelves of gadgets, which means lost revenue because people love gadgets. Especially kitchen gadgets. They'll lure your customers farther into the store, which will increase the likelihood they'll see something they think they need. Same with customers looking for paint. Having to walk all the way to the wall means they'll get a good look at everything else you have on display. The longer you keep your customers in the store, the higher your sales. Just a thought."

She set her shades in place and set the cowbell to clanging again. Outside, she strode purposefully along the sidewalk until she was out of sight of the store windows. Releasing a shaky breath, she leaned a shoulder against a rough brick wall, unmindful of her sweater.

From the day of her arrest, she'd been planning this trip to make things right with her father. Never had she expected she'd be accused of plotting to bump him off.

With a low moan, she pushed off the wall and rushed to the corner. Five steps into the alley, her belly rejected her breakfast.

At least she'd made it outside first.

KERRY TURNED OFF her car and stared through the gathering shadows at the brick house across the street. It was a tidy one-story, with man-size lilac bushes anchoring each front corner and a covered porch in between. Lantern-style lights on either side of the door illuminated a sad-looking potted tree and a massive redwood rocking chair.

She closed her eyes. That there was only one chair on the porch struck her as incredibly lonely.

Stop that. She'd promised herself she'd be practical about this. If she approached her father in tears, he'd shut her down faster than the Liquor Control Board could shut down a bar serving alcohol to minors. Besides, maybe one chair didn't mean he was lonely. Maybe one chair meant he was…thrifty.

A trait she wished it hadn't taken her so long to embrace.

She opened her eyes again and squinted through the gloom, distracting herself by trying to identify the true color of the pansies that sprouted along both sides of the driveway. The same driveway she hadn't been able to pull into because of the vehicles crowding it.

An old Jeep, three pickups and a minivan. Her stomach rolled. She wouldn't be doing her popularity any favors by disturbing her father when he had guests.

Then again, maybe he'd find it tough to turn her down in front of an audience?

Except she really didn't want to do this in front of an audience. Especially this audience. One of the vehicles was a silver F-150 she could swear had been parked in the alley she'd puked in. Chances were good the truck belonged to Gil Cooper.

Hadn't she created enough hate and discontent there?

She reached for the ignition of the beat-up sedan she'd been driving since her late-model SUV had been repossessed. The aged car served as a constant reproof of the terrible choices she'd made, but it was also the one thing she could rely on. As the engine shuddered to life, she glanced back at the house and caught a shadow crossing in front of the large picture window that overlooked the military-precise yard.

Had her father spotted her? She bit her lip. He wouldn't call the sheriff on her, would he?

She sagged back against the seat. They were all feeling better about Eugenia, who had been released from the hospital Thursday afternoon. Kerry had given her father the entire weekend after to cool off. Meanwhile, she'd welcomed the bar's steady pace. She had only a few more days to learn what she could of Snoozy's routine before he gave her temporary custody of the bar—and Mitzi.

With a flick of her wrist, she turned the car off again. If she truly wanted to rebuild a relationship with her father, she couldn't chicken out now. And if the sheriff showed up, she'd do her best to talk herself out of a stalking charge.

She strode up the sidewalk, the steady click-clack of her boot heels drumming into her a confidence she sorely needed. *Got this. Got this. Got this.* A deep breath as she climbed the steps rewarded her with the sweet scent of lilacs, and an alien swell of hope.

When her father opened the door and a flash of gladness brightened his face, hope gave a fist pump. Even when the gladness dimmed to confusion, then disappointment, hope made the decision to hang around.

He had opened the door, after all.

"Hello, Da—umm, hello." Kerry clenched her keys tighter, as if she feared they'd make a break for it. "How are you?"

His eyes narrowed as he swiped crumbs off his shirt. The tangy odor of chili powder hanging in the air hinted the bits had probably belonged to a corn muffin. "Shouldn't you be at work?"

"It's Monday night. The bar's closed."

"What're you doin' here?"

"You're thinking I should have called first. But I figured if I did, you might tell me not to come over."

"Right." He folded his arms over his chest. "Because I already have people here. People who were invited."

"I actually came to ask you to breakfast."

As her father stared, someone called out from behind him. "Harris, man, who is it? If it's someone packing cash then for God's sake, send 'em in."

That sounded like Joe Gallahan. Of course. Poker night.

She pushed her lips into a smile. "I'd ask you to dinner, but that would have to happen at the bar and we wouldn't get much of a chance to talk."

He was shaking his head. "We've already said all we have to say."

"You've said a lot. Me, not so much."

A hoot of laughter sounded somewhere behind him. Were his friends listening in?

Harris scowled. "I have company I need to get back to."

"Take your time," someone yelled. "We haven't finished stacking the deck."

That would be a yes.

"I apologize for interrupting your game," Kerry said. "Will eight tomorrow morning work for you?"

"Cal's place will be crowded."

"Then it's a good thing we're eating at my place."

His eyebrows shot up. "You're cookin'?"

"Pancakes, home fries, sage sausage and biscuits with apple butter." All of his favorites, once upon a time.

He glanced over his shoulder, then back at her, and rubbed his palm over his head. "Why so determined to make this happen?"

"There are a few things I should tell you. Things I'd rather you not find out on your own."

From behind her father came a rattling crash and Gil's name shouted in protest. She caught her breath. So Gil was inside. Had he overheard? Was he worried she'd tell her father about their... time together?

It wasn't kind of her, but she almost wished she had the courage to do exactly that. She wouldn't, though. She had enough hostility to deal with.

"Somethin' to tell me, huh?" His jaw worked. "What, you go and get yourself arrested again?"

Her chest squeezed. The man's head was harder than marble. "If I did, I wouldn't be standing here talking about it. By the way, why didn't you tell me about your heart condition?"

"This isn't the time to be discussin' it."

"Over breakfast, then." She could be just as hardheaded.

"Harris!" someone yelled again. "Ask her in and give her some chili."

"That'll just scare her away," another voice said wryly.

Joe again. Their attempts to welcome her were touching, but saddened her at the same time. Though Gil wasn't seconding any invitations.

No surprise there.

Her father started to swing the door shut. "I have a delivery to make first thing in the mornin'."

"Maybe you could come by the bar afterward."

"I doubt Snoozy's payin' you to talk."

"Wait." She slapped a palm against the door to hold it open. "I'm staying in the apartment above

Eugenia's shop. But it's only until I can afford something on my own."

His head went back and the door went wide. But not to let her in. He stepped out onto the porch and let the door thud shut behind him.

"She's seein' someone else, did you know?" he demanded. "Some financial wizard. She and I were doin' great till you decided to pull your little scam and now she's dating a man with more manners than personality. Did you ever consider how all the trouble you got yourself into might affect other people? No, you did not. So I'll tell you. From here on out, my priority is Eugenia Blue."

Kerry switched her keys to her left hand since the fingers of her right had gone numb. "You want her back."

"Damn right I do."

"That's why you and I need to talk. If we can at least try to move past all this hostility, it would go a long way toward repairing your relationship."

"You two in on this together? She already tried settin' that condition."

Dear Lord, she wanted to pinch his head. "We're not 'in' on anything. She doesn't know I'm here."

"Good. 'Cause fixin' things with you shouldn't be a prerequisite to being with the love of my life."

Kerry drew in a sharp breath.

Her father looked stricken. "I shouldn't have said that. You know I loved your mother."

"I know you did," she said woodenly. "Just not enough." She resisted the urge to press her palm against the gash in her chest. "But I'm here to talk about Eugenia. If you would just try to honor her feelings, and show her that you're trying, she'll be much more open to the idea of a second chance."

Quite an assumption, Kerry Mae. But it was obvious Eugenia still had feelings for Harris. If he'd meet her halfway, they'd have solid odds of getting back together.

Now if he'd only meet his daughter halfway...

"No woman likes to be dismissed out of hand," she said gently.

That earned her a suspicious glance, and a gruff, "I'll think about it."

"That's all I ask."

He frowned at the little tree in dire need of re-potting. "Guess maybe I could stop by Snoozy's one night this week."

"That would be nice," she said, as calmly as she could manage, and said good-night.

But on her way back to her car, her smile broke free.

Progress. It was a beautiful thing.

AT THE SOUND of Harris's front door closing, Gil pushed his half-eaten bowl of chili aside. When Seth made a successful grab at the beer Gil nearly toppled, he shot an absent grin to his right. He'd lost his appetite.

For a moment there, he'd thought Kerry was about to come clean. He wasn't sure how Harris would react, but he'd prefer the older man's too-spicy chili to a knuckle sandwich for dinner, thank you very much.

In the corner of the dining room a decades-old TV was playing Monty Python's *Life of Brian*. Harris had lowered the sound, but Gil sat in full view of the screen, and he'd been thinking of Kerry from the moment he'd sat down. He'd told himself she'd laughed at his lame jokes because it was all part of the schmooze, but the pleasure in her eyes had seemed sincere.

Harris ambled back into the room and Gil scooped up his cards without looking down. The older man's irritation at being interrupted by the doorbell had been replaced by a somber thoughtfulness. He exhaled loudly as he resumed his seat between Noble Johnson, Castle Creek's blond giant of a librarian, and Joe Gallahan, the marketing shark turned motel owner who ran Sleep at Joe's.

"Where were we?" Harris picked up his cards and thumbed them into a fan. When no one answered he looked up and met the four expectant pairs of eyes trained on his face. His brow puckered. "I don't suppose we could just get back to the game?"

When no one said anything he exhaled a curse word, tossed down his cards and folded his arms.

Joe rested his elbows on the battered pine table. "Why didn't you invite her in?"

"You know damned well why."

Seth shot Gil a sideways glance. Gil swigged his beer, which suddenly tasted a hell of a lot like guilt.

"It's because of me, isn't it?" Noble dropped his spoon into his empty bowl. As metal clattered against ceramic, he flushed and patted his belly. "I can't help what chili does to me. That's what air freshener's for."

"You could help it by not eating the chili," Seth said, his expression deadpan. He scratched at his short beard. "If it causes you so much distress, why don't you just give it a pass? Eat a sandwich instead?"

"I do give it a pass. And when it brings tears to your eyes, I get my best shot at the pot." Noble nodded at the pile of chips in the center of the table. "It's my secret weapon."

"Tell you what." Joe slid a stack of chips across the table. "I'll pay you not to eat any more secret weapon."

"Oh, yeah." Noble leaned over the table and used both arms to pull the small stack in, as if he'd won the jackpot. "Come to papa." When he sat back down, his chair groaned under his bulk and Harris winced.

"Okay, gents," Seth drawled. "Let's figure out

where we are. Noble dealt, Harris bet five, Joe raised five, I put in ten. It's on you, Coop."

Gil shifted in his chair. Everyone grabbed their drinks and held them steady until he'd stopped moving.

After a fresh assessment of his cards he tossed them facedown on the table. "I'm out."

"Bummer." Noble added two chips to the pile, then two more. "I'm raising another ten. And a question. So, Harris. No one here has met your daughter?"

"Gil met her," Seth said. After Harris tossed in his three chips, Seth hesitated, eyeing his own stack. "Didn't you, Coop?"

Gil was going to kill him. The next time they visited Hubbard Ridge, he was going to push him over the edge. He peered over his glasses at Harris. "She waited on me at Snoozy's."

Harris smacked his cards into a stack in his hand and passed a glower around the table. "Hands off, all of you. She's smart and she's pretty, but she's also spoiled, and way too ready to go for the easy solution, whether it's legal or not. Best thing you bunch of blockheads can do is steer clear."

Gil traced the design on the back of a card. *Too damned late.*

Seth gave a sly sort of cough. Gil aimed a kick his way and his foot connected with the table leg instead. Poker chips clinked and clattered as the table rocked. Tea sloshed over the edge of Joe's glass.

Gil bit back a whimper. Son of a *bitch*, that hurt.

"What the hell?" Noble demanded.

Harris had a chip between his index and middle fingers and was tapping it on the table. "I'm not getting any younger over here."

Joe raised his hands. "I'm out. Noble's too cheap to keep raising for no reason."

"I hear that." Seth slapped his cards on the table and sat back.

Noble gave Harris the side-eye. "Call."

"Hold on." Gil leaned forward, gaze trained on Harris. "You were a little hard on her, weren't you? When she came to the door?"

"My door. My kid." Harris scowled. "What's up with you, anyway?"

Gil was feeling guilty, that's what, for talking to her like he had at the store. As boneheaded as it was, he also couldn't stop thinking about what'd he'd said at the bar, when he'd begged her to let him tell another joke.

"'Cause everyone deserves a second chance."

He shrugged. "She didn't come across as a spoiled kid at the bar. That's all I'm saying."

Harris tossed his cards onto the table. "You don't know her. She'll stay long enough to convince herself I don't need what she owes me and take off again. I'd put money on it if she'd left me any. Well, her and this joker to my right because whatever he has sure as hell beats a pair of sevens."

"Yet you kept betting." Gil didn't take his eyes off Harris. "Why?"

"Because," Seth drawled, the word dripping in *duh*, "that's how the game is played."

"No." Gil pushed at his glasses. "Because there's always the possibility that the risk will pay off. Sooner or later, the odds will turn in your favor."

Joe groaned. "We're not going to get another lecture on probability theory, are we?"

"Just saying." Gil held up his hands. "Doesn't make sense that you'd give up on your own kid. Even Snoozy's taking a chance on her."

Jesus, what was he saying? She hadn't told him who she really was because she'd known he wouldn't want anything to do with her.

He picked up his spoon and poked at the remains of his chili. Maybe she wasn't conniving after all. Maybe she was just lonely.

Or maybe she was conniving *and* lonely. He let go of his spoon and it clanged against the side of the bowl.

Harris sniffed. "Her job at Snoozy's was Genie's doing."

"How is Genie?" Noble got the full blast of Harris's former drill sergeant glare and quickly corrected himself. "Eugenia. Ms. Blue. How is she doing?"

Harris rubbed two fingers over his chin. "All right, I s'pose."

Gil exchanged a glance with Seth. Yeah, that was pretty much code for "I wouldn't know since she's not talking to me."

Seth finished a swig of beer and pointed his bottle at the old man. "You don't believe Snoozy hiring your daughter is a good idea?"

Harris eyed Noble's cards. "Think I'm looking forward to Snoozy kicking my ass when it all goes south?"

Joe got up and grabbed the platter of cookies. "Doesn't he already want to kick your ass?"

"That he does. Which is why I had to make my own chili."

"What exactly did she do?" Gil asked quietly.

Harris's mouth tightened and relaxed. "Her husband was running some kind of insurance scam. When she finally realized what he was up to, instead of turning him in, she tried to cover it up. Ended up being part of it. And that's all I'm saying about that." He turned his glower on Noble, who still had his cards pressed to his chest. "You ever plannin' to show us what you got?"

"Pass me a cookie and I'll consider it."

Harris stretched forward, snagged the platter and pulled it close. One by one he picked up the cookies and gave them a lick.

Noble made a tsk-tsk sound and fanned out his cards on the table in front of him.

Harris slapped both hands to his head. "You beat me with a pair of *nines*?"

"Look at that." Joe bumped knucks with Noble across the table. "Way to bluff."

Noble beamed. "Those aren't nines, boys, they're balls, and we all know a pair of balls beats everything."

Gil swallowed a sigh. Exactly what he would need. A pair of balls, if he had any idea of coming clean to Harris and starting things up again with Kerry.

Except that wasn't entirely his decision, was it? He doubted she'd agree to tell her old man what had happened between them. Why should she? She hadn't even wanted to give Gil her number. Which meant he'd be risking the friendship of the man who'd basically been his mentor—albeit a grumpy one—ever since Gil's own father had died. And he'd be risking it for nothing.

He glanced across the table at Harris, who was stuffing cookies in his mouth while Noble loudly counted his winnings.

When you had too much to lose, it was time to deal yourself out of the game.

KERRY WAS REALLY starting to appreciate her day off. Monday was her sleeping in day. Ten in the morning and she'd only just decided she should probably get out of bed. Eight hours of sleep? A beautiful thing.

That's where the appreciation stalled, though. Once she'd hauled herself out of bed, hit the shower and polished off her usual breakfast of oatmeal and coffee, the day stretched out in front of her like one big, long, soon-to-be-missed opportunity.

Three weeks ago she'd arrived in Castle Creek and she still hadn't made much headway with her father. He'd stopped by the bar once, but Snoozy had given him the stink-eye, so he didn't stay long. He'd made good use of that perfect excuse and hadn't come back.

Neither had Gil Cooper.

She rolled over in bed, rested her cheek on her stacked hands and gazed through the unshuttered window at the sun-limned treetops hiding the view of the lake. She'd seen Gil twice since she'd asked for a truce, but only on her way to work. Once he'd been loading cans of paint into a customer's trunk, and once he'd been sweeping the sidewalk in front of his store. Remorse had filled her each time, but she'd gotten exactly what she'd deserved.

If she'd been honest with him, maybe he'd have eventually realized she truly did mean to patch things up with her dad. Maybe he'd have given her a chance.

Now it seemed she'd be lucky if he ever acknowledged her again, let alone flashed a dimple.

With a disgusted sigh, she heaved herself out of bed and stood wavering between comforts—coffee first, or a shower? She moved toward the kitchen, where she could see the enticing blue of the lake out of the window above the sink. And if she turned ninety degrees, she could see the front of the hardware store.

Which was why the shower won out.

And also why she felt a sudden sense of purpose. She hadn't been to the lake yet. Today was the day she'd check out the beach. Maybe even take a picnic. And a book.

She pulled off her T-shirt and hurried into the bathroom.

Twenty minutes later, she reached around to fasten her bra clasp and winced as the lacy fabric of the cups rubbed across sensitive skin. She frowned. Her bras were wearing out, but she'd have to make do. No way she'd spend her precious paycheck on lingerie.

She pushed the lacy bra into the back of the drawer and selected another of her favorites, a pretty purple, velvety-soft thing. But when the fabric brushed her nipples, she winced.

Holy Hannah. She'd been having some erotic dreams about Gil, but had she actually been touching herself in her sleep? Pinching her nipples like he had, and—

She backed up, and dropped abruptly onto the bed. Pressed the heel of one hand to her forehead as she stumbled through a few calculations.

She'd missed a period. Two weeks ago.

Oh, dear God, no.

No, no, no.

CHAPTER SEVEN

KERRY LEANED FORWARD and hugged her arms around her waist. Her bra straps dropped from her shoulders and tapped her arms in a gentle rebuke. The pristine white carpet blurred at her feet and she covered her mouth with a trembling palm.

This was what they got for using borrowed protection. Gil had been about to go back to his place for condoms when Kerry had remembered what he'd said about Eugenia being the perfect hostess. They'd opened the drawer in the bedside table and sure enough, found their permission to get busy. They'd checked the expiration date, but something must have gone wrong.

Terribly, horribly wrong.

Somehow Kerry managed to stop rocking and work her way to her feet. It took her five tries to put on her jeans. Her feet kept missing the leg holes.

Two hours later, after a dazed trip to Erie for a pregnancy test—the last thing she needed was to run into one of her regulars at the local drugstore—and two back-to-back trips to the bathroom, Kerry's suspicions were confirmed.

Dreadfully, doubly, life-changingly confirmed. She was pregnant.

Though she hadn't really needed either set of twin pink lines to tell her so.

"Kerry Mae," she whispered to the blurry white blob staring back at her from the bathroom mirror. "What have you done?"

Everyone knew condoms weren't one hundred percent effective. She'd have to tell Gil.

Nausea struck. Plastic clattered against ceramic as the indicator hit the sink. She whirled around and slumped to her knees, fingers scrabbling at the toilet seat.

So much for proving she could be responsible.

So much for making her dad proud.

So much for her "truce" with Gil.

Oh, God. *What am I doing to do?*

She crossed her arms on the toilet rim and dropped her forehead to her wrists. "What a crap-fest," she whimpered to the blue-tinted water below. "How am I going to be able to afford a baby?" Or an abortion, if that was the way she decided to go?

But she already knew she wouldn't. A tiny portion of the panic was already starting to subside, and in its place flickered an enchanted, wondering warmth. She pushed up onto her knees, and pressed both palms to her belly.

A baby. She wouldn't be lonely if she had a baby.

A split second later, fresh panic chilled her insides. Even if she could afford to raise a child, how would she do it? She couldn't bring a kid with her to the bar six days of the week. And if they stayed in Castle Creek, how could they live in Eugenia's apartment? The last thing her customers would want to hear was a crying infant above their heads.

But if they left Castle Creek, they'd have no support at all. And she'd never make things right with her father. In fact, this…this could be the nail on that particular coffin.

Should she—*could* she—give the child up for adoption? Let the child grow up in a financially stable home with a mother who didn't have a criminal record?

With a whimper, Kerry pressed her hands to her face. She was getting ahead of herself. She couldn't make any of these decisions without talking to Gil first. He'd probably tell her to go to hell, but she had to at least try to do the right thing.

She got up off the bathroom floor, drank a few sips of water and padded back into the bedroom, where she burrowed under the covers, deep enough to hide from the sun.

TUESDAY MORNING, WHILE Gil restocked light bulbs, windshield washer fluid and the old-fashioned candy machine just inside the front door, he kept telling himself the reason he was feeling off-kilter had nothing to do with Kerry Endicott.

Right. And he could bench-press Audrey Tweedy's cranberry-colored late-eighties Lincoln.

He scratched his head as he headed toward the restroom for its daily once-over. No, he couldn't stop thinking about their night together, but it was more than that. Before flouncing out of the store, she'd tossed out that advice about moving the paint display, and damned if it hadn't paid off. Several people had asked when he'd started stocking "the fun stuff." Another customer had thanked him for relocating the paint because she hadn't liked the feeling of having an audience while picking out a color. She'd walked out with four gallons.

In the weeks since Kerry had made her suggestions his sales hadn't skyrocketed, but they'd certainly picked up.

When his cell rang, he stuffed the roll of paper towels under his arm and frowned at the screen. His brother again.

No. *Hell*, no.

Gil crammed the phone back in his pocket and set the paper towels aside. He strode toward the office and got down to making a fresh pot of coffee. If he didn't keep his hands busy, he might break something. On purpose.

He slapped the filter into place and peeled the lid off the red plastic container. Poured water into the machine, slammed the lid closed and pressed the power button.

He was not in the mood to spar with Ferrell again. Nor did he want to hear any more about how he was screwing up his own life. He'd spent far too much time fuming over that last conversation.

"You don't want to be there at the store any more than I like being poor."

As the hollow, gurgling trickle of coffee filled the small kitchen space, he braced his hands on the counter. His palms were so sweaty, they almost slid right off.

His heart raced as he pushed upright. Wouldn't that be something. Hit his jaw on the edge of the counter and end up knocking himself out or worse, all because he couldn't think about his brother without losing his shit.

Gil wiped his hands on his jeans and contemplated the coffee he no longer wanted. Who was he kidding? Not Seth, and not Ferrell. Himself, maybe.

Wake up and smell the coffee, asshole.

He didn't want to be here. He didn't want this responsibility. He wanted to do research, not retail. He wanted to teach. Help people think. Share the import and charisma and myriad applications of math.

The clank of the bell signaled a customer and he set his jaw. Maybe he should make an appointment with Valerie Flick after all. The thought left a bad taste in his mouth, but it also lent his heart a buoyancy he hadn't felt since…

He grimaced. He couldn't even remember. He'd felt the stirrings of it with Kerry, but that had lasted about as long as… Another grimace. It hadn't lasted much longer than he had, the first time he'd been inside her.

Way to kill the mood, Coop. He headed out to the front, already mentally comparing his assets and liabilities. The numbers imploded into a smoldering glob of nuclear waste when he saw who waited for him by the register.

Kerry Endicott.

It pissed him off royally that some small part of him was pleased to see her.

Though if she'd come to manipulate him some more, you'd never know it from her face. Her faded jeans and dark gray sweater, sleeves pushed up to her elbows, did nothing to add color to skin nearly as white as Sheetrock. Her hair was scraped back into its usual ponytail, emphasizing eyes weighted with purple shadows. Maybe that was her plan, to rouse his sympathy.

"Why are you here?" he asked bluntly.

"We need to talk."

He snickered. "That might scare me, if we meant anything at all to each other."

"Could we talk in the back, in case someone comes in?"

He frowned. She didn't sound smug or the slightest bit dastardly. Instead she sounded… worried.

Oh, shit.

"Everything okay with your dad?"

"As far as I know. He's still not talking to me."

"Eugenia?"

"This isn't about anyone else, okay? Just…us."

A sense of foreboding made his heart rate pick up. He pushed at his glasses. "Want to tell me what this is about?"

"I'm trying to."

"Fine." He led her past the small break area and into his office, leaving the door open so he could hear the bell out front. He leaned his hips against the edge of his battered metal desk and gestured to a chair in the corner.

She remained standing. She shoved at the sleeves of her sweater, and he felt a sudden burst of self-sympathy because whatever she was about to say was sure to make this day suck worse than the day he'd learned she was Harris's daughter.

"To be honest…" she started.

"That would be refreshing." When she sucked in a breath, he tugged at his ear. "That was uncalled for," he muttered. "I apologize."

She didn't rail at him. Instead she raised her chin. "I'm pregnant."

"What?" He grabbed at the edges of the desk so he wouldn't end up on the floor. *"What?"* He scanned her face, which showed nothing but sincere trepidation. He wild-eyed her stomach. "Are you sure?"

"I need to schedule a doctor's appointment, but I took two tests. I'm sure."

"Jesus," he said. *Pregnant.* He raised both arms and stacked his hands on the back of his head. Paced out to the breakroom and back. Finally he lowered his arms and met her gaze. "How do you know it's mine?"

She flinched, but when she spoke, her voice remained even. "Because you're the only man I've had sex with in well over a year. But I have no objection to a paternity test."

Her reasonableness shamed him. Then again, she'd had more time to absorb the news. This frickin' unbelievable, heart-stopping news.

He dug his fingers into his hips.

"When did you find out?"

"Last night."

Carefully he blanked all emotion from his expression. "What do you want to do about it?"

"I was hoping," she said slowly, "we could figure it out together."

"You must have some idea."

She moved then, shifting sideways to stand behind the chair in the corner. She gripped the back as if she needed help staying upright. Her knuckles paled.

"I want to keep this baby. I want to raise him or

her on my own, here in Castle Creek. I've done a lot of dumb things, but I'm smart enough to know I'll need a support system. I'm hoping you'll want to be involved. With the baby, I mean."

When he said nothing, just stared, she spoke again, in an unruffled tone that served as a stark contrast to the panic in her wide green eyes.

"You're freaked out. I get that. I am, too. I didn't take advantage of you and I'm not trying to trap you. Since it seems at least one of the condoms was defective, the only way we could have prevented this was to abstain from having sex that night." She didn't say what they both knew. They would have had sex even if the apartment had caught fire.

Hell, when they'd had sex, it had felt like the apartment was going to burn to the ground.

He rubbed a hand over his face. "You're going to keep the baby."

She nodded.

"You're going to raise the baby alone."

Another nod, a little less decisive than the first.

"Here in Castle Creek."

The motion of her head barely qualified as a nod. She must have picked up on the skepticism that was so thick in his throat, he could practically taste it.

"And how am I supposed to trust you'll really do that?" he demanded. "Your father told us something about what landed you in prison.

You're reckless and irresponsible and at the first sign of trouble, you bury your head under the covers."

She paled.

"And I'm supposed to trust you with my child?" His chest throbbed. His heart was breaking. For the baby, for Harris and for his own dreams, which he'd only just goddamn finally acknowledged. Now they had as much chance of being realized as he had of winning a throwdown with Seth.

And Kerry. If she'd truly meant to pay off her debts, she'd never manage it now.

Raise the baby alone. She had no frickin' clue.

She came out from behind the chair, shoulders rigid, eyes sparking in protest. "I would never do anything to hurt my child."

"Yeah? Look what you did to your own father."

She faltered, then snapped into perfect posture. "I'm not that person anymore."

He started to laugh, but the sound was all ugly. He ran both hands through his hair and dropped back down onto the desk. "I can't believe we're having this conversation."

She pulled at the sleeves of her sweater, hiding her hands. Or maybe warming them.

"You don't have any other family to go to? Anyone else who could lend a hand?"

"My father is all the family I have. I can't help hoping he'll come around. If he doesn't, well, then, this baby and I will create our own family. It's just… I don't ever want my child thinking she's the reason he and I never reconciled."

"She?"

A glimmer of humor softened Kerry's mouth. "I would think you'd appreciate a statistical probability. But in my head, I've been alternating pronouns."

He managed a nod. *His* head was starting to pound.

"Gil?"

"Yeah?"

"I need a job."

"You have a job."

"I won't when Snoozy gets back." Her gaze couldn't have been more earnest. "You've seen for yourself I'm a hard worker. I don't know anything about working in a hardware store, but I know about retail. And I'm a quick learner."

"You expect me to trust you with my store, too?"

Another ghost of a smile. "What's that compared to trusting me with your child?" She sobered. "I had a hard enough time getting the job at Snoozy's. It'll be even harder to find work now, once any potential employer learns I'm pregnant."

"Shit," he said tiredly.

"I'll leave you alone so you can process." She stopped at the door, and reluctantly turned back. "You deserve to know what I did to earn a felony conviction. Not even Dad knows all of it. He didn't want to. But if we're going to make this work, we have to be honest with each other."

He couldn't help a snort.

"It was selfish not to tell you who I was," she said. "I already apologized for that."

He rubbed his forehead. At least she hadn't said she'd never lied.

"My ex-husband, Trent, was a car salesman. When I realized we were living beyond our means, I didn't question it. Trent kept telling me about these big commissions he had coming, so I started borrowing money to cover the bills. I was desperate to get us back into the black. Neither of our families had been thrilled about our marriage in the first place, but I was determined to prove them wrong."

"What was really going on?"

She pushed her hair behind her ears, her fingers trembling. Gil sat, deliberately impassive, resolved not to let her manipulate him into sympathy.

"He was recruiting wealthy women to report their sports cars stolen," she said, "then shipping the cars to China, where luxury vehicles command much higher prices. The women would get the insurance money and half the proceeds from the sale. When I discovered the truth, I didn't report him. I tried to cover it up. Even worse, I used my expertise in database and online research to help locate other car owners he could pull into the scheme."

The office fell quiet, the only sound the rustle of paper as Gil shifted on the desk.

Kerry shoved her sleeves back up to her elbows. "I was convicted of receiving stolen property and conspiracy to commit fraud. Trent was furious that his sentence was so much longer than mine, but when they approached me with a deal, I didn't hesitate to take it."

"And despite all that, you expect me to trust you with a job?" He didn't wait for a response. "Would you, if you were me?"

Her chest rose and fell. "I have to get to the bar."

She left. The clank of the cowbell echoed through the vacant store.

Damn it, he was still paying for all the crap his brother had pulled. And here he was, about to invite another thief into his life.

Gil's vision blurred and his pulse grew loud and jagged. No room for air in his lungs, as if he'd breathed in a truckful of sawdust. He pushed his index finger and thumb up under his glasses and pressed them to his eyes, counted to ten before letting go.

A baby.

He pushed a half-hearted laugh through his nose. His mom would be ecstatic.

He shifted sideways and lay down on the desk,

hands behind his head. The tape dispenser bit into his shoulder blade so he shoved it, and it hit the floor with a satisfying *crack*.

How the hell was he going to pay child support, let alone wages for Kerry? And what about doctors' bills? He didn't even know if she had insurance.

Diapers, food, crib, clothes… He took off his glasses and pressed the heels of his hands to his eyes.

A baby. His lips curved on their own accord.

He wouldn't be lonely if he had a baby.

A muffled ringing from under his ass alerted him his brother was calling again. He had every intention of ignoring the summons, until Kerry's words floated back into his brain.

I don't ever want my child thinking she's the reason he and I never reconciled.

Shit. Not only was Gil going to be a dad, but Ferrell was going to be an uncle.

Would it kill him to try again? He'd let things lie for six years. Punished his brother and his mother both. Ferrell, for doing his damnedest to drive the store into the ground and his mother for not being more bitter about it. But they'd all been grieving for his father, and for their crumbling family, and Gil had played the martyr long enough.

Maybe he should follow Kerry's example and get back to working toward a reconciliation.

Provided Ferrell was off the drugs. That shit he would not have around his kid.

He jerked upright and slid to his feet, taking half the items on the desk with him. Frowning, he put his glasses back on and answered his phone.

"Guess you got my number, now, don't you, G?"

Yeah, in more ways than one. "You sound sluggish," he said. "You still using?"

"No. But that doesn't mean I'm not struggling."

"I'm sorry to hear that."

A beat of silence on his brother's end. "You almost sound like you mean it." Then the note of wonder in his voice soured. "Valerie Flick says you're not returning her calls."

Gil kicked at the papers he'd scattered on the floor. "Give it up. I'm not selling."

"I wanted to give you one more chance to reconsider."

"Or what?" When Ferrell didn't answer, Gil sighed. "What's going on with you? Why the sudden urgency?"

"Now you care. You hear what sounds like a threat, and—"

"Was it? A threat?"

"Geez, bro. You're getting uptight in your old age."

Gil stooped to pick up the stapler. When his lower back protested, he rolled his eyes at himself. "It has less to do with old age and more to do with the fact that our legacy is going under because my baby brother got hooked on drugs and started robbing the family business to fund his habit."

"Legacy? It's a goddamned hardware store."

"Did you want it to fail?" When his brother went mute, Gil exhaled. "You haven't contacted me in half a dozen years and now I've heard from you twice in one month. What kind of trouble are you in?"

"You sound like Dad. Before he bailed on us, you know?"

Yeah. He knew. Their father had bailed on them in more ways than one. Much of that had been due to his deepening depression. Every now and then Gil got a too-close-to-the-edge glimpse of what that might be like. Fifteen minutes ago, for example, when Kerry had delivered her little bombshell. But Gil had always been one to dig in his heels instead of running away.

"I can't give you any money," he said. "You OD and that's on me."

"I said I was clean. Why won't you believe me?"

"You know why." He crouched and started gathering papers. "I've heard it before."

"Maybe this time you could try and listen."

Gil did try, but by the time they put the conversation out of its misery, he was no closer to figuring out how to be a better brother.

Or how the hell he was going to make a halfway decent father.

AGAINST HER BETTER JUDGMENT, Kerry glanced up. Two more people pressed up next to the bar, necks craning, eyes riveted on her fingers as she carefully garnished the chocolate martini with a long coil of orange peel. She completed her "snake" by adding a destemmed half strawberry for a head, the wide end already decorated with a pair of googly eyes made out of icing.

Someone clapped, and despite a sleep deficit that was making her feel like she was trying to function underwater, Kerry couldn't help a grin.

She buried her sticky fingers in the towel beside the cutting board, swiped her hands down the front of her apron and pushed the drink across the bar. "There you go. One Mitzitini."

She'd lost count of how many she'd fixed that evening. Fifteen? Twenty? That was the good news. The bad news? She was in very near danger of running out of the caramel and chocolate syrups she'd piped in meandering rings around the inside of the glass to represent Mitzi's markings. They were also almost out of strawberries. And whipping cream. And chocolate liqueur.

The only thing she had plenty of was the googly eyes she'd assembled at dawn, thanks to her insomnia.

She rang up the drink and smiled her thanks at the tip the customer left in the jar. Another reason to appreciate the success of her special martini.

More tips meant a faster paydown of her debt, which meant she could start saving for the baby.

Her mind shied away from actual figures. She'd promised herself she wouldn't do any more calculations. They only depressed her.

She rotated her shoulders. "Who's next?"

"We are." A pair of ladies somewhere in their seventies trotted sideways along the bar until they stood across from Kerry. Their smiles were bright, their makeup brighter. They had matching pixie haircuts, but the taller lady's hair was snow-white, her friend's silver. The white-haired lady had paired purple eyeshadow with flamingo-pink lipstick. Baby blue served double duty on the silver-haired lady.

Purple, pink and blue. Like cotton candy. Another cocktail idea for Snoozy's new and improved menu.

*Im*proved, not *ap*proved. She was taking a chance, serving drinks he hadn't signed off on, but she couldn't bother the man on his honeymoon, could she? Besides, she was hoping to surprise him with some impressive sales numbers, on the off chance he'd ask her to stay. She was still hopeful Gil would come through with a job, but things were already tense enough between them. Working together just might push one of them over the edge. And she suspected she could make more money at the bar.

Though how far into her pregnancy she'd be

able to manage fourteen-hour shifts—on her feet—was anybody's guess.

Her stomach lurched and she gripped the edge of the sink. Pregnant. Holy Hannah. She still couldn't wrap her mind around it.

One single irresponsible night had changed her life—and Gil's life—forever. She'd come to Castle Creek to make amends and had only ended up making more trouble. She pressed a hand to her belly. *Forgive me, baby.*

Pink Lips Lady pointed at the sign Kerry had propped on the bar. "Try the Mitzitini, Snoozy's newest cocktail." "We'll take two of those," she said. "To begin with."

Kerry wanted to hug her for the distraction. "Coming right up," she said.

Her friend plucked a credit card from a zebra-striped wallet. "Make mine a virgin, please, dear heart."

Kerry was already assembling ingredients. "I like to use coconut crème and lemon-lime soda, if that's all right with you."

Blue Lips Lady bounced on her toes. "Sounds delicious."

After mixing the drinks in the shaker, she poured them into prepped martini glasses. She palmed an orange and cut thin strips of zest. She coiled the strips over each drink, to capture any escaping oil, then positioned the peel and added the half strawberry with icing eyes to finish off the garnish.

Struggling not to panic at the number of customers waiting to order mixed drinks, Kerry finished off Blue Lips Lady's mocktail with a cinnamon stick and set both glasses on the bar. "Here you are, ladies. Virgin gets the cinnamon."

"Thank you, hon." Pink Lips Lady took a dainty sip and beamed her approval. "Welcome to Castle Creek. We're the Catlett sisters."

"Thank you. I thought you two might be related." She smiled politely against a wince as the customer behind them sighed loudly. Then the penny dropped. "Oh. You're the co-mayors."

"Mayor Hazel at your service." Pink Lips Lady raised her glass. "I had big plans for this place, you know."

"But it's a lot cheaper to come up with a clever new cocktail than it is to install a stripper pole." With a double wink, Blue Lips Lady accepted her credit card back from Kerry. "I'm June. So nice to meet you, dear heart. Your table decorations are adorable. Listen, we're having a fund-raiser for the community center next month. You'll lend us your artistry, won't you? Wonderful. We'll be in touch." To her sister she said, "Now let's get out of the way of these poor thirsty people."

More clapping. The Catletts took it well, managing a pair of elegant, good-natured curtsies despite balancing drinks and oversize handbags as they made their way to a table.

Wide-eyed, Kerry watched them go. Apparently she'd just been recruited for a decorating committee.

With a bemused smile, she turned her attention to the next person in line.

Kerry couldn't pour drinks fast enough, which meant Ruthie was stuck taking orders as well as cooking them up. The poor woman pushed in and out of the swinging doors to the kitchen so often and so fast, they had no need of the overhead fans Ruthie kept the air circulating all on her own. She did manage to take a break every now and then, to linger at the pool table and flirt with her boyfriend. Burke Yancey was a tall, lean man with shaggy, near-black hair who liked his beer.

A little too much. Kerry frowned. Probably time to cut him off. He was starting to list to the side.

A while later, as she guzzled a quick glass of water, she spotted Dylan just inside the door, wearing jeans, a too-big sweatshirt, and his faded yellow high-tops. He dropped his backpack and scratched his head as he surveyed the mostly female crowd. None of whom had shown any interest in the real Mitzi, which warmed Kerry's chest with a sweet swell of sisterhood.

Though Snoozy's pet did deserve credit for inspiring the bar's first specialty cocktail.

Kerry stopped pulling a draft long enough to give Dylan a wave. He caught her eye, frowned and kept both hands in his pockets.

Uh-oh. Bad day at school?

Ruthie burst out of the kitchen, face flushed, frilly blue apron hanging off one shoulder, the bun holding her bright red hair off her face askew. The moment she saw Dylan, she clutched his skinny arm and hauled him into the kitchen.

Kerry sighed. So much for recruiting the kid to help prep garnishes.

For the next twenty minutes, she served drinks nonstop. Snoozy's male regulars had made themselves scarce, which made her wonder how long it would take them to start lobbying for a Men's Night.

Dylan pushed through the kitchen doors, slid onto the nearest stool and thumped his elbows onto the bar. He'd pulled his red hair back into a short ponytail at his neck and his freckles shone with sweat. In case Kerry hadn't managed to divine his mood, he heaved a lung-unloading sigh.

She scooted the tub of dirty glasses down to the end of the bar, closer to the kitchen. "What's wrong?"

"Nothing."

His response shocked her. Not.

"Ruthie talk you into washing dishes?"

"I don't mind." He shot her a crafty glance. "She said you'd pay extra."

She nodded. Thank goodness for tips. "Is it school? Having trouble with one of your classes?"

"No. Well, yes, but…no."

"Would you like me to make you a drink and we can talk about it? Bartenders are great listeners."

"What kind of drink?"

"How about a cran-dandy cooler? That's basically ginger ale mixed with four fruit juices."

"Whatever," he muttered.

"I'm going to take this to the back and let Ruthie have some dinner. Then I'll be out to fix your drink. Don't go anywhere."

Five minutes later, she presented Dylan his mocktail. He took a cautious sip and nodded. "Thanks."

"My pleasure."

Without another word, he pushed his glass to the side, leaned over and grabbed his backpack. While Kerry poured a pitcher of beer for two of the handful of men who'd braved Ladies' Night, Dylan set out a textbook, a notebook, a pencil, an eraser and his cell phone. She finished the sale, replenished her garnish tray and refilled her ice bin, all while watching Dylan grimace and write and erase and grimace some more.

She cleared away his empty glass. "How you doing?"

"It's too noisy in here."

Kerry scanned the room. The crowd had thinned, which explained why the music seemed louder. A pop country beat kept the energy high as customers emptied their glasses and plates. Several women and a few men surrounded the pool table, doing more trash-talking than playing. Another group watched a reality show on the television that usually broadcasted national sports. Surprisingly, the men weren't complaining.

She stuck her head into the kitchen to request an order of fries for her and a sandwich for Dylan. Ruthie lifted a spatula in acknowledgment but never lifted her head.

Kerry rubbed her eyebrow. She'd have to find a way to get into Ruthie's good graces. Kicking her boyfriend out of the bar was probably not the best way to go about it, so hopefully it wouldn't come to that.

"We need to talk."

The deep, familiar voice shot starch into her muscles. Her breathing roughened as she turned her back to the swinging doors. Dylan must have heard the word she muttered under her breath because his eyes went wide.

CHAPTER EIGHT

Eyeing a grim-faced Gil, Kerry snatched up a towel and started wiping her hands, just to give them something to do. It had to be a good thing, didn't it, that he'd shown up at the bar, and before closing time? He wouldn't chew her out in public. Gil was too reserved to do something like that, and anyway, he wouldn't do anything to hurt Snoozy's sales.

As he nodded a greeting at Dylan, Kerry studied him. He didn't look like he was out for blood. He did look good. With his hunter-green Henley, clean-shaven jaw and careless hair, he looked very good. He also looked like he hadn't gotten any more sleep than she had.

She moved behind the bar, grateful for the physical and professional barrier. She kept going, all the way down to the cash register, where they'd be out of earshot of Dylan. After pulling a draft, she set it on the bar, then snatched up her towel/security blanket again.

Gil tapped the mug. "What's this for?"

"A bribe. Maybe you could reconsider that truce."

She stretched across the counter and plucked

a ten out of her tip jar. "Don't worry. I'm paying for it."

"I came to apologize. This isn't your fault, but I acted like it was."

She froze. "That's generous, but untrue. If I'd told you who I was, we'd never have slept together."

"But we did, and that decision was as much mine as yours." He watched her ring up his beer and deposit the change back in the tip jar. "If we're going to make this work, we have to come together." The tips of his ears reddened. "*Work* together. But here's the thing."

Her head shot up. "Are you involved with someone?"

"No," he said indignantly.

She had no right to the warm rush of relief that eased the cramping in her chest. "See how easy it is to jump to conclusions?"

He ignored that. "Your dad is a good friend of mine. He doesn't trust you. He does trust me. You start working at my store and he won't trust either one of us."

"After he finds out why you hired me, distrust will be the last thing we'll need to worry about."

When Gil adjusted his glasses, she hid a smile. Surely he knew her father's bark was worse than his bite?

"We should tell him together," he said. "It shouldn't be all on you."

Oh. He'd been worried for *her*. Her ponytail felt suddenly too tight, and she reached back to adjust it. "Does this mean you're offering me a job, after all?"

He glanced around. The bar had begun to empty. "We can iron out the details later," he said finally. "Thing is, I can't afford an employee. Especially now, with…extra expenses." He glanced at her stomach. "But those suggestions you gave me about rearranging my displays did make a difference over the last few weeks. And what you're doing here seems to be working. Help me out a few hours a day, provide some more retail advice and the profits should cover your wages, maybe leave us with some extra." He wrapped his hand around his mug, though he had yet to take a sip. "Maybe we could start a fund. You know. For college."

Her breath caught. "That's a lovely thought. Count me in. But I can work more than two hours a day."

"I don't see how, when you're putting in so many hours here. At some point your health and the health of the baby will mean more to you than earning a few dollars toward your debt."

She couldn't look away as he lifted the beer to his mouth. The onset of a full-body flush had her scooting closer to the ice well. "We don't know much about each other," she said, "but I can already tell your love of logic is going to bug the hell out of me."

She grabbed a rag and a spray bottle full of vinegar-and-water solution. Turned away and busied herself cleaning the mirror at the back of the bar.

One minute he's doubting he's the baby's father and the next he's talking college fund. This was all so hard to take in, and she didn't even *feel* pregnant.

When Gil lowered his mug, she caught his eye in the mirror. "I should tell you that when Snoozy gets back, I plan to ask him to consider keeping me on. I know more about tending bar than selling power tools, and the tips are decent."

"Makes sense," he said. "But keep in mind that working at the hardware store means automatic day care."

Carefully she set the spray bottle down before turning to face him. "You mean you?"

"Whichever one of us isn't waiting on a customer. Surely I can figure out how to change a diaper." He cleared his throat. "I would appreciate your help getting my store back into the black. But that help has to be the legal kind."

Kerry's chest actually throbbed from the impact of his words. "I understand," she managed.

"And no more snark about rat poison."

She nodded once. "Thank you, by the way."

"For believing you?" His lips tightened. "I do want that blood test."

"Understood. But no, I meant for not trying to talk me out of keeping the baby."

He opened his mouth, closed it, picked up his beer for another healthy swig.

Kerry turned back to the mirror and barely resisted sticking out her tongue at her own reflection.

She was pathetic. She and her lovesick-teen reaction to his killer smile and kind face, those black-rimmed glasses that gave him a naughty professor vibe any woman would find irresistible.

Damn it.

Here she was, so far in the hole she'd practically tunneled all the way through to the Indian Ocean, with an unexpected pregnancy, a father who wanted nothing to do with her and a temporary job that would barely cover the needs of a newborn, let alone thousands of dollars of debt.

Yet she couldn't stop having sex dreams about a man who considered her as appealing as a case of typhoid fever.

With a vicious squirt of cleaner, she blurred his reflection and moved on to the next section without rubbing the spray away. Behind her Gil guzzled the remainder of his beer.

The sound of paper ripping brought their heads around. Dylan balled up a scrap from his notebook and threw it behind the bar. Kerry picked it up and tossed it into the trash.

"I'm fine," Dylan snapped before she could ask.

He snatched up his pencil again, and she held up her hands to show him she'd keep her distance.

Ruthie popped out of the kitchen. She set a plate mounded with fries and what looked like a turkey sandwich in front of Dylan, produced a bottle of ketchup and plunked it down beside his plate.

"I know you're being run ragged tonight," Kerry said to Ruthie. "Thanks for hanging in there."

"I can't quit." Ruthie shoved a hank of hair behind her ear. "Not until the pool game's over, anyway. I bet twenty dollars on Burke."

Kerry flinched. "Please tell me you're joking."

Someone called Ruthie's name and she scurried away without responding.

Crap. If Burke wasn't leaning over the pool table, he was loitering outside the kitchen doors, waiting for Ruthie and the occasional plate of leftovers. Maybe Kerry needed to start providing the couple with a better caliber of leftovers because if Ruthie quit Snoozy's, no one in Castle Creek would ever talk to Kerry again.

She tipped her head at Gil. "Are we done? I need to start cleaning if I'm going to send Ruthie home early tonight."

"And close up yourself?"

"You do it six nights out of seven."

WHEN SHE PURSED her lips at him, Gil's head went light and he pressed his ribs against the bar to steady himself. Maybe it was the word *nights*, or maybe it was the phrase *"do it,"* but something had him suddenly desperate for another handful of Kerry Endicott. He didn't even care what he ended up palming. Her neck, her shoulders, her ass—okay, maybe he did care, because her breasts were frickin' amazing—but the urge to touch her was so strong, his arms started to shake.

This despite the scowl twisting her features.

You are unbelievable. She'd cheated so many people, including her own father, and Gil found that a turn-on? What was wrong with him?

Yeah, she'd paid the price. That didn't mean she was suddenly an honest person.

And she was pregnant. With his child. Except…he couldn't make her any more pregnant, could he?

Unless she wasn't.

"Did you make a doctor's appointment?"

She glanced around before answering. "Eight o'clock Thursday morning. You're welcome to come, if you'd like to hear the results for yourself. The doctor could administer the paternity test while you're there."

"Wouldn't that be awkward?"

"Not as awkward as you trying to decide if I'm making it all up."

"I hate this stuff!" Dylan slammed his textbook closed and jabbed once at the cover with his mechanical pencil. *Snap.* The tip broke. He stared down at the pencil, suddenly aware of people watching, his freckles drowning in a sea of red.

Gil felt for the kid. Being the center of attention because you did something right was bad enough. Being the center of attention because you acted like a jerk was a full-on nightmare.

He tipped his head in Dylan's direction. "What's he working on?"

"Math," she said, and her face cleared. "Do you think you could help?"

He said yes only for Dylan's sake.

Two minutes later, Gil slid onto the stool next to Dylan and handed him a tall glass.

Dylan peered doubtfully down at the contents. "What is this?"

"Iced tea and lemonade. It's called an Arnold Palmer, after the golfer."

Dylan shrugged, then sipped. "Not bad." He cut a glance Kerry's way. "That was kind of a girly drink she gave me before."

Gil hid a smile. "She tells me you're Mitzi's wrangler."

"Nah. I just keep her cage clean and stuff."

"That's pretty brave. I know a lot of guys who wouldn't take money to step foot in that pen. Me included."

Dylan's thin chest swelled. "It's not that big a deal. And there's always someone around to help if she ever did decide to attack."

Gil didn't have to fake a shudder. While Dylan

fought a grin—though he didn't put up much of a fight—Gil tapped his notebook. "So, what're you wrangling with here?"

The grin evaporated. "Quadratic equations."

"Cool."

"These problems aren't cool. They're impossible."

"Maybe think of them as challenging instead. And what's life without a challenge?" Gil couldn't help glancing at Kerry, who was pouring Crown Royal into a cocktail shaker. He winced. Whatever else she planned to mix in there, it was a waste of good whiskey.

"I don't need a challenge," Dylan grumbled. "I need a passing grade."

Gil's fingers tingled at the prospect of putting pencil to paper. "Maybe I can help."

"Why would you do that?"

"I like math." When Dylan scoffed, Gil bristled. "You know what math is, right?"

"What?"

"The only subject that counts." When Dylan made a puking sound, Gil chuckled. "Seriously, though. Chicks dig guys who do math."

"Get real."

"Let me put it this way. Guys who do math become things like game designers and robotics engineers and fighter pilots. Jobs like that pay pretty damned well, which means the guys who do them can afford things like nice apartments and fast cars. Make sense?"

Dylan returned Gil's knuckle bump. "Totally."

"So we're going to knock this out?"

Dylan nodded once and pulled his notebook close again. What seemed like only minutes later but was probably closer to an hour, the teen put down his pencil and sat back. "I need another drink."

"So do I." Gil stretched and glanced around. In the hour or so they'd been at it, maybe half the patrons had cleared out. He had his own stuff to get home to, but no way was he leaving this kid in the lurch. Dylan was smart, but he had a long way to go to catch up to the text. And final exams were right around the corner.

Gil tapped the rim of his glass. "Same again?"

Dylan checked his phone and swore. He jumped off the stool and scrambled to gather his things. "I'm late. I have to go."

"Want to meet again tomorrow night?"

Dylan hefted his backpack over his shoulder. "I don't have money for a tutor."

Gil pressed a hand to his chest. "You think I'm good enough to be a tutor? I'm touched."

"You could be better," Dylan said with a straight face. "Your zeroes look like flat tires and you hog the pencil."

Gil mock-punched him in the shoulder. "Next time I'll bring my own. Anyway, I thought we were just hanging out. I do you a solid now, you do me one some other time. Deal?"

Dylan thought about it, and offered a nod. "Deal."

Liz Watts walked up to the bar. "Hey, Dylan. Hey, Coop."

Everyone said their hellos as Kerry moved to their end of the bar to serve Liz. Gil had to give Kerry credit. She didn't look the least bit wary.

Liz's smile, on the other hand, was as stiff as the do on a grandma's hairspray-loving head.

"Diet soda, please," she said.

As Kerry fixed the drink, Gil nudged Liz. "How's the rug rat?"

Her smile turned all kinds of tender. She started to answer, then had to wait for a chorus of cheers at the pool table to die down before she could make herself heard. "He's wonderful, thanks. Marcus wanted him all to himself tonight, so he chased me out of the house for a few hours."

Gil turned his tea glass around and around. What would that be like? How long would it take before he felt comfortable enough with his own baby to do something like that?

His own baby. Jesus.

Kerry set Liz's drink on a coaster and pushed it across the bar. "Would you like a cherry with that?"

"No, thanks." Liz made a face, then motioned with her chin at the Mitzitini sign. "What does Snoozy think about these new cocktails you're offering?"

"He hasn't actually tried them. I'm hoping when he gets back—"

"This isn't some trendy city bar." Liz crossed her arms and leaned forward on the polished wood. "It's a place where good old boys gather to drink beer and brag about who has the biggest—" she shot a glance at Dylan and visibly regrouped "—fish mounted over their fireplace. Can you really see Snoozy mixing Mitzitinis once you're gone? Or taking the time to put tea candles on every table?"

"Maybe not." Kerry picked up Dylan's empty glass. "But Liz, that's between Snoozy and me. I'm the one he hired to manage the bar."

Damn. Gil gave Kerry a mental thumbs-up.

Liz shot upright and flipped her long blond hair over her shoulder. The ends whipped across Gil's cheek and he flinched.

"Just offering some friendly advice," she said, her voice pitched high. "Not that I care." She snatched up a cocktail napkin and scrunched it against her nose. "Must be a cold coming on," she said thickly, and turned away.

Harris came through the door as Liz hurried toward it. He frowned as she stopped to talk then pulled her into a one-armed hug. They left without looking back.

Dylan was right behind them.

"Pretty sure it was something I said," Kerry muttered. She stood with her hands braced on the bar, shoulders as rigid as a concrete wall.

Gil made a wild guess. "You haven't told your father yet."

"Not yet. When I do, I have a feeling it'll be a one-sided conversation. And a very brief one."

"Don't put it off too long," he said quietly. No one knew how much time Harris had left.

Her eyes filled, and she nodded.

He cleared his throat. "Something up's with Liz. She's not normally so defensive."

"It's me. She's afraid I'll take advantage of Snoozy."

"Maybe." He couldn't say much about that, since he shared Liz's concern. Funny how he was more worried about Snoozy's business than his own.

It probably had a little something to do with Kerry's concern for Dylan and her regret over her father, not to mention the guilt that tended to follow Gil around.

But he had a baby to think of now. And the fact that the woman carrying his child was not only a convicted felon but the last woman he could see himself having an enduring relationship with pissed him off no end.

Run away. A scene from a Monty Python movie entertained his brain—a handful of crusaders fleeing a killer rabbit. *"Run away!"* they panic-shouted to each other.

"You can start tomorrow," Gil told Kerry brusquely. "We open at nine."

SIX O'CLOCK IN the morning and Gil was so restless he was actually considering his second run in a week. If only this unfamiliar edginess was about the meatloaf special he'd brought home for dinner the night before, or the coffee he'd made at three in the morning.

But no, these jitters were all about his new employee. The one he couldn't afford to hire. The one he couldn't stop thinking about.

The one he should stay away from but couldn't because, hello. They'd been smoking hot in bed together.

They'd be working together.

They'd be having a baby together.

Coop, Coop, Coop. What the hell have you gotten yourself into?

After chasing down and turning off his alarm clock, he impressed himself by managing fifty push-ups while watching *The Twilight Zone.* When he was done, he pulled on his sweats and snarfed a granola bar.

Another peek through his blinds showed the lights were on above the shop across the street. Looked like Kerry was getting as much sleep as he was. Was she panicking about the future? Worrying about today? Maybe she was still pumped from the success of Ladies' Night.

Or maybe she was missing a boyfriend. Maybe at that very moment she was on the phone with the guy. Or Skyping with him. They could be having Skype sex.

She'd asked Gil if he was involved with someone. He'd never returned the question. He released the blinds and they snapped back into place.

He was out the door and down the stairs and pounding the sidewalk by quarter after six, but he slowed to a walk after the second mile.

So much for impressing himself.

Hiring Kerry had been a rotten idea. Not only was he going to piss off Harris and wear himself out keeping close track of what was going in and out of the cash register, he was going to torment himself working alongside a sweet, smart-alecky woman who had the kind of curves a man wanted to sink into. Wrap himself around. Lose himself in.

Been there, done that.

Which was exactly why he wanted to do it again.

It was also why he found himself suddenly facing fatherhood. Without a father of his own to hit up for advice.

Gil pushed himself back into a run. Just outside town he veered off the road and jogged to the far side of a gravel lot. In the thinning shadows, he found the path that led through a grove of scraggly pines down to the lake. He stopped at the edge of the bank, lungs laboring, shoes and socks damp from dew-heavy grass.

The lake mimicked his restiveness. Or maybe it was the other way around.

Foam-tipped platinum waves smacked into the rock-strewn beach below, over and over. Water hissed and stones rattled. Gil sucked air and traced the rippling origin of the waves all the way across to Canada. A seaweedy, dead fish smell clung to the back of his throat.

Torment. Maybe that was the key. He was punishing himself for all the years he'd punished his father and his brother, all because he'd resented his own choice to stay with the hardware store, AKA the sinking ship. He'd punished his mother, too, postponing trip after trip to her place in Florida because she'd never managed to treat Ferrell with the tough love he so desperately needed.

Who was Gil to judge?

The sun edged higher, misting the lake with amber. Gil headed back to the path.

You got this, Coop. As long as he set the right tone from the start. Kept things distant. Professional. They had plans to make, and those plans couldn't include getting naked.

He had to put his business first.

By the time he got back to the hardware store he was ready to drop, but he hadn't managed to pound out the unrest. A cold ending to his hot shower didn't do the trick, either. Nor did forking down a carb-heavy breakfast of oatmeal pancakes.

Somehow he managed not to nick himself while shaving, but that was the extent of his good luck. He spritzed himself in the eye with toothpaste spit while brushing his teeth, broke a bootlace—twice—while lacing up his Timberlands, and when he pulled a shirt free of its hanger, he pulled too hard and somehow ended up with the hook end stuck in his hair. After spending several minutes untangling his carefully combed hair from the twisted wire, he yanked the damned thing out. Now he had a bald spot.

Jesus. He was lucky he made it downstairs without puncturing a lung. How the hell was he going to manage putting clothes on a baby?

A sudden pang for his mother had his vision blurring.

Half an hour later, Gil stood behind the cash register, rearranging the pens in the china creamer and the apples in the basket and reminding himself over and over again that this wasn't a frickin' date. This was serious business. Kerry had debts to pay, he had a save-the-hardware-store strategy to develop, and they had money to put aside for the baby Kerry planned to raise on her own.

Like hell.

Still, his brain kept returning again and again

to the image of Kerry behind the bar, reaching for something high off a shelf, or bending to scoop ice for a drink. Thick ponytail swinging, green eyes shining.

Brow scrunching as she watched Dylan struggling with his homework.

Face brightening as a customer complimented a drink.

Someone knocked on the glass. Gil jumped, and gave himself a mental fist bump when nothing dropped, cracked or collapsed. It was Kerry.

He adjusted his glasses, ran a hand through his hair—*good job, Coop, now she'll be able to see the bald spot*—and strode over to let her in.

CHAPTER NINE

"GOOD MORNING," HE SAID. "Welcome to Cooper's Hardware."

Jesus, could he sound any more awkward?

"Good morning." She walked past him and took off her shades.

He shut the door behind her and held off on turning the Open sign toward the street. When he got a load of her face, sympathy stirred.

"Jitters again?" he asked. "Or just plain old-fashioned insomnia?"

She sputtered a laugh. "I look that bad?"

"Nothing a little spackle won't fix."

She rolled her eyes and followed him across the store. "Maybe we could try coffee first."

"Did you bring any?"

She stopped. "Was I supposed to?"

She seemed so stricken, he couldn't help a chuckle. "Just kidding. Not only can I offer you coffee, I ran by Cal's Diner earlier and picked up some cinnamon rolls. You interested?"

He walked backward into the small break room just outside the office.

She trailed him in and set her purse on the chair

in the corner. "The ones as big around as a sixty-tooth, fine-finish circular saw blade?"

He whistled softly. "Somebody's been doing her homework."

"I saw the sign out front. You're having a sale."

"*We're* having a sale." He was ridiculously pleased. That she'd noticed. That she was in his store. That she'd be around his things. Touching them. Learning them. Talking them up so people would buy them.

Gilbert Cooper, you're right where you should be. With all the other tools. She's only here because she's carrying your baby.

He kept conveniently forgetting how she'd brushed him off when he'd asked for her number.

"It was because of your father," he blurted.

"What?" She splashed milk onto the counter instead of into her coffee. Damn. She was as nervous as he was.

"After we…hooked up. You gave me the brush-off because you knew I'd find out who you were."

"I suppose I could have told you then, but I didn't know how. 'Thank you for the great sex and by the way, I'm an ex-con and chances are you know my father'?"

It had been pretty great, hadn't it? Somehow he managed not to say that out loud. Instead he said, "Sounds melodramatic when you put it that way. Wait. Can you drink coffee?"

She smiled midsip. "As long as I keep it to one

cup. Believe me, that was one of the very first things I looked up."

"One might get me through to lunch, but then I'd be falling asleep in my tuna sandwich. Although..." He set his mug down. "Maybe I should cut back, too. A solidarity type thing." When she gave him a look, he frowned. "What?"

"You're different today."

"Just trying not to be an ass."

"I appreciate it." She picked up her purse and went into the office. "Okay if I stash this in here?" When he made a noncommittal noise, she dropped her bag in the bottom drawer of the filing cabinet.

"We'll save all the pesky new employee paperwork for later," he said. "How about a tour?"

"Sounds good."

There wasn't much to show, so Gil took his time. No sense in rushing when they had no customers to wait on. Kerry paid close attention and she liked to straighten things, poking this into place, prodding that into alignment. He liked that she was trying.

All the while, his pesky inner voice demanded to know how he could be so cheerful about calling a truce with a criminal.

After he'd shown her around hand tools, power tools, building materials, plumbing, electrical supplies, cleaning supplies, housewares, lawn and garden products and all the miscellaneous sections in between, they ended up back at the cash register, where they leaned against the wooden counter and munched on apples.

She smelled good. Like a spicy, high-dollar dessert.

Someone get me a fork.

"So, what do you think?" he asked casually.

"It's a wonderful store. Sweet, old-fashioned and fun. You stock everything from tennis balls to Dutch ovens to lumber."

"The eclectic inventory is what gives the place its charm. It's also the source of the high operating costs."

Arms crossed, tapping the apple against her chin, Kerry pushed away from the counter and paced in front of the windows. "You know what this place is missing?"

"Besides customers? And clean windows?"

Her expression turned sheepish. Oh, yeah, she knew at least one of those smudges had her name on it. "The social factor," she said.

Gil swallowed a bite of apple. "I have a Facebook page."

"Not social media. Face-to-face-type social."

"So, what, you're suggesting I hold some kind of open house? Offer guests cheese and wine to enjoy as they contemplate toilet plungers?"

"What I'm suggesting is that you give people a reason to hang out. The longer they stay, the more likely they are to buy something." She gestured toward the corner by the stairs that led to his apartment. "You could fit a few café tables over there. Bring your coffee station out here and set up some games. Work a deal with Cal's Diner and offer fresh pastries. Invite a few retirees to play some checkers. Get a few kids in here after school to do their homework."

She was thinking of Dylan. "How am I supposed to do that?"

"Offer them a discount. Bring in some kittens. Offer free tutorials on all those power tools you sell. You'll figure it out."

"You want to turn my hardware store into a community center?"

"I want to turn your hardware store into a place people want to go. I want to turn it into a viable business."

He took off his glasses, closed his eyes and pinched the bridge of his nose. "You're supposed to be helping me make money, not spend it," he said.

"You know as well as I do you have to spend money to make it. You're just being stubborn." She tipped her head as she considered him. "Or is it something else?"

The bell over the door jangled. Gil tossed his apple core in the trash can under the desk and held out his hand for Kerry's apple. "Finished?"

She handed it to him carefully and together they faced their first customer, volunteer firefighter

Burke Yancey. Gil didn't know him well, but he'd shot pool with him a time or two at Snoozy's.

As Gil threw away what was left of Kerry's apple, Burke grinned and rubbed a hand over his chest. "Well, now. Don't you two look cozy."

Gil frowned. There was just enough slur to Burke's words to tell him the firefighter had been drinking. Or maybe he hadn't stopped, after leaving the bar last night. He was wearing his uniform, though it was wrinkled as hell. Surely he wasn't on shift today? "Burke." Gil greeted him tersely, then turned to Kerry. "Why don't you start taking inventory? The clipboard's on the desk in the office."

Gil didn't like the look in Burke's eyes as the firefighter watched Kerry walk away. "She tends bar at Snoozy's. She's working for you, too?"

"Just started today."

Burke punched him on the shoulder. "Didn't know you had it in you."

Knocking back beers hadn't affected the firefighter's strength any. Gil barely resisted the urge to rub his shoulder.

"Why are you here, Burke?" he asked tightly. "Can I help you find something?"

"Ruthie says that chick's trying to take over the bar. She doesn't like her much." Burke jabbed his chin in the direction Kerry had taken. "You and she…?" He gave his hips a leisurely pump.

Gil shoved his hands into his pockets before he

did something stupid. Something that would involve having to buy himself a new pair of glasses. "If there's nothing I can help you with, I need to get back to work."

Burke snorted. "Yeah, didn't think so. She's way out of your league. But dude, you don't seem to realize the opportunity you have here." He gestured for Gil to come closer, and spoke in a whisper no softer than his regular speaking voice. "She's been in prison. Missing out on… you know." He poked Gil with a sly elbow. "I'm thinking she'd be hella grateful to any guy who paid her the right kind of attention, if you know what I mean."

Rage licked fire into his veins and Gil flexed his fingers. After a few deep breaths he found himself channeling Seth and cracked his knuckles. "Yeah, I know what you mean. You'd better get the hell out of here before I kick your ass."

Burke responded with a slow blink. "What?"

"What's the matter with you, disrespecting a woman like that? I don't want you back in here until you've learned some manners."

Burke rolled his red-rimmed eyes. "No way you can kick my ass."

"You're drunk. Sure you want to find out?"

The firefighter hesitated then held up his hands in an unsteady surrender. "Look, I just came in to get some string for my weed whacker."

Gil herded him toward the door. "Get it online."

"You suck, dude. And so does your store."

Gil watched the firefighter barrel down the sidewalk, back toward the firehouse. He took out his phone and fired off a quick text to a buddy on the day shift, suggesting he convince Burke to hit his bunk and sleep it off.

"You didn't have to do that for me."

Damn. Gil swung around. "You heard."

"It's not the first time I've heard something like that." Her shrug was far from the casual gesture she was probably going for. "Not from him, though. He drinks a lot, but he's never caused any trouble."

"He's a decent guy when he isn't drinking. Seems like lately there's a lot more drinking and a lot less decent, though." And that was enough talk about Burke Yancey. He jerked a nod at the clipboard she held. "Question?"

"Would you mind showing me where you keep the soft copy? I need to add some items."

"Sure." Before she could turn away, he touched her arm. Beneath his fingertips her sweater was fuzzy and warm.

"We should talk."

"About?"

"The cash register."

She hugged the clipboard to her chest. "As in, I'm not allowed near it? Don't sweat it. I didn't expect anything else."

He shook his head. "One advantage to having you here is that it frees me to work in the office or run errands. I can even make deliveries again, which would be a big boost to my bottom line. Not allowing you near the register would mess all that up." The muffled slam of a car door pulled his attention to the front. A middle-aged man wearing a bright yellow windbreaker was making his way toward the store.

Gil checked the time on his phone. "When do you need to head to Snoozy's?"

"Ruthie's opening for me, so I can stay until noon."

Gil began backing toward the office. "Then for the next hour, you're it. Come get me if you need me."

"Wait, what were you going to tell me about the cash register?"

"You need to type in a code before you can use it." The cowbell clanged and Gil quickly recited the numbers.

Kerry narrowed her gaze. "You're planning on pouring yourself another cup of coffee, aren't you?"

With a mock innocent look, he spread his hands. "Someone has to drink it."

He had a feeling he'd be having a lot of secret assignations with the Cap'n in the future. At least he'd be having assignations with someone.

KERRY SPENT HER entire shift at Snoozy's half hoping, half dreading Liz would show. She never did. When she wasn't stressing about Liz, she was second-guessing her decision to tell Gil she was pregnant. Why hadn't she waited until a blood test confirmed it? If it came back negative, she'd have freaked them both out for nothing, and Gil would be sure to withdraw his job offer. Which meant Kerry would probably end up commuting to Erie after Snoozy got back.

Not that the time away from her father seemed like it would be a big deal after all. Not when he couldn't bring himself to talk to her. Doing dumb things like hurting Liz's feelings wasn't helping her cause any.

No wonder she managed to shatter four whiskey sour glasses and her lunch plate before her shift ended. Good thing Snoozy wasn't around to see it. Ruthie was, though. Kerry had sent her home early just so she wouldn't have to see the disgust on the redhead's face. And of course the breakage meant the tip jar took another hit.

Her evening was saved from being a total disaster when Dylan walked in. He was later than usual, and she'd been petrified he wouldn't show because she had no idea who to recruit to look after Mitzi. One of her customers had suggested she call the Castle Creek librarian, a guy named Noble Johnson, but that had to have been some sort of joke.

Dylan did his python caretaker bit and set up his usual homework station at the end of the bar, moments before Gil walked in.

Just one glimpse of his dimples had her stomach trembling and her fingers tingling with the need to touch him again. Her disgust with herself matched Ruthie's. How could she continue to crush on a guy who had such a low opinion of her?

He had put her off-kilter that morning with his friendly attitude. And trusting her with the cash register. What was that about? Maybe he hoped if he stopped growling at her, she wouldn't rob him blind?

Funny not funny, girlfriend.

He slid onto the stool next to Dylan's and made a big deal about showing the teen his set of retractable pencils. Dylan was more interested in teasing him about the pocket protector he kept them in.

Kerry was trying hard not to smirk about the aforementioned pocket protector as she approached them for their drink order.

"Dude," Dylan was saying. "What happened to your hair?"

Gil's face was the color of the maraschino cherries Kerry had just finished stocking. "Nothing," he said, and shot a weak smile at Kerry. "Why?"

"Did your girlfriend cut off a hunk of it for a bracelet? That's what my brother's girl did to him.

Whacked off a piece to weave into some sort of keepsake, she said, and left a bald spot over his ear. He didn't text her for like, a whole week." He eyed Gil's hairline and shook his head. "Love sucks."

Kerry could have kissed Dylan for banishing all the awkward out of the encounter. "What can I get you? Another cran-dandy cooler?"

He made a face and tipped his head sideways at Gil. "Nah. I'll have what he's having. You know, that golf drink."

She donned a crafty expression. "Actually, I was going to pour him a mix of everything I have on tap. You know, the draft version of a suicide."

Gil's head jerked back and his jaw flexed. He bent his head and took his time selecting a pencil from his collection, finally mumbled something to Dylan and opened his notebook.

"I'll have an Arnold Palmer, too, please," he said, his voice all sand and gravel.

Kerry bit the inside of her lip. She'd struck a nerve. A sinking sensation chilled a path from her chest to her belly.

Apologizing would only make things worse. She fixed and delivered their drinks and moved to the opposite end of the bar to give them their privacy.

As she worked her way through her bar space, cleaning and taking inventory, she realized they were talking about Dylan's family. She couldn't help herself. She moved closer.

"He doesn't let me do anything," the teen was saying. "It's like he's scared something's going to happen to me, too. I can't go anywhere."

"He lets you come here."

Dylan squirmed. "That's 'cause I need money for lunches and stuff, and a lot of times he doesn't have it."

"Your mom's care must be very expensive," Gil said quietly.

"I guess." He didn't look up from his textbook.

Gil met Kerry's gaze, and something bleak passed between them.

"Hey, you hungry?" Gil asked Dylan. When he nodded, Gil turned back to Kerry. "Too late to get Ruthie to fry up a couple of burgers?"

"She shut down the grill and went home," Kerry said apologetically. "But I can put together a couple of ham and cheese subs if you're good with that."

"Cool with you?" he asked Dylan.

Dylan nodded and exchanged knucks, and Kerry fought another bout of tears all the way to the kitchen.

Only three weeks pregnant and she was pretty much crying at the drop of a hat. What would three months be like? Or six?

Gil and Dylan continued working for about an hour. The sight of their heads together—one blond and one red and yes, the blond did seem a little patchy—had her heart in perma-melt mode.

She couldn't wait to go home and indulge in a good cry. Get it out of her system. Until the next day, anyway. So much for not feeling pregnant.

Gil offered to drive Dylan home and they left together, after Kerry reminded Gil she might be late the next morning because of her doctor's appointment. He gave her a thumbs-up and, with a hand on Dylan's shoulder, guided him out the door.

The moment her last customer left, Kerry locked the door, turned off the neon blue Snoozy's sign and retrieved her cell from behind the bar. She pulled up the number Ruthie had reluctantly recited and sent the text it had taken her all night to draft.

Could we meet for an early breakfast Friday?

She'd rather meet tomorrow morning and get it over with, but her doctor's appointment made that impossible. She set down her phone and gave her fingers a quick cross for good luck. She didn't expect Liz Watts to answer anytime soon, if at all. According to Eugenia, Liz had a nine-month-old boy at home—chances were the entire family was already in bed. Even if Liz were still awake, Kerry doubted she'd respond.

Who could blame her for blowing off the woman who'd made her cry? In public?

She tugged the clip out of her hair, gathered it up again along with all the pieces sweat had glued to her neck and replaced the clip. Then she got down to her favorite part of the shift—closing up. Setting everything to rights. Making everything fresh for a brand new day.

She'd already covered and stored all her mixers and juices and restocked her glasses. Before she could leave for the night, she had to restock the beer cooler and check for liquor empties, wash her blenders and utensils and soak the soda gun nozzles, wipe down the bar area, the tables, and the bar stools, sweep and mop the floor and finally, close out the register.

She was just settling down at Snoozy's desk when her phone pinged. Liz had responded to her invitation to breakfast.

Do you plan to apologize?

Kerry rolled her eyes, but found herself smiling, too.

Meet me and find out.

Liz replied,

Can't manage breakfast. Come by the greenhouses for coffee. Any time after 7.

Kerry considered Liz's words. Chances were she'd run into her father at Castle Creek Growers, but she might as well get it over with. Two for one. Such a deal.

Be there around 8.

Kerry's phone lit up a few seconds later with Liz's reply.

Bring coffee. Your dad makes it too strong. It takes me half an hour to pour a cup and with every sip I expect a fossil to bubble up to the surface.

Heartened by Liz's joking tone, Kerry set aside her phone and turned back to the computer. She glanced at the clock and grimaced. Despite having been through closing a number of times, she was still a slowpoke. She'd be lucky if she made it out of the bar before three.

But within half an hour she'd finished updating the sales spreadsheet and the comped drinks and waste log, made notes about inventory, and prepared the bank deposit. She was getting better at this. With a record-setting yawn, she pulled on her sweater, grabbed her purse and conducted one last walk-through.

"Good night, Mitzi," she called, then scurried out the front door, still not thrilled with the idea of being locked in with a ten-foot python.

THE NEXT MORNING, Kerry completed her outfit by shrugging into her favorite navy sweater. The look wasn't exactly chic, but she needed all the support she could get. Although she was ninety-nine percent certain what the outcome would be at the doctor's office, she couldn't help the nerves that made it impossible for her to even consider eating breakfast.

She pulled her hair back into a loose bun, swiped a pink gloss across her lips and let herself out of the apartment. She stood at the top of the metal staircase and prayed her legs wouldn't give out. At the moment, they felt as sturdy as a pair of those cheap plastic sword picks Snoozy used for garnishes.

She was halfway down the stairs when she realized that big silver blob she'd been seeing out of the corner of her eye was Gil's pickup. He stood beside it, looking dressier than usual in khakis and a blue button-down shirt.

He spread his hands. "Might as well get used to going to these things together."

She didn't know whether to salivate or cry. A few deep breaths eased the pressure in her chest and she managed to blink back a small surge of tears. The spit thing was already a done deal.

She swallowed. "You'll be late opening the store."

"I put a note on the door. I doubt anyone will even notice."

She walked the rest of the way to the truck and hesitated at the tailgate. "Part of me is relieved I'll have someone to keep me company. The rest of me resents that you're here because you don't trust me."

He grunted. "Where was all this straightforwardness when you were helping your husband commit insurance fraud?"

His words smacked the warm and fuzzy right out of her. Wordlessly she followed him to the passenger side and accepted his help stepping up into the truck. After he settled himself into his own seat, he pointed to a travel mug in the center console.

"That's for you."

Still smarting from his words, she poked at it. "Doesn't smell like coffee."

"Because I figured you'd already had your one cup. That's orange juice. No pulp."

She swung her head around. "How'd you know I don't like the pulp?"

"Lucky guess."

"Thank you."

"You're welcome." He started up the truck and pulled out of the parking lot. She gave him directions and settled back with her juice.

The butterscotch rays of sunlight filtering through the windshield warmed the cab, and—along with the steady drone of the engine—lulled

Kerry into a state of sleepiness. Through slitted eyes she glanced over at Gil, and tried to imagine what it would be like if they weren't on their way to finding out whether their one night of passion had a consequence that would bind them together forever.

Maybe they would be on their way to a day of shopping, or breakfast with Harris and Eugenia. *Errrrrt.* Her fantasies halted with a mental squeal of brakes. It would take a miracle for her father to forgive her. Especially now. And Gil was understandably disgusted by the things she'd done. Her shoulders sagged under the weight of hopelessness.

How frustrating, to have your intentions constantly questioned. And she had no one to blame but herself.

"Help me understand why you did it," Gil said.

She opened her eyes and sat upright. What was the point? she wanted to ask. Nothing she could say would mitigate what she'd done. Nothing would make him feel better about taking a chance on her. But he'd asked, and she would answer, if only as part of her penance.

Gently she placed the cup back in its holder. "I don't know that I understand it myself," she said. "I loved my husband and I was scared our life would change. I ignored my conscience and betrayed a lot of people."

"Did he threaten you?"

Her fingers curled together in her lap. "There weren't any extenuating circumstances. I did a terrible thing for selfish reasons. I did wrong because it was easier than doing right. I was not a good person, Gil." She turned her head, and let her gaze rest on his strong, long-fingered hands. She ached for the privilege of lifting one of his hands from the wheel and joining it with hers. "I'm not that person anymore."

"Do you still love him?"

"I started falling out of love the moment I learned about the fraud." Shame delivered heat to her face. "Makes no sense, I know, considering I helped, but there it is. When I found out he was having affairs with most of the women he recruited, that was the end for me."

He slowed the pickup, bent his head to peer through the windshield and flicked on his turn signal. "We're here."

"Don't you have an ultimate regret?" she asked thickly. "That one huge, dark, smothering regret you'd give anything to be able to off-load?"

He killed the engine and stared through his side window. "Yes."

Her inhalation was so sharp, she wondered if she'd sliced her windpipe. "It's not me, is it?"

"No." His fingers weren't quite steady as they

worked his seat belt. "I have bigger regrets than you and me."

Without another word Kerry got out of the truck.

An hour later they were climbing back in. Doors thudded, seat belts clicked. Then nothing.

The sun had climbed higher. Instead of soothing, its amber rays irritated. Kerry's eyes watered, and she sneezed.

"God bless you," Gil murmured.

"Thank you."

He stared at the keys in his hand, making no motion to fire up the pickup. "What are you feeling?"

"Overwhelmed. Scared. Excited." She shot him a sideways glance. "Guilty. You?" When he didn't say anything, she swallowed hard. "I wanted to *want* it to be negative. My life's a mess. Bringing a baby into it would not be doing anyone any favors. But I wanted that negative even more for your sake than mine."

He sorted through his keys. "You're glad you're pregnant."

"As backward as it is, I found myself rooting for a positive result. I'm going to have somebody on my team now. Somebody who will love me unconditionally."

"Until they grow up to be a teenager."

"Or until they find out I'm a convicted felon. Whichever comes first."

He slid the key into the ignition. "I don't think unconditional love works that way." He let his hand fall to his thigh. "I'm not disappointed, either."

Her stomach flipped in a long, slow cartwheel. *"What?"*

"I expected to be. But being responsible for another human being puts a lot of things into perspective. I know it won't be easy, working out how exactly you and I are going to handle this. But we'll figure it out. Maybe setting our dreams aside to raise a kid will help us off-load some of that regret we talked about."

She frowned. "What do you mean?"

"You are staying, aren't you? Castle Creek's a friendly place. People care about each other here. They look out for each other."

"You sound like a real estate agent."

He cast a sideways glance as he started the truck. "I know there's a lot you want to accomplish here. I'd hate to think you'd let anything— or anyone—chase you out of town."

"You're saying my father won't take this well. I think you're right. But who can blame him?" She put on her sunglasses. "I came here to pay what I owe him, and hopefully get him to consider forgiving me. So far I haven't proven much except I'm open to having sex with strangers."

"You're trying to make it easier for me." He pulled onto the road. "You want me to dislike you. Or at least make everything about the fact that you're a felon."

"It would make things easier for me, too."

"That ship has sailed, don't you think?"

Right. Because they'd called a truce.

She toyed with a button on her sweater. "Now that we know for sure, do you mind if we go by Eugenia's house before opening the store? I realize it's early to tell anyone, but knowing she won't mind if I stay put will take so much of the stress out of planning."

"She's not at the store?"

"She told me last night that she'd be opening late today. I guess she didn't want me to worry."

"She thinks a lot of you."

For whatever reason, she did seem to. What she'd think of this latest development, though, Kerry had no idea. Her throat thickened at the thought of losing Eugenia's regard.

"Have you eaten?"

She blinked at the subject change. "I was too nervous."

"There's a couple of granola bars in the glove compartment. Help yourself."

She selected a peanut-butter-flavored bar and savored the first bite. "Thank you. I didn't realize how hungry I was." She chewed and swallowed her second bite. "I have to say, you're taking all of this remarkably well."

He shot her a grim smile. "Inside, I'm already halfway through my second fifth of Jack."

"January," she said under her breath. Was that a good month to give birth? She gave Gil a considering glance. "You have any experience in this sort of thing?"

"If you mean have I ever been pregnant, the answer's no."

"Ha." The commercial part of the town transitioned to vineyards and roadside produce stands, and the sharp, nostalgic smell of fresh-cut grass sweetened the air. "What I meant was—"

"I know what you meant." Gil glanced in the mirror and shifted lanes to pass a hay-laden tractor. "When I was a kid, our cat had two litters of kittens. Does that count?"

"Of course it does," Kerry said wryly. "That counts double. Thank you. I feel so much better now. Dr. Dolittle to the rescue."

He reached over and squeezed her knee. "Don't worry. You'll be fine, and to make sure of that I'll be right there with you, every step of the way."

"You will?"

"Someone has to scratch behind your ears and sing 'Soft Kitty' to you."

"'Soft Kitty'?"

He lifted an incredulous eyebrow. "Sheldon's lullaby? From *The Big Bang Theory*?"

Oh, for God's sake. "Tell me something. Is there any geek box you haven't checked?"

"Not that I know of," he said contentedly.

"This baby is in big trouble," she muttered. But when Gil started whistling an unfamiliar tune, one she assumed was this "Soft Kitty" lullaby, she had to turn her head away so he wouldn't see the gratitude that dampened her cheeks.

EUGENIA SHIFTED THE picnic basket to her left hand and pulled her front door closed. A small bird erupted from the dried peony wreath on the door and Eugenia shrieked. Hand to chest, she watched the bird—a chickadee, maybe?—dart over to one of the apple trees bordering her property.

Uh-oh. She stood on her toes and carefully checked out the wreath, but saw no sign of a nest. With regret, she unlocked the door, removed the decoration she'd hung just last week and set it on the table in the foyer. Allowing a family of birds to nest on her front porch would not bode well for the babies. Christopher Robin, her serial killer cat, would not let them survive.

As a lazy drift of air ruffled her bangs and cheered her with the scent of lake water and pine, she took a quick inventory. Basket, purse, keys, sunglasses, outgoing letter for the mailbox. She had it all.

Except for courage. She'd left that behind on the kitchen table, in a not-quite-full bottle of Jameson. Indulging in a cup of Irish coffee had seemed the perfect way to prepare for the meeting ahead, but considering the condition of her stomach, she wished she'd skipped the whipped cream.

Eugenia put her sunglasses back on, slid the envelope into the pocket of her gray linen pants and tugged at the hem of her thin sweater. She was reaching for the handle of the picnic basket when a vehicle appeared at the foot of her driveway.

Her belly tumbled sideways and she vowed then and there to give up dairy.

Harris Briggs.

Six burly feet of lumberjacky deliciousness stepped out of an aged pickup truck, and Eugenia mentally chastised herself for every single time she'd ever rolled her eyes over the word *swoon*.

He ambled up to the bottom of the steps, took off his shades and gave her a nod. "Eugenia."

"Harris." She poked her hands into her pants pockets so she could dry her palms. Paper crinkled as she ended up wiping sweat on her letter. "I wasn't expecting you."

"I can see that." His face settled into its normal scowl as he eyed the basket at her feet. "Let me guess. Cold chicken, chardonnay and fruit tarts you'll pretend you made yourself. No blanket, though, since that Vincent character you're datin' wouldn't be caught dead sittin' on the ground."

"'That Vincent character,' as you so charmingly call him, has a first name. It's Sutton. And there is a blanket in there—"

"Bet you five dollars you won't be usin' it."

"You're right. We won't."

Harris grunted, but the sound didn't carry a lot of triumph.

Somehow Eugenia resisted the urge to bounce down the stairs and kiss him on his hairless, clueless head. She crossed her arms. "Sutton and I won't be using the blanket," she said, "because he and I aren't dating anymore."

"What?"

Eugenia waited patiently while Harris processed that.

Three. Two. One.

His face cleared, and he blustered a moment to hide a smile. Then his scowl returned as he started slowly up the stairs. "So, who's the picnic for?"

"Before we get into all that..." Eugenia picked up the basket, backtracked to the wrought iron table in the corner of her porch and set the basket in the center. She brushed off a lavender-colored cushion and sat, gesturing at the chair opposite. "Why don't you have a seat and tell me why you're here?"

"Don't want to make you late."

"It's fine." Actually, she was early. She'd grown tired of trying to make time go faster by fluttering around the house.

With a hesitant nod, he joined her at the table. He pulled out a chair and cast a dubious glance at it before gingerly lowering his bulk. When the chair held, his shoulders eased downward. The basket partially obstructed his view across the table so he gave it a shove.

"I went by the shop," he said. "Not often you close on a weekday."

"Everyone deserves a break now and then," she said briskly, and hated herself for sounding defensive. Hated herself even more for the thrill that zigzagged through her because he'd come looking for her.

"I agree." He gave the basket the side-eye. "And sometimes breaks can last too long."

"What are you going on about, old man?"

"I'm not going on about anything." His voice was gruff. "Kerry told me she's livin' in your apartment."

"And you came to tell me that under no circumstances should I allow her to stay there."

"No, I came to thank you for looking out for her."

Slowly Eugenia sank against the back of her chair. "What?"

"You offered her a place to live and helped her find a job. I want you to know I appreciate that."

"You're welcome. It's what you should have done."

His cheeks went ruddy. Still he held her gaze. "You're right, but I couldn't bring myself to do it."

"I'd ask why, but I'm not the one you need to explain yourself to."

"I plan to. She invited me to breakfast. I'll take her up on it sometime soon and we'll clear the air."

"Well, it's about time." Waving away a curious bee, Eugenia sat forward. "You should have gone to see her when she was in custody, Harris. At the very least, when she was in home detention. She's your daughter."

"I didn't want to see her like that."

"I'm betting you didn't bother to explain that to her."

His brow furrowed. "I told myself, and her, too, that I resented having to be vetted to see my own daughter. She saw right through that, of course. I took the easy way out and I finally got to thinkin' that's why I've been so hard on her—because I'm disgusted with myself."

Eugenia reached across the table and clasped his hand. Reveled in the sturdy warmth of his grip. Yearned to tug him to his feet and lead him to her bed, where they could remind each other of the companionship and the tenderness and the damned fine orgasms they'd been missing for months.

But even if Harris stepped up, they still had problems to work through. And the last time they thought they'd worked through them, they'd learned the hard way that they'd only gone around them. Then circled back to pick them up, like a group of dusty, road-weary hitchhikers.

"Your daughter needs to hear this," she said gently. "Tell you what." She patted the basket. "Why don't you take this to Kerry at Snoozy's? Share an early lunch before the regulars descend? Save her from eating that god-awful chili?"

"That where you were goin'? To see Kerry?"

"No, I was coming to see you." When he brightened, she held up her free hand, even as her heart shuddered with regret. "Now don't go mixin' your pickles with your peppers," she teased lightly, borrowing one of his favorite expressions. "You might not like what I have to say. I need to make sure you understand that I intend to do everything I can to persuade Kerry to stay here in Castle Creek. Right now, you two have the option of reconciling. What if—" Her gaze dropped to his chest and her fingers tensed around his. The strong, massive chest that protected an ailing heart. She swallowed. "What if something happens and you two never made peace?"

"Now, don't go gettin' your dress over your head. She and I, we will get this figured out." He shifted in his chair. "Although things got a little complicated the other night."

Oh, dear Lord. Eugenia reclaimed her hand and sat back. "Tell me."

After Harris related what had happened at Snoozy's, with Liz and Kerry having words and Liz leaving in tears, Eugenia shook her head. "Something's going on with that girl. Maybe Liz is feeling overwhelmed. New husband, new baby, new boss?" She hiked her chin at him. "I've heard he's a real hard-ass."

"Jackass, you mean. That seems to be your pet name for me these days."

Eugenia felt the flush begin at her ankles. "I prefer the one I had before."

His nostrils flared. "Me, too."

The chickadee came back, wings flapping a gentle beat as it fluttered around the front door in search of its peony perch. After leaving a disappointed deposit on Eugenia's welcome mat, it darted off again. Harris and Eugenia sat in silence for several moments, breathing in the faint scent of lilac, breathing out sorrow.

Harris ended the quiet. "Anyways, Liz told me this morning Kerry contacted her. Asked if they could meet for coffee. Sounds like to me she wants to work things out."

"Sounds like to me you're feeling better about the situation."

"With Kerry?"

"Yes," she said softly. "The situation with your daughter."

"I'm feelin'…" He scratched the top of his head. "Confused."

"It's a start. And the fact that you came over today to thank me? I'm impressed."

"You shouldn't be." His gaze dropped to the porch floor and he shrugged his thick shoulders.

"I meant what I said, but bein' here has just as much to do with us. I'm findin' it harder and harder to stay away."

It was thrilling to hear. At the same time, she'd heard it before.

When she didn't respond, he lifted his gaze and lowered his brows. "What? You're impressed, but you're not happy?"

She crossed her legs, heard the rustle of the envelope in her pocket and pulled it out. She smoothed it over her knee. "I'm sad, but not about seeing you. Nothing with us is easy anymore. It won't ever be easy. We've rejected each other so many times that getting one of us to take a chance again is as likely as Parker naming her baby boy after you."

Harris bristled. "Parker likes my name just fine. She uses it all the time. You're the one who likes to get creative with it."

Eugenia snickered. "Does she know your middle name is Marion?"

"Does she know your middle name?"

Eugenia narrowed her eyes. "You wouldn't dare."

"Share this picnic with me—" he tapped a knuckle against the basket "—and I'll take it to my grave." When she sucked in a breath, he grimaced. "Sorry, Genie. Poor choice of words."

She managed a smile. "Make it up to me by letting me have the extra fruit tart."

"Like I was ever going to get it anyways." He scratched his chin. "Genie?"

"Yes, Harris?"

"If there's a chance I can fix things with Kerry, that means there's a chance I can fix things with you. If you're willin' to try."

The rush of hope in her chest kicked the breath from her lungs and left her dizzy. She'd waited a long time to hear those words. How sweet it would be to let loose their love again, with all their ghosts laid to rest.

With *most* of their ghosts laid to rest.

"Harris, I—"

The rumble of another engine interrupted her. Another pickup, this one bigger and newer, started up her driveway.

"By the time we eat, my belly will be kissin' my spine," Harris grumbled.

Eugenia stood and shaded her eyes. "Who is it?"

"Gil Cooper." Harris twisted around farther in his chair. "He has Kerry with him." Grunting, he pushed to his feet. "Why isn't he at the hardware store?"

"And why isn't she at Snoozy's?" Eugenia dropped the envelope on the table and hurried down the porch steps. Kerry made it out of the truck before Gil did, and uneasiness pricked at Eugenia's spine as she noted the strain behind the young woman's smile.

CHAPTER TEN

"Is everything all right?" Eugenia asked.

"Yes." Kerry didn't seem to know what to do with her hands. "I wanted to discuss something with you, but I can see this is a bad time."

Harris thudded down the steps behind them. He and Gil reached the women at the same time but Harris didn't so much as look at his daughter. "Gil Cooper," he blustered. "Why are you here?"

"I'm playing taxi," Gil responded easily.

"Well, I'm playing hooky." Eugenia tugged at Harris's shirt with a wordless appeal to back off. "We're about to go on a picnic, but that doesn't mean we don't have time for you two. Would you like to come up and sit on the porch? I have some lovely raspberry tea in the refrigerator."

"Thanks, Eugenia, but we can't stay long." Kerry cast a nervous glance at Gil. "I'm glad you're both here. I have something to tell you."

Gil stepped forward and cupped Kerry's elbow. "*We* have something to tell you."

It was all Eugenia could do not to squeal with glee and launch into a celebratory dance. But one glance at Harris's face and she settled for a mental *yee-haw* and a couple of toe bounces. Maybe it wouldn't be so hard to keep Kerry in Castle Creek, after all.

"You're dating? You haven't been in town for what, a month, and you're dating? *Him?*" Harris glared at Gil. "The man can't win a poker hand to save his life. And he's going bald, did you see that? You really want to date a bald man?"

"It's one spot." Gil spoke through clenched teeth. "It'll grow back."

"Oh, yeah?" Harris bent at the waist and slapped at the naked top of his head. "That's what I used to think."

"Oh, for Pete's sake." Eugenia fisted the pearls around her neck. "Harris Briggs, stop acting like an ass."

Harris shot upright, revealing a beet-red complexion, whether from embarrassment or hanging upside down, Eugenia had no idea.

He jabbed a finger at Kerry. "You said you were goin' to prove you weren't the same person. You said you were goin' to focus on correcting your mistakes. How can you focus if you have a boyfriend?" He gave Gil an unfriendly side-eye. "Or whatever you want to call him."

"I call him my employer," Kerry said in a not-quite-steady voice. "I work for Gil. Part-time, at the hardware store."

"Oh." Harris passed around a scowl.

Eugenia sighed. She was disappointed, yes, but

Kerry had trusted Gil to bring her here, and Gil was having a hard time keeping his eyes off her. Hope springs eternal, and all that. She glanced at Harris and sighed again. Even when spring had long given way to winter.

Then she shifted her gaze back to Kerry and went still. *Uh-oh.* There was more to this. The apprehension on Kerry's face gave it plain away.

Harris pushed back his shoulders, looking as contrite as Eugenia had ever seen him. "Sounds like you're workin' hard to keep your word," he said to Kerry. "I'm sorry I accused you of letting yourself get distracted."

Kerry's cheeks were a pale green. Either her skin was reflecting the grass at her feet or the proverbial poo was about to hit the fan. And they were all standing close enough to get splattered.

"There's no need to apologize," Kerry said faintly. "There's more."

"More?" Harris demanded.

"More," Gil said firmly.

More. Eugenia held a hopeful breath.

Kerry clasped her hands in front of her. The sleeves of her sweater fell to her wrists. "I'm pregnant," she said.

Gil fumbled for her hand. "I'm the father."

"Oh," Eugenia breathed. "A *baby.*" She spun toward Harris and clapped her hands. "You're going to be a *grandfather.*"

He wasn't as thrilled. In fact, he looked down-right livid.

Eugenia refused to let go of her smile. "Harris—"

Everything above the old man's neck turned the color of merlot. With a furious shake of his head he charged toward his pickup, shouldering Gil out of the way in the process.

"Harris Briggs," Eugenia yelled after him. Oh, this was bad. Very, very bad.

The jackass made it worse by running over her tulips as he roared out of her driveway.

THE NEXT MORNING, GIL leaned against the jamb of the office door, sneaking a cup of coffee, watching as Kerry cleaned the outside of the front windows. She was working that rag like the windows were coated with gasoline and someone was running at her with a burning torch.

It killed him, how hard she was taking her father's reaction to yesterday's announcement. Understandable, since Harris couldn't have made his disgust more obvious. That had to hurt like hell. Still, Gil wished Kerry could find a way to shrug some of that off. The stress couldn't be good for the baby.

She hadn't said a word on the ride back to Cooper's. When they'd arrived, she'd thanked him for taking her to her appointment, then made a bee-line for the broom closet. He'd tried to send her home so she could chill for an hour before her shift at Snoozy's, but instead she'd swept the entire store, wielding the broom as frenetically as she was now cleaning the windows.

She stopped suddenly. Shoulders heaving, she slid her phone from her pocket. Whatever she read was not welcome news because she sagged against the window and lightly banged her forehead. Again. And again.

Gil ditched his coffee cup and strode to the door, telling himself his urgency was more about the potential damage to her brain than the smudges she was making on the freshly washed windows.

He shoved open the door, took her arm and coaxed her upright. "What's going on?"

Her teeth snagged her lower lip and he felt like a frickin' creepster but he couldn't look away.

"I forgot to cancel my coffee date with Liz." She swept her hair away from her face and tucked her phone back into her pocket. "I'll call her later. She can't resent me more than she already does."

Not a bet Gil would take.

"What about Eugenia?" he asked. "Did you get a chance to check in with her?"

Kerry nodded.

"Want to talk about it?"

"Not even a little." After brushing past him to enter the store, she whirled around. "I shouldn't have come."

"Go home," he said. "Get some rest. It's not like I'm neck-deep in customers here."

"No, I mean, I shouldn't have come to Castle Creek. The more I try with my dad, the more I damage our relationship. I'm not sure we can come back from this."

"You're feeling sorry for yourself."

"Don't you think I've earned it?"

"A few minutes' worth, maybe." He glanced at the faded blue Dutch Boy Paints clock on the wall behind the cash register. "Time's up."

"He thinks I'm after Eugenia's money."

"He *what*?"

She offered up a faint smile. "I'm grateful the thought hadn't occurred to you, too. But according to Eugenia, my father's convinced I got pregnant on purpose so I could appeal to her maternal side. Once she takes me under her wing, I'm set for life."

"Son of a bitch." What the hell was wrong with the old man?

Gil's boots smacked a pissed-off rhythm as he swung away and strode through the stockroom. He shoved through the back door into the afternoon sunshine of the loading dock and inhaled.

Spring flowers. Engine exhaust, from the truck that had delivered his shipment of ladders that morning. Plus something dicey from the Dumpster that squatted twenty feet to his left.

He descended the concrete steps, gripped the

handle on the Dumpster's shoulder-high access door and slid it shut. *Clang.*

Harris had never talked much about his daughter as a child, though he had related the occasional story. Gil's favorite was the one about the "monster spray" Harris and his wife had invented to help their little girl deal with her fears of the dark. Despite Harris's reticence about her, Gil had never gotten the impression that his relationship with his daughter had been a strained one.

Until Kerry got married. Then things had taken a deeper dive after her arrest.

Once she'd served her sentence, she could have stayed in North Carolina and sent money to her father electronically. She'd have had an easier time finding a job in the city. But she was after more than a paycheck. She was determined to mend a rift and she'd put up with prejudice and unkindness to try for it.

And Harris wasn't cutting her one inch of goddamn slack.

The back door squeaked open and shut. He turned. Kerry stood on the concrete apron, arms crossed. She squinted in the sun.

"I shouldn't have told you," she said. "Eugenia's already given up on him and I'm sure he'd be crushed if you did the same. Please don't. You have to understand I've hurt him deeply. He's barely had time to adjust to my being in town and now I'm expecting him to deal with a pregnancy, too. I knew it wouldn't be easy to convince him to forgive me. I just have to give him more time."

Her struggle to be understanding touched him. It also pissed him off.

"No." Gil shook his head. "He's had plenty of time."

He jumped up onto the concrete apron and got close enough to make her nervous. She dropped her arms and her eyes went wide.

"Enough with being passive," he said. "Find a way to talk to him. Make him listen to you." Like Gil should have done with his own father.

"This is Harris Briggs we're talking about. No one makes him do anything."

"Do you really want to go through pregnancy, and birth, without the support of the only family you have left?"

When her eyes went liquid, his chest went hollow.

He stared at his own hand as it reached out to her. It was as though his arm had suddenly disconnected from his brain. *Wait.* They'd agreed not to touch. Not to flirt.

But his traitorous hand gripped one of hers, curled around it and squeezed.

All neural wiring was spontaneously reconnected. He knew because the sticky warmth of her skin was screwing with his breathing.

She stilled, neither leaning toward him nor leaning away. He knew he affected her, though, because he swept his thumb across her wrist and her pulse tapped an agitated beat.

He took one step closer, leaned down and lightly touched his lips to her ear. She shuddered, and he clenched his teeth against a groan. She smelled like vanilla. He couldn't imagine a more captivating scent.

"The more you leave unforgiven," he murmured, "the less you'll sleep at night."

"You said you were the father."

That did not compute. "What?"

"The results of the paternity test haven't come back yet, but you told my father the baby is yours."

He lifted his head, and with the forefinger of his free hand stroked the hair out of her eyes. "You haven't given me any reason to distrust you. Not since the night we met, and I get why you made that choice. The person I know now…she's not the type to take advantage of other people." He stopped when she let loose a shaky breath. "What?"

"Nothing, I—" She looked away, then back. "That's the nicest thing anyone has said to me in a very long time."

Gil swallowed. Yeah, it had been a nice thing to say. Where the hell had it come from? Where was his resentment? His suspicion? The regret that they'd ever hooked up?

Christ, he was getting soft.

Quietly he huffed at himself. No, he was getting used to the notion that she was having his baby.

He was *liking* the notion that she was having his baby.

He pulled off his glasses and rubbed his eyes. *Face it, Gilbert. You're falling for her. You're falling for them both.*

"You're right," Kerry said.

He lifted his head, blinked at the fuzzy-edged version of her and slid his glasses back into place.

She'd turned toward the chain link fence that stood about forty feet away. That, and the thick row of pines directly behind it, separated the rear of Cooper's from the rear of the drugstore.

A small squirrel scampered along the top of the fence. It stopped, chittered a greeting, then went along its bouncy way. Something spooked it and the squirrel sailed off the fence and up the nearest pine tree, soft green spikes jiggling in its wake.

"I do need to make my father listen. Maybe..." She ran a trembling hand through her hair, dislodging her ponytail. "Maybe by not pushing the issue, he thinks I don't care. I don't know. What I do know is that if I keep taking advantage of Eugenia's generosity, I'll keep driving a wedge between them." She pushed up her sleeves. "You know what I'm going to do? I'm going to ask him if I can move in."

A kick of regret made Gil catch his breath. That meant she wouldn't be across the street anymore.

He wouldn't be able to jog over to see her. And if Snoozy offered her a full-time gig? She'd be giving up her job here at the store. He wouldn't see her at all unless he went by the bar.

He opened his mouth to invite her to move in with him instead, then closed it before he could manage the first word. When had he become so eager to sacrifice his privacy? Kerry moving in with Harris would be the best thing for both of them. For the baby, as well.

He repeated the words to himself, in a failed attempt to ease the pressure in his chest.

GIL'S AFTERNOON WAS blessedly busy, leaving little time to stew over the situation with Kerry. He held a class on installing a ceiling fan, and made the mistake of high-fiving someone while descending the ladder. That led to an unscheduled class on ladder safety. After that he had gadget shelves to restock, and after that, an uneventful tutorial on the use of a drywall screwdriver (uneventful if you didn't count old Mr. Katz driving a screw into a wall and hitting a live wire. The resultant sparks demonstrated quite nicely the importance of wearing eye protection). Still, Gil managed to close an hour early, in the hope that he'd catch Seth before he closed his own place. Fifteen minutes later, he parked his pickup in front of Tweedy's Feed and Seed, relieved to see that one of the bay doors remained open.

He strode inside the old firehouse Seth had painstakingly renovated a few years earlier, resurrecting in the process the feed store once owned by Audrey Tweedy's father. The fact that he'd kept the original name had earned Seth big points with Audrey and her co-mayor besties. But Seth hadn't been trying to schmooze—he'd simply felt it was the right thing to do.

Gil took a second to let his eyes adjust to the dim interior. Quiet surrounded the rustic plank shelves laden with pet food and livestock supplies and birdseed and beekeeping equipment and pretty much everything a home- and landowner would need that Gil *didn't* carry.

He drew in a breath, appreciating the rich, grainy smell of sweet feed. This much quiet had to mean Seth's kids weren't around. Gil moved to the cash register and tucked under the counter the handful of stick candies he'd brought, just in case.

"Walker," he called out. "You here?"

"Storeroom" came the response from the rear of the building.

Gil found him in the back, stacking bags of feed onto a pallet, each bag hitting the pile with a *crunch*. Seth straightened and swiped his forehead with the back of his canvas glove.

"Hey, man. Good timing. I got a big-ass order to fill." He grabbed a spare pair of gloves off a nearby shelf and tossed them over. "Make yourself useful."

Gil snagged the gloves out of the air but didn't put them on. "I can't," he said, injecting a decent amount of regret into the words. "I just ate."

Seth glanced at him with a *yeah, right* expression. "I'm not asking you to swim, just toss around a bag or two."

"You remember what happened the last time."

"Grab the bags by the middle, not the pull tab, and that way we won't end up with twenty pounds of pellets all over the floor."

Gil rolled his eyes. "But I'm wearing my glasses."

"Don't make me kick your ass, Coop."

Reluctantly Gil pulled on the gloves. "I'm having a baby."

Seth snorted as he let fly another bag. "Nice try. Now start stacking. List is taped to that shelf there." He pointed, glanced at Gil and did a double take. "What's that goofy-ass grin for?" His jaw dropped. "Shit, are you serious right now?"

Gil nodded.

"You got Harris's daughter pregnant?"

"Not on purpose."

Seth yanked off his ball cap and slapped it against his thigh. "You kept me out of the loop, man. That's bullshit."

"I've only known for two days but I can catch you up in one sentence." Gil crossed his arms. "She's tolerating me because we're going to have a kid together while all I can do is picture playing house."

Seth settled his hat back on his head. "No wonder you ditched poker night this week. I thought you were pissed at me for telling you who she really was."

"I'm sorry. Things have been... My brother called. Twice."

"And?"

"Remains to be seen." Gil shrugged. "Thing is, I need to know that something in my life will stay the same."

"You won't get rid of me that easily. Jackass." Seth stretched a closed fist across the pallet.

"Jerkwad." Gil returned the knuckle bump.

"One last thing."

"Hit me."

"You sure you want this?"

Gil didn't hesitate. "Yeah. I am. Kerry's made mistakes, but she's determined to start fresh. And it's my kid. So...yeah."

Seth nodded. "Then just take care of her. Be with her. Something pulled you two together in the first place, right? If it's meant to happen, it'll happen. And if you need anything, let me know. Now, you going to help with this order, or what?"

Gil puffed out his cheeks in a noisy exhale and scowled at the bags stacked at his feet.

What if it wasn't meant to happen?

His gut went hollow.

Dylan had it right. *Love sucks*.

KERRY FINISHED OFF the orange juice she'd cut with too much water and the toast she'd left too long to brown and headed back to the bedroom to get dressed. She scowled at the bed that looked so inviting yet had failed so completely to lull her to sleep.

No wonder she had a headache. Or maybe it was simply the stress of not knowing where she stood with Snoozy. Or her father. Or her bank account.

Or Gil. He'd eased up on her. More than that, he was actually being kind. But she wanted more. That near-kiss yesterday morning hinted that he might, too, but she had no idea how much of that was motivated by sympathy, or a misguided sense of baby-daddy responsibility.

The last thing she needed to do was complicate an already chaotic situation by sleeping with him again. She needed to talk to her father. Moving into her dad's house would put Gil out of desperate-dash-across-the-street range.

Kerry's head continued to throb as she dressed in jeans and a plum-colored top. She eyed her navy sweater, then decided to wear something with a little less wear to it. After spending too long staring at the contents of the closet, she grabbed the sweater after all and headed into the bathroom for a couple of ibuprofen.

But once she had her medicine cabinet open, she changed her mind about the pills. According to her doctor, one dose was acceptable in the first trimester, but why risk it? She'd do her best to tough it out.

She called Gil's cell number. "I'm heading over now," she said with forced cheerfulness when he answered. "I'm letting you know so you can unlock the door. I'd hate to have to knock on the glass and smudge your windows."

He chuckled, and her headache eased. If that was one thing she'd learned, it was that fingerprints on the storefront windows drove Gil crazy. Like Snoozy, who was the reason Ruthie cleaned the plexiglass on Mitzi's pen twice a day.

Gil was waiting for her as she crossed the street. He held the door open, wearing the lopsided, endearing grin he'd worn the night they'd met. Her pulse quickened from a stroll to an all-out run.

Damn those dimples.

The quiet enveloped them as the door closed. It made the rasp of her breathing sound that much louder. She hurried back to the office, but of course she couldn't outrun her breathlessness.

"You've been busy." She stashed her purse in the file cabinet and draped her sweater over the back of the chair. She inhaled deeply and smelled the usual coffee, but also bleach and lemon cleanser. "Couldn't sleep?"

"Not so much." He gave the coffeepot a questioning heft and poured her a cup when she nodded. "You?"

"I did okay." She toasted him with the May the Froth Be with You mug and sipped. Though she hadn't had her coffee yet, she didn't really want any, since her stomach had decided to pick a fight with the toast she'd forced herself to eat. Still, maybe the infusion of caffeine would calm the pounding in her head.

Despite her stomach's advice to set the coffee aside, she was grateful to have something to keep her hands occupied. Something besides smoothing Gil's rumpled blond hair or grabbing the collar of his dark green polo and pulling him in for a good-morning lip-lock. What she wouldn't give for another chance to taste his skin.

She dropped her gaze. "What's on the agenda for today? Want me to continue taking inventory?"

"How about we finish what we started yesterday?"

Kerry's hand jerked and coffee sloshed. Luckily she'd drunk enough that none made it over the rim. "What do you mean?"

"Discussing your ideas for improving the sales

floor." There was a smugness in his eyes, but a vulnerability, too. "What did you think I meant?"

He knew very well her first thought had been about that near-kiss. She shook a finger at him. "Keep that up and I'll spread the word that Gil Cooper's a big fan of lipstick imprints on his front windows."

"Diabolical. But all I have to do is spread the word that I clean the windows with water from the toilet."

"That's disgusting."

"But effective."

"How about we get down to business?"

"How about?" he said softly.

Even as hot sparks of awareness bounced around in her chest, she ignored the innuendo and led him back out front.

"You could use a couple of speed bumps," she said. When he lifted an eyebrow, she explained. "Displays that grab a shopper's attention. Slow him down, so he'll spend more time in the store. Or her, of course."

"Got any specific ideas?"

"Display a few of your smaller projects. Like a wooden welcome mat, or a wine rack. Impress the woodworkers who come in, make them feel like they need to compete. They'll ask you what you used and voilà. You have a sale."

"That's clever."

"That's retail." She led him over to the electrical aisle. Damn it, she should have taken that ibuprofen after all. "Then there's the butt brush problem."

"The what?"

She gestured with the mug. "This aisle isn't wide enough. Studies have shown that shoppers will avoid an item, even if it's the only thing they came in for, if checking it out brings them too close to another customer's butt."

"You're making that up."

"No, I'm not. It's real. I swear. I can get you the links to a couple of online articles if you want to—"

"Kerry. I believe you." He was smiling as he pushed at his glasses. "By the way, Eugenia called and asked about you this morning."

"She did?"

"She wanted to make sure you were okay after the other morning."

After the way her dad had reacted to the news of her pregnancy, he meant. "That was sweet of her."

"You don't know the half of it. She asked if we'd decided where we were sending the kid to college. She was teasing, but when I told her about the baby fund she said she'd like to contribute."

"That's—" Her chest hitched. "Gil, that is so thoughtful."

"Right?"

Right. Absolutely. And of course Eugenia wouldn't expect to be reimbursed. Still, the weight of Kerry's debt threatened to smother her. She clutched at the neckline of her top and yanked, giving herself room to breathe.

As Gil scrunched his brow, the cowbell sounded. They both turned to see a small elderly woman walk in. She wore a brown wool coat, a pink crocheted beanie over chin-length gray hair and bright purple sandals that matched her sunglasses.

"Gilbert," she said. "Did any stepping stones come in?"

"Yes, they did, Mrs. Yackley." To Kerry, he said, "Why don't you get back to taking inventory while I handle this? I'll check in with you later."

Relieved, Kerry nodded. While Gil went off to help Mrs. Yackley, Kerry went back to the office to get rid of her coffee and pop those pills.

GIL LOADED THE last of Mrs. Yackley's terra cotta flagstones into the back of her SUV—how such a tiny woman could climb into the driver's seat without a step stool, he would never know—and thanked her for her business. He jogged back inside and stopped, just inside the door, listening to the tones of the cowbell fade.

When was the last time he'd been so pumped about the store?

Easy. It was so long ago he couldn't remember.

And of course the reason he was eager to be back on the clock had nothing to do with hardware.

He rubbed his hands together. He had invoices to pay and an order to build, but he felt like doing a little inventory instead.

"Kerry?" No answer but the muted rumble of a car passing outside. She was probably in the restroom.

Then he heard a sound at the far end of housewares. Something that sounded a lot like a whimper. *What the hell?*

At the end of the aisle he found Kerry in a crouch, her hand to her head, her hair hiding her face. The clipboard lay beside her, the pages loose and scattered.

"Jesus, what happened?" He squatted beside her. "Kerry. Did you hit your head?"

She was pulling in deep, shuddering breaths. Slowly she tipped forward until she was on her knees, one hand braced on the floor, the other still pressed to her head. "Just…give me a minute," she whispered. "I'll be okay."

He placed a hand on her back. "Are you crying?" He popped up and passed a scowl around the store. "Did someone say something to you?"

She huffed a feeble laugh. "No, it's just…sometimes I get these headaches."

Shit. He grimaced. "You have a migraine?"

"Something like that," she whispered, and bent

lower, as if wanting to rest her head on the floor. "If I could just stay here a minute…"

"Screw that. You need to be in bed."

"Yes," she said faintly. "Okay." She started a slight rocking motion. "Could you grab my purse for me, please?"

His blood went cold. "Is the baby okay? Do you need to go to the hospital?"

She shook her head, then moaned. "I'll be okay, I just need to lie down. Could you get my keys?"

"You're in no shape to walk to the door, let alone cross the street." She was forgetting he didn't need her keys, anyway. "Come on. Let's get you up."

He pulled her to her feet as carefully as he could. She slapped weakly at his arm.

"I can do it," she snapped. She straightened, took one step and sagged into a rack of gardening gloves.

"Like hell," Gil snarled. He braced one arm behind her back and the other behind her knees. Despite her protests, he lifted. He grunted, lurched sideways, and pushed himself upright with a shoulder to the wall.

Really frickin' heroic, Coop.

Kerry whimpered, and closed her eyes.

"I won't drop you," he said.

"Even when I throw up?"

He paused, and eyed the distance to the bathroom. "Do you need to?"

"It could happen."

"Can you wait until we get upstairs?"

Her eyes shot open. "You're not taking me home?"

"I can keep an eye on you here."

"I need my own bed."

He took a moment to hoist her higher, then strode toward the stairs. "If we continue to stand here arguing then I will drop you."

As he started to climb the stairs she dropped her head to his shoulder. Tenderness, and a sharp need, spiraled through him. Jesus, he was in trouble.

"You're sweating," she said.

"You're heavy," he shot back.

She stiffened, then hissed in a breath, and he knew his words weren't the problem. He hated that she was in so much pain. He hated even more that if he didn't put her down soon, they were both going to end up hitting the floor.

At the top of the stairs he kicked open the door and staggered across to his bed. He set her down on the unmade sheets, on the side of the mattress closer to the bathroom. Immediately she rolled to her side and hung her head over the edge.

Frantically he glanced around, then lunged at the gift his ex had given him the year before, a peace lily the size of a bar stool. He turned the pot upside down, dumping the contents on the floor, and placed the planter within spewing distance of Kerry.

"There," he said, brushing his palms. "Let loose."

She laughed weakly. "You did not just do that."

"I'd rather clean up dirt than puke. Especially if the puke has chunks."

She moaned and dug her fingers into the sheets.

Okay, so no more vomit jokes.

He pushed a hand through his hair and crouched beside the bed. "What do you need?" he asked. "Should I call your doctor?"

"No," she said faintly. "I took some ibuprofen. I just need to keep it down. Do you have ginger ale?"

"I'll check." Before frisking his kitchen cupboards, he took a detour to the bathroom and wet a washcloth with cold water. When he placed it gently on Kerry's forehead, the small, relieved sound she made had him feeling like he could carry her up and down the stairs a dozen more times.

Okay, fine. Ten.

Make that two.

If he had help.

Five minutes later, he'd unearthed a bag of stale pretzels. If he tried to feed her those she'd hurl for sure. Instead he made her a piece of wheat toast and added that to the glass of lemon-lime soda he'd already arranged on a meat platter.

He set the "tray" on the nightstand and brandished a straw. "Thank God for fast food," he said. He unwrapped the straw and dropped it into the glass of soda. "Sip of soda, bite of toast. Let's start out slow."

Obediently she sipped, then took a small bite of toast, the look on her face as she chewed making it obvious she wasn't enjoying it. Finally she swallowed and lay back down, wincing as her head hit the pillow.

"What about the store?" she asked.

Screw the store, he wanted to say. "I'll go back downstairs as soon as you're settled," he said. He returned the glass to the tray and knelt at her feet. He untied her shoes and slipped them off one by one, and peeled off her ankle socks.

She flexed her toes and sighed. "Thank you," she murmured.

"You're welcome." He lined up her shoes by the bed and tugged at his ear. "I don't suppose you'd let me have your jeans, too?"

She answered with a half-hearted snort.

"Another time, then. Ready for some more toast?"

All in all, she managed four bites and half a dozen sips. They were awkward ones—she ate and drank while lying on her side, her head half off the bed. When it looked as though the toast and soda would stay down, Gil freshened the washcloth on her forehead, closed the blinds on either side of the bed and jogged downstairs to retrieve her purse. Which weighed a frickin' ton.

Back upstairs, he tucked her phone under her pillow. "I'm just a call away," he said.

"Thank you," she whispered, her voice thick with tears. "I should be fine in an hour or so."

Right. And he wouldn't spill anything on himself today.

He worked the blanket and sheet free and pulled them up to her shoulder, then backed away from the bed. She looked so miserable. He wanted to stay. He wanted to hold her until she felt better.

But what he needed to do was leave her the hell alone so that time, and the ibuprofen, could do their thing.

He moved toward the stairs. He'd give Ruthie a heads-up. Kerry might be feeling better in a couple of hours, but no way she'd be up for the lunch shift. Dinner, maybe. Though he hoped she'd stay put. She needed the rest.

Yeah, that's why you want her in your bed.

He grimaced at his own thoughts and swung around. And froze.

A man stood at the top of the stairs, in dress pants, a shirt and tie, one hand in his pocket, the other holding a can of orange soda.

"Jesus Christ," Gil gasped, hand to his chest.

"Yo, G." With a grating *snick* his brother popped open the can. "Is this a bad time?"

Gil hovered at the bottom of the stairs, reluctant to move further into the store in case Kerry called out. His brother meanwhile wandered the aisles, poking at inventory and adjusting displays, much as Kerry had on her first day of work. Except her expression had been more thoughtful than derisive.

"You've made some changes, but I'd recognize this place blindfolded." Ferrell ran a hand down his bright blue tie. "You almost didn't recognize me, though, right?"

Gil narrowed his gaze, but his brother's hand remained tremor free. His eyes looked clear, his body lean but not gaunt.

Hope, sharp and sweet, made his shoulders feel suddenly lighter.

"Not with that moustache, no." He pushed out of his inertia and moved toward Ferrell, his hand outstretched. "You look good."

"So do you." Ferrell tested Gil's grip and grinned. "You've been working out."

"Trying to get back into a routine."

"Because of her?" Ferrell motioned with his chin at the stairs. "Who is she?"

Gil wasn't ready to go there yet. "A friend."

"Uh-huh." Ferrell flashed a sly smile before spreading his arms, indicating the empty store. "Looks like you've got some time on your hands. How about you show me how much Snoozy's has changed?"

"How long will you be in town?"

"Just passing through." Ferrell made a show of tugging at his cuffs. "I have a job interview in Cleveland tomorrow, but what do you say to a couple of brewskies, for old times' sake?"

Gil hesitated. He hadn't seen his brother in years, and their most recent conversations had been hostile and unproductive. Yet here they were, politely and casually talking face-to-face.

Something was up.

"Ferrell."

"Yeah, G." He turned his back on the rack of gadgets he'd been studying, and that's when Gil saw it.

Ferrell was scratching his right arm as though he'd been attacked by a ravenous swarm of mosquitoes.

"What's up with your—" Before Gil could even get the question out, Ferrell was digging at his neck. When he realized what he was doing, he dropped his hand, but it was too late.

Son of a bitch.

Gil caught his breath at the sudden bruise-like ache spreading across his chest. "You are still using."

Not quite pulling off a sneer, his brother shrugged. "So I take the occasional hit. I told you I have an interview tomorrow. I go in there all stressed and cranky and no way I'll get the job."

"You get behind the wheel like this and chances are you won't make it to Cleveland alive." Gil concentrated on unclenching his molars. "Stay here. Let's get you some help."

"Screw that."

"Ferrell." Gil shoved his hands in his pockets so he wouldn't start grabbing things off the shelves and heaving them at the floor. "I want to help."

"No, you want to make the rules. I don't need help, I need money."

And there it was.

Gil looked him square in the eye. "You can shake this."

"I don't know, bro." Ferrell propped an elbow on the cash register. "Can you shake your 'friend' upstairs?"

"That's different."

"She's a drug, same as heroin. Eventually she'll wreck you."

Gil yanked his hands from his pockets and strode toward the counter. His brother's eyes widened as Gil approached, but he didn't move.

"Is there really a job?" Gil demanded.

Ferrell scratched his ribs. "I'm not in a good place for the whole nine to five, you know?"

"You're not in a good place, period. What can I do to help you get clean?"

"You can let me figure out my own goddamned life." He pushed upright. "I'm out of here."

"Ferrell—"

"No. I'm done."

But he didn't move, and Gil knew he was holding out for cash. He cleared his throat. "I love you."

Ferrell snorted. "I can tell." He pulled a set of keys from the front pocket of his khakis. "But that won't put gas in my car."

Nice try. "At least let me know where you're going."

"I was thinking the Everglades. You know, taking a one-way trip on one of those airboats."

Gil jerked to attention. "Don't do anything stupid."

"You mean, like Dad?" Ferrell grimaced. "I know better. He didn't end his pain, he just passed it on."

They both fell silent.

Then Gil swore.

"Wait a minute. The Everglades? You're headed to Florida to bum off of Mom, aren't you?"

"At least she's always glad to see me."

Gil faced the counter, both hands gripping the edge. "You know damned well she can't afford to help you out."

"She has friends, doesn't she?" He rounded the far end of the counter and eyed the cash register.

"Ferrell. Don't do this."

"You're remembering why it's been so long since we saw each other, am I right? Don't feel guilty." He pressed a button and the cash register pinged, but the drawer didn't open. "We all make our choices and we all have to live with 'em."

"We can make new choices."

"Don't you lecture me, G." Ferrell stabbed at another button. When he got the same protesting ping, he scrubbed at his moustache and pointed a finger at Gil. "Don't you goddamn dare. At least I tried with Dad. At least I cared. Now tell me the damned code so I can get some gas money and get the hell out of here."

Slowly Gil straightened. "I made a mistake with Dad. I just…let him go. I don't want to make the same mistake with you."

"I'm not interested in some frickin' family game night, I'm interested in some funding." He banged his fist on the cash register keys. "You giving all your money to that bitch upstairs? Is she the reason you don't have any left for me?"

Even as Gil reminded himself that was the addiction talking, he couldn't stem the surge of fury behind his breastbone. "You have two minutes to walk out that door," he said grimly. "Two minutes before I call the cops."

"So this is you practicing tough love?" Ferrell gave his head a disgusted shake, but it was the register he had his eye on. "Damn it!" he yelled, and stomped back around the counter. "I came here looking for my brother, not some sanctimonious drill sergeant prick." He stalked to the door and rammed it open with a ninety-degree kick. The glass cracked under his shoe and the cowbells hit the floor with a mournful clatter. "Thanks for nothing, G."

Ferrell stormed off. Gil closed his eyes and held his breath. Seconds later he heard a metallic *whump* outside—the exact sound a man's boot might make when it connected with the side panel of a silver F-150.

Gil rubbed his chest. At least his insurance was paid up.

KERRY ROLLED OVER onto her back and slowly opened her eyes. She blinked into the dimness, and gradually registered the absence of pain. No more headache, no more nausea.

Thank you, God.

She yawned, and frowned up at the raftered ceiling high above her. Where was she? She moved her legs, and felt the twisted, uncomfortable drag of her jeans. She was still dressed. Right. She'd never left Gil's. He'd carried her upstairs.

Holy Hannah. The man was lucky he hadn't put his back out. A humiliated, full-body flush had her kicking off the sheet.

A muttered curse and a rhythmic brushing somewhere to her right brought her up onto her elbows. Through the gloom she could make out Gil working a brush and dustpan as he cleaned up the dirt he'd dumped earlier. Something rattled and he swore again.

Kerry cleared her throat. "Wouldn't that be easier with the light on?"

He dropped the dustpan and straightened. "Hey. Feeling better?" He took a step toward her, hissed in a breath and jerked up his knee. "Ouch, damn it." He hopped over to the bed, sat down and leaned over his foot. Two seconds later, something clattered against the opposite wall.

"I forgot there were rocks in the planter," he said.

"And now it's out there lurking, just waiting for you to step on it again."

He shifted around on the bed so he faced her. "You *are* feeling better."

"I am, thanks." She sat up and scooted back against the headboard. His eyes gleamed at her out of the shadows as she ran both hands through her hair.

"So," she said. "I heard Mrs. Yackley call you Gilbert."

He grunted. "What did you think 'Gil' was short for? Emperor of the Known Universe?"

"I was thinking more along the lines of 'Gilligan.'"

His face scrunched in a mock scowl. "You're lucky you're carrying my baby."

"I was thinking the same thing," she said softly, and blushed. "Thank you for taking such good care of me."

His scowl disappeared, but he didn't say anything.

She put a hand to her forehead. "I must have really been out of it. Was someone else here?"

He got to his feet. "Let me get you a glass of water. Mind if I turn on a light?"

She shook her head, and watched as he moved away and hit a switch. Soft light filtered out of his kitchen and stretched across the bed.

Holy Hannah, his place was huge. It was all one room, with dark wood floors and planked walls the color of oak, like the rafters that supported the roof, which had to be a good twenty feet above her head. To her left was the door he'd told her opened into the bathroom, and the door on the other end of the wall led back downstairs to the store. To her right a black metal staircase spiraled upward to a catwalk adjoining a wall of jam-packed bookshelves, and beneath that, the kitchen, a cozy space with teal accents.

Gil, barefoot in steel-blue sweatpants and a tight-fitting tee, stood at the sink, wrestling an ice tray. The muscles in his back and arms flexed as he twisted the white plastic tray, and Kerry's brain began to sputter, like an engine on its last drop of gas.

"Wow," she said, suddenly wishing with all her might that she had the freedom to reacquaint herself with those muscles.

He glanced over with a grin. "Some place, right?"

Well, yeah, that too.

He opened a cupboard and grabbed two glasses. She should get up. She should not make him serve her. Not any more than he already had. But a distant pounding in her head signaled that her headache hadn't entirely given up on her yet.

"Thank you," she said, as Gil handed her a glass of water.

"You're welcome. Want to take your clothes off?"

She choked and spewed water. Gil reached behind him and grabbed something off a chair, a T-shirt, and brushed at the droplets.

He tossed the shirt aside. "I only meant you might want to change into something more comfortable. I can loan you a T-shirt—not that wet one—and a pair of boxers if you'd like."

Her pulse started to race as she eyed his outfit. "Is that what you wear to bed?"

"Too much?" He slid his thumbs behind his waistband. "Want me to take something off?"

CHAPTER ELEVEN

Yes.

"No! I mean…" Kerry threw back the sheet and sat up. Ignored Gil's protest and glanced around for her phone, a clock, anything. "What time is it?"

"Around six."

"Six?" She shot to her feet and instantly felt like her head was about to float away. She dropped back down onto her butt. "Oh, my God. The bar. Who's at the bar?" She glared up at Gil. "Why did you let me sleep? Now Snoozy will let me go for sure."

"Because you needed it." He lowered into a squat and put a hand on her knee. "I called Liz. She's handling it. She said not to worry, that she and Ruthie have it covered, and they'll see you for your shift tomorrow if you're feeling up to it."

"She'd have had to ask my dad for time off, which means he knows I blew off the bar today."

"Hey. You didn't blow it off. You're sick." He gave her knee a squeeze. "How about some soup and crackers? Afterward you can lie back down and get some sleep."

It sounded divine. It was humbling, the way he was taking care of her. And not something she was used to. But the fact that she enjoyed his care-giving so much was the very reason she couldn't accept any more of it.

Well, maybe the soup. But that was it. After the soup, she'd be on her way.

"Something to eat sounds wonderful," she said. "But after that I need to go."

"Not to the bar."

She hesitated, then shook her head. As much as she wanted to, she wasn't feeling up to it. She wasn't feeling up to Liz, either.

"No," she said. "Home."

He slapped his hands on his thighs and stood. "You stay put while I work my magic with the can opener. After dinner I'll walk you across the street."

Canned chicken noodle had never tasted so good. They ate on the couch, their bowls balanced on their knees, in the gloom that wouldn't aggravate the ache in Kerry's head.

She ate slowly. She didn't want to spill. She didn't want to leave, either.

Neither spoke. The only sounds in the loft were the clank of metal against ceramic, the occasional slurp and the gentle whirring of the overhead fans.

When Gil leaned forward and placed his empty bowl on the coffee table, then turned to face Kerry, she held her breath. If he asked her again to stay, she didn't know if she could find the energy to refuse him.

"You did see someone," he said. His clasped hands hung between his knees. "Here, I mean. You weren't dreaming. It was my brother."

"Your brother? I didn't know you had a brother. Is he still here?"

Gil shook his head. "He's part of the reason I lost it when you came looking for a job. That comment you made, about entitlement…it reminded me of my brother. He and I don't get along."

Somehow she managed to scoot back on the couch and tuck herself into the corner without spilling a drop. "Tell me about him."

"Another time."

She lifted her bowl. "As much as you can until I'm done."

He gave her a look over the top of his glasses. He knew what she was up to, but he didn't call her on it.

For appearance's sake, she lifted the empty spoon to her mouth. "Does he live around here?"

"No." He turned and collapsed against the back of the couch, his thigh inches from her feet. "I don't know."

Kerry suppressed a wince. There had to be a lot of unhappy history behind those three words. "What happened?"

He took off his glasses and rubbed his eyes. When he opened them again, he didn't put his glasses back on and Kerry couldn't look away. The intimacy of the moment made her feel outside herself, as if she were watching someone else connect with Gil.

It was familiar, yet not. If they ever hooked up again, there would be no bubbly wonder about the possibility of love. They would be two people connecting because they'd made a baby. Which meant hooking up again would not be a good idea. Reading more into that bond meant certain heartbreak.

"My parents invested everything they had in this store," Gil said. "When the economy took a nosedive, their relationship did, too. Running a business—it's tough. It made my mom hard. It wasn't a complete surprise but it hurt like hell when we found out Dad was cheating on her. My mom kicked him out. He moved two states away and I never saw him again. I talked to him on the phone a few times, but...it never went well."

The weariness in his voice pinched at her heart. She touched a foot to his thigh, and his hand came down to rest on her ankle.

"He wanted her to sell the store, but she always thought he'd come back, and she wanted Cooper's to be here for him when he did."

"He never did?"

"After his girlfriend left him, he fell into a depression. My brother talked with him a few times, but every day I was faced with the mess his leaving had made and I refused to speak to him. Ferrell mentioned Dad seemed down, but we didn't realize how bad off he was until we got the call that he'd shot himself."

God. "Gil. I'm so sorry." She set her soup aside and squeezed his arm. "How long has it been?"

"Six years. I see it now, that he needed an escape, but at the time Ferrell and I were in our early twenties, wrapped up in our own lives and always griping about not having any free time." He shrugged. "So here I am, fighting to keep the store open because the Cooper family has put so much into it. Time, money, heartache... Mom lives in Florida now, with her sister, but if she ever comes back, the store will be waiting."

Kerry bit her lip. She was here to listen, not judge. "That explains your reaction that night at the bar when I made that stupid joke about pouring you a suicide."

He stroked her ankle. "You didn't know." He put his glasses back on and pointed at her bowl. "Finished?"

She shook her head and picked it up again. There were maybe two spoonfuls of soup left. She swallowed one. "Is that why you and your brother don't get along? Because you wouldn't talk to your father?"

"That's one reason. Mostly it's because he was stealing."

Kerry blanched.

"He'd found a buddy who could turn inventory into cash. It took us a while to figure it out and even when we did, Mom didn't want to believe it. Turned out he was using the money for drugs."

"So with your dad gone, your mom struggling with her new reality and your brother on drugs, you were the one holding it all together."

"Not very well. I should have handled the situation with Ferrell better. He left not long after my dad died. He wanted us to sell, but only so he could get his hands on his share of the proceeds. Considering the hole we were in, there wouldn't have been anything left. He took off in the middle of the night, sent us a postcard a couple months later, saying he'd found a job working construction. I didn't hear from him again until…well, around the time you and I met."

Kerry twisted her lips. He hadn't spoken to his brother in six years? "Is he still on drugs?"

"Yeah." His hand tightened on her ankle. "He said he was clean, but he lied."

"Maybe he hasn't hit rock bottom yet," she said softly. After a couple beats of silence, she asked, "So he won't be back?"

"No. I can't have that around my kid."

His response reassured her and saddened her at the same time. "You and I seem to have family estrangement in common."

Abruptly Gil sat up and held out a hand for her bowl.

She passed it over without protest, and watched as he stacked his bowl on top of hers. "Actually, I guess I have more in common with your brother, since he was the source of the estrangement."

"Can I get you anything else?"

Hurt collected in her throat. That was a dismissal if ever she'd heard one.

A swallow scattered the ache as she stood and walked stiffly back to the bed. "Did you ever involve the police?"

Gil spoke over his shoulder as he moved into the kitchen. "My mother made it clear that if I did she'd never talk to me again. I figured I had to leave her one family member in her life."

"But you don't keep in touch with her."

"Not as much as I should."

Kerry sat on the end of the bed and pulled on her socks. "You should call her. I'd give anything to be able to talk to mine."

Dishes thunked into his stainless-steel sink. "I'll keep that in mind."

With a sigh Kerry finished tying her shoes, then gathered up her purse. She opened her mouth to ask Gil about her phone, then remembered he'd tucked it under the pillow. As Gil stood at the sink, hands braced and arms stick-straight, she retrieved her phone and crossed the loft to the outside door.

"Gil, I'm sorry. This is none of my business. It's just...having someone do what you did for me today, and sharing a quiet meal…it's been nice. But in a false way. I get that." With her shoulder, she pushed her hair away from her cheek. "Thank you for getting me through a tough time. I won't make sick days a habit, I promise. As long as the baby cooperates, anyway. I'll see you in the morning."

"Yes" was all he said. He didn't try to talk her into staying, or insist on walking her across the street, or even advise her to watch out for traffic.

That casual yes neutralized the closeness they'd established. Which was a good thing, right? She had to focus on the reason she was here in the first place.

But the words were practically slamming against her teeth, so she opened up and let them out. "Can I ask you something?"

"Kerry." A two-syllable warning.

She ignored it. "You seem to really love the hardware store. The work, not so much."

He straightened and faced her. "What do you mean?"

"You're distracted. I know you're worried about finances, and now there's the baby to complicate things, but I was wondering if you're happy running Cooper's."

His gaze narrowed. "It pisses me off when my buddy Seth says things like that. Imagine how it makes me feel when you say them."

Okay, then. "It's just that you seem more passionate about math, and teaching."

"I'm not cut out to be a teacher."

"How can you say that? You are a teacher. All that online mentoring you do? All that time you spend with Dylan? All the people you teach downstairs to use tools and finish projects?"

He looked away, shaking his head.

Dread, heavy and frigid, expanded in her chest, making it hard to breathe. "This is about the baby, isn't it?" she whispered.

"Let's just say it's not the best time to consider changing careers."

"Oh, Gil. You thought about it, didn't you?" That's what he'd meant, that time he'd spoken about setting dreams aside.

He didn't say anything, but she had her answer.

"How do you not hate me?"

"How could I hate you for making the same choice I made? Besides, you're having my baby. You said something once, about unconditional love. That's what I want, too."

"But it's costing you your dreams."

"That's what parents do, right? They sacrifice." He jolted back into movement, skirting the dustpan and the rest of the mess on the floor as he walked toward her. "They also teach their children to stand up for themselves."

She folded her arms over her waist. "Why do I get the feeling that's a slam?"

"Yesterday, out on the loading dock, you said you were going to talk to your father about moving in with him. You haven't done that yet, have you? Which makes me wonder whether you came to Castle Creek to make amends or to distance yourself from what you did in North Carolina."

He was deflecting. But these were things that needed to be said, so she let him get away with it.

"Mostly the first, some of the second." She fought to keep her lips from quivering. "I actually convinced myself I was earning your respect. Satisfying you that I'd changed. But that's not the case at all. You've been easing up on me because of the baby."

"If we're going to raise a child together, we might as well get along."

"I'm thinking your definition of 'getting along' includes having sex, but that's not going to happen. And no, it's not about payback. It's about self-preservation. I'm half in love with you already."

His eyes went wide, then he slid his hands into the pockets of his sweatpants and curved his shoulders inward. "How am I supposed to trust that's not just you taking the easy way out again?"

"What is that supposed to mean?"

"It would be convenient, wouldn't it, if you and I ended up together? Then your housing problem is solved—"

"I don't have a housing problem."

"—and we don't have to hash out custody—"

"Wait." Her hand went to her throat and she felt the blood leave her face like islanders fleeing a volcano. "Custody? Are you planning to take me to *court*?"

An ugly sense of betrayal clawed at her heart. Dear God, no. Yes, she was the baby's mother and she was intent on getting her life together, but she was also a broke ex-felon surviving solely through the kindness of others. Her own father didn't even want anything to do with her.

She stumbled back a step. If Gil took her to court, she couldn't count on her dad to testify on her behalf. And the rest of her life would speak for itself.

"Kerry, no. I shouldn't have said that. I didn't mean it." Gil was suddenly standing in front of her, hands fumbling for hers. "Look at me. Please."

Strong fingers gripped her wrists. She looked up, but couldn't focus on his face. Tears, she realized. She could taste them.

Lightly he shook her arms. "I'm sorry I said that. I would never take the baby away. We'll figure something out. We'll do it together. Okay?"

Panic resonated in his voice. He was just as scared that she'd keep the baby from him. Two days ago, they'd been dreading the positive test result. How had they gotten here so fast?

She drew in a shuddering breath, and nodded. "Okay," she managed. "Okay. I have to go."

He was right. It was way past time to talk to her father.

She let Gil pull her into a brief hug, agreed she'd see him in the morning and let herself out of his apartment. All the while she could barely breathe, as if her lungs had been ironed flat.

That Gil could hurt her so deeply made one thing clear. She wasn't just halfway in love with him. She was gone, baby, gone. Meanwhile, he might have given her access to his cash register, but he still didn't trust her with what really mattered.

IT WAS AFTER eight when Kerry stepped up onto her father's front porch. The outside lights were on, but she didn't hear the TV inside. Fingers crossed she wasn't about to drag the old man out of bed or he'd probably egg his own porch just to get her off it.

She bounced on her toes a few times and shoved her hair behind her ears. After pulling in a deep breath, she raised her hand to knock lightly on the door, thought better of it and leaned on the doorbell. She wasn't going anywhere until she had a chance to talk with him, so she might as well make some noise.

He took so long to answer, she wondered if he'd peeked through the blinds, seen her standing there and gone to arm himself with some eggs, after all. Then the door swung open, his hands were empty, and the overpowering scent of just-applied aftershave told her he'd hoped to find Eugenia on the other side.

She prayed she managed to keep the pity from her face.

He didn't quite manage to keep the disappointment from his. But she'd take disappointment over outrage any day.

"Hi," she said. "I'm sorry for coming by so late."

He hesitated, then stepped back and waved her inside. "Guess Gil told you I called."

"What? No." She glanced around, caught a quick impression of browns and plaids and dirty dishes on the coffee table before turning back to face her father. "You spoke to Gil?"

"This mornin'. Liz told me you were sick and I wanted to see how you were."

Wait, had she just stepped into an alternate universe? Who was this man and what had he done with her father? "He didn't tell me," she said. "But that was nice of you. Thank you."

"How are you feelin'?"

"Much better. I should. I slept all day."

He gestured at the couch, and once she'd dropped down onto the plaid, he settled in the recliner. "I remember you gettin' those headaches. I'm sorry you're still dealing with them."

"I don't get them as often as I used to." Holy Hannah, this was awkward.

He must have thought so, too. He rubbed his palm over his head and tipped forward in his chair. "If you didn't know I called, then why are you here?"

"Because I need something."

He squinted at her. "What do you need?"

"Advice." She gazed at him steadily. "Maybe even a place to live."

He frowned. "What's wrong with Genie's place?"

"Not a thing. It's perfect. But I haven't asked her if it's okay to have the baby there. And being there at all…" She looked down at her hands. "I feel like this is driving a perpetual wedge between you two. I didn't bother to ask you if it was okay." She raised her head. "I haven't bothered to include you in any major decisions I've made in the past ten years."

His cheeks were reddening and she braced herself. But when he spoke, his voice remained level. Gruff, but level.

"The only one drivin' a wedge between us is me. She let me have it and she let me have it good after I stormed away the morning you told us about the baby. She wasn't too happy about the tulips I ran over, either. You didn't ask me about livin' here for the very same reason. You knew I'd blow my top."

Bull's-eye. "The rest of it was about being

ashamed of the decisions I made. It was about punishing you, too."

"If you're ashamed of that, then you know how I feel, 'cause I've been punishin' you."

Kerry stood and clasped her hands behind her back. "I'm sorry about your heart condition," she said thickly. "Sorry you're having to deal with something like that, and sorry I haven't been around to help."

Harris's shoulders went rigid. Slowly he rocked forward, and pushed to his feet. He didn't look at her, and he didn't speak.

Kerry gulped, the sound obscenely loud in the strained silence. "I know I haven't been a part of your life for a long while, but I'd like to change that. Just…please tell me what I have to do to earn your forgiveness. Because, Dad—" her voice broke "—I don't think I could stand it if you died without forgiving me."

He reached out, and when she stepped forward he patted her into a hug. "I'm so sorry, Kerry girl," he choked out. "I've been makin' you wait for forgiveness I gave a long time ago."

Kerry lifted her head from his shoulder and swiped her palms across her cheeks. "You forgave me?"

"Course I did." He wiped his face on his shirt-sleeve. "You're my daughter."

"Not much of one."

"You've been more a daughter than I've been a

father. I admit I've been pushin' you away. I knew you weren't stayin' long and I didn't want to care so much when you left." He gave the back of his neck a good, long rub. "Then you said you were pregnant, and—" He began to sob, big, coughing gulps of air scraping in and out of his throat. His blue flannel shirt trembled around his body.

Kerry realized with a shock that he'd lost weight since the last time she'd seen him. Fresh tears streamed down her face as she wrapped her arms around him. They both held on tight, until the emotion faded to self-conscious sniffles.

"I'm ashamed of myself," her father said.

She handed him a clean napkin she'd unearthed from the clutter on the coffee table. "I hope you don't mean for crying."

"For making you believe I don't care."

Crumpling her own now-soggy napkin, she shook her head. "You were just returning the favor."

He finished wiping his face and tossed the napkin on the table. Sheepishly he pulled a pack of gum from his shirt pocket and offered it to Kerry.

With a strangled laugh, she accepted a stick. "Most people think of tea as the cure-all. You always did believe in the power of cinnamon gum."

"It helps me think." He patted her on the shoulder and dropped back into his recliner. "Cryin's hard work. I'm exhausted."

She eyed him closely. "You okay?"

"Fine, except for bein' a jackass. Genie calls me that for a reason, you know." He exhaled. "You said you were looking for advice. If it's the romantic kind—"

"It's not."

He heaved a sigh. "Good, 'cause you don't go wishin' on a clover you ain't found yet. Especially when you're searchin' in the dark."

She perched on the arm of the sofa. "I have no idea what that means."

"It means despite my asinine tantrum, I'm pleased as punch I'm goin' to be a grandpa."

"You are?"

"After the way I acted, I was afraid you'd leave town and I'd never see you or the baby. I promise you this. I'll be a better grandfather than I was a father."

She leaned forward and patted his knee. "I promise you this. You won't have to try so hard."

He hesitated. "You and Gil…"

"It was a one-time thing. We were both lonely and reckless and…" She shrugged. "We took precautions, but obviously something didn't work the way it was supposed to."

"So you won't be raising the child together?"

"We won't be living together, if that's what you mean. But we'll both be involved in the baby's life. We just haven't worked out the details yet." Her mind shied away from the word *custody*.

He turned his attention to the small table beside

his recliner, and poked at a stack of catsup- and mustard-smeared plates. Kerry winced. Looked like he'd been eating a lot of hot dogs.

"You're welcome to move in here, if you'd like," he said, too casually.

"I appreciate that. Very much. But what about the baby?"

He lifted an eyebrow. "I'm assuming you'd be bringin' the baby with you."

She couldn't help a laugh. "No, I mean, are you sure you're up for middle-of-the-night squalling and mashed peas in the carpet and the lingering aroma of dirty diapers?"

"You talkin' about you, or the baby?"

"Very funny, Dad." Though she could definitely picture herself indulging in the midnight squalling bit. She wrenched her mind away from thoughts of Gil and stood.

"I'll let you know, okay?" If she didn't move in, at the very least she could start bringing him some healthy meals. "I never wanted to ask your help again. I wanted to make you glad I showed up."

He squinted up at her. "I am. I love you."

Her breath snagged wetly in her throat. "I love you, too, Dad. I want you to know that *I* know I have a lot to make up for."

"You came, and despite all the baloney I've put you through, you stayed. You've already made up for it all." His expression turned sly. "Course, you are just as stubborn as your old man, so I'm bettin' you'll insist."

She hid a smile. "I do insist."

"In that case—" he leaned around her and stared pointedly at the dishes scattered across the coffee table "—I do have a plate or two that could use a little scrubbin'."

BUSINESS WAS DEAD.

Like, call-the-coroner dead.

Kerry stood in the doorway to the supply room, a package of cocktail napkins cradled to her chest as she surveyed the nearly empty bar. No one leaned over the pool table or squinted up at the TV. No one stood vigil by Mitzi's pen, eager for an eye to eye with the Burmese. No one spilled their drink and yelled "My bad!" or crowded the bar asking when the fresh popcorn would be ready.

A few more shifts like this would suck up all the profits from Ladies' Night.

With a sigh, Kerry ripped open the package of napkins and rounded the end of the bar.

Luckily it had been a different story at the hardware store that morning. They'd been so busy that beyond their initial awkward greeting, she and Gil had barely had a chance to talk. They'd had customers waiting outside the door at nine, and Gil had run a router demo at ten.

Kerry knew they had things to discuss. At the

very least she needed to let him know she'd finally talked with her father. *Reconciled* with her father. But she was still smarting over that custody threat.

She was bent down, sliding fresh stacks of cocktail napkins into place, when someone slapped the bar top.

"You stood me up."

Slowly Kerry straightened. Hand on hip, Liz Watts faced her across the bar.

"We need to talk," she said brusquely.

Okay, then. If Liz was going to let her have it, at least she'd picked a slow night to do it.

"I know," Kerry said. "I apologize for not getting back to you. To make up for it, when we do get together for coffee, I'll bring you a box of those cinnamon rolls everyone's raving about." When Liz perked up, Kerry smiled. She never had gotten around to trying one, though both Eugenia and Gil had set her up. She really had to remedy that.

"I can't thank you enough for what you did for me yesterday," she continued. "You and Ruthie rocked it. The place was spick-and-span when I got in this morning, with all the receipts and records in perfect order."

Liz bristled. "I worked here for years. Of course everything was in order."

"I wasn't worried about the bar," Kerry said

gently. "Just what Snoozy would think of me for ditching work."

"I spoke to Gil. He said you were really sick. That's not ditching." Liz gathered her crinkly hair up off her neck, then let it go again. "Look, my gripe is the assumption that you and I would get along simply because my husband, Marcus, spent time in prison. No one said it outright, but I know Snoozy and Eugenia were thinking it." Her eyebrows drew together. "Marcus and I don't like to be reminded of that."

Kerry gave the ice in the bin a few stirs with the scoop. "I get it," she said, and left it at that, since Liz seemed to want to talk.

Liz slid onto a stool, and ran a palm across the smooth surface of the bar top. The wistfulness in her expression finally got through to Kerry.

"This is about the bar," Kerry said. "You wanted to be the one to run it while Snoozy was away."

Liz's shrug was casual. Too casual. "I do miss my job here. I had fun yesterday."

"What do you do for Parker?"

"A lot of different things. I prep the soil, spray and harvest the plants, pot and label the seedlings, and keep the digital records. But since we mostly sell in bulk, there's not a lot of customer interaction."

"And that's what you miss?"

"That's one of the things."

"But working here means being inside all day."

"It also means spending a lot less money on sun block."

Kerry eyed Liz's fair skin and nodded in understanding. "Why don't you come back?" It was a natural suggestion, but Kerry found it tough to make.

"It's not as easy as it sounds. I made a commitment to Parker and Harris and the greenhouses. Ruthie has my old job here and even if Snoozy would let me take it away from her, I wouldn't. I make more money working for Parker and besides, working evenings isn't optimal when you have a small child."

"Maybe you could split your time between the two." Kerry poured her a diet soda and added a slice of lime, since Liz didn't seem to care for cherries. When she held it out, she received a genuine smile in return and the entire bar seemed to brighten. "You know, work mornings at the greenhouse and afternoons here."

"I couldn't do that. That would cut into Ruthie's hours."

"It might be worth it to ask." Kerry hesitated. "But you and me. Are we good?"

Liz considered. "Shove that bowl of popcorn my way and we're golden."

The door opened and Dylan slouched in. Despite the fifty-something degrees outside, he wore his customary long-sleeved tee over basketball shorts. Tonight the shorts were lime green.

"Hey, Dylan," Liz said. "Good to see you again." She slid off the stool and lifted her drink and the popcorn bowl. "Mind if I take these back to the kitchen? I want to tell Ruthie that Dylan's here. He was such a huge help last night, we promised him a treat tonight, didn't we, Dyl?"

He blushed.

"The biggest banana split this side of Lake Erie. Ruthie went out and got the sprinkles special this morning." Liz's expression turned long-suffering. "Better get my visit in before Burke shows up and Ruthie doesn't want anything to do with me."

Kerry resisted the urge to indulge in an I-hear-you-sister eye roll. After what he'd said about her at the hardware store, Burke Yancey was not her favorite person. He was a well-behaved bar regular, though, and she had a business to run.

Well. Until Snoozy got back.

Liz headed for the kitchen. Kerry reached across the bar and gave Dylan a friendly shove on the shoulder.

"Look at you. Impressing the ladies left and right. By the way, I missed you yesterday."

"Me, too," he mumbled. "And Gil."

"I know. I'm sorry. I was sick and he was kind enough to take care of me. Did you get your homework done?"

He nodded, but it was a lackluster motion.

She peered closer. He was looking a little green. "How about you? Feeling okay?"

"Yeah."

"You sure? Want some ginger ale?"

Another nod, but when she placed the glass in front of him, he did nothing more than toy with the straw.

A regular came in, waved and headed for the pool table. Kerry set about pouring his usual Jack Daniel's, neat. "Is someone bothering you at school?"

"No," he mumbled, then "Yeah. But I'm used to it."

"Boys your age?"

"Mostly."

"Want to talk about it?"

He wagged his head, though his expression remained more despondent than mutinous.

"It's okay if you don't want to talk," she said lightly. "I have paperwork I need to tend to, anyway." She moved away long enough to greet her regular, surrender his drink and take his credit card. When she returned, she was relieved to see Dylan had taken a swig of his ginger ale. "But hey, if you're determined to be the strong, silent type tonight, once you're finished taking care of Mitzi you could move a few boxes for me, back in the storeroom."

His chin moved and Kerry's throat went thick. What had the poor kid so upset that he was nearly in tears? She ran the credit card, wondering how Dylan would react if she rounded the bar and gave him a hug. As she returned the card to its owner, Dylan pushed to his feet. "It's just that I have this big history test Monday and if I don't pass it I'll probably have to go to summer school."

"I can see why you'd want to avoid that."

"But I don't have anywhere to study."

Kerry frowned. "Is something happening at your house?"

"Gil didn't tell you?"

"Tell me what?"

He pulled his lips in, then shrugged. "It's too quiet there."

That was code for something, but what, she didn't know. She hadn't asked Gil about Dylan's confidences because she hadn't wanted to pry. Maybe she should have.

"It's not quiet here." She looked around and made a face. "Not usually, anyway. You can't do it here?"

"Ruthie's always dragging me to the back to do dishes."

"Good point. How about a friend's house?"

"My friends aren't into studying," he said scornfully. "They're into gaming and TV and stuff."

Kerry rested her elbows on the bar. She was running out of ideas. "Could you hang at the library?"

"You're not allowed any drinks and stuff."

"You definitely need drinks and stuff when you're trying to study."

He shoved at his ginger ale. "I don't know why we have to learn about the stupid Jazz Age, anyway. Who cares if I have to go to summer school? At least then I won't be stuck at home with—" He broke off.

With who? An abusive parent? But wouldn't Gil have said something, if Dylan had told him about it?

She stood straight and slapped the bar. "Tell you what. How about hanging out at my place? I mean, if you can find a way there and back."

Dylan stared. "For real?"

"You need a ride somewhere?" Liz was back. She leaned on the bar beside Dylan and bumped shoulders with him. "I can take you."

"Dylan needs a place to study. I told him he was welcome to my apartment."

"Oh?" Liz wrinkled her brow. "Alone?"

"Gil's right across the street," Dylan said excitedly. "And I'll lock the door, and I've got my phone. I could get my brother to come pick me up when he's done his shift at the diner."

Liz straightened. "Sounds like you have it all worked out. I'll ask Ruthie to make that banana split to go."

Kerry pulled her purse out from under the bar and rummaged for her keys. "Just lock up and leave the key under the mat when you go." She separated the apartment key from the rest of the keys on the ring and held it out to Dylan. When he reached for it, she pulled it back. "No wild parties, no X-rated movies, no deciding it'd be neat to see the view from the roof. You stay inside the apartment and your books stay open. Deal?"

His lips twitched as he nodded soberly. "Deal."

"One last thing. You need to get your parents' okay first."

He exhaled. "Just my dad's."

"Your mom's not around?"

"She's sick."

Kerry's heart sank. That explained the quiet he'd described.

While Kerry waited on another customer, Dylan called his father, who seemed too distracted for much of a conversation. Dylan hung up with a Christmas-came-early expression that revealed he hadn't expected his father to give permission.

He finished taking care of Mitzi's needs just as Liz banged out of the kitchen, carrying a takeout bag. "Ready?"

Burke Yancey strolled out behind her, eating a bowl of what looked like macaroni and cheese. Kerry blinked. She hadn't even realized he was here tonight.

While Liz and Dylan were walking out, Gil walked in, and Kerry's stomach knotted.

He spoke to them briefly, then turned toward

the bar. He looked tired, but fresh. His hair was slicked over to the side, and he wore the same khakis and button-down he'd worn to her doctor's appointment.

He must be going out.

She wished she had the right to ask him where.

His expression remained casual as he joined her at the bar. "Dylan seemed pretty excited about having your place to himself."

"His mother is sick, apparently."

"She has cancer."

Oh, no. "I'm sorry to hear that."

"I guess his dad likes him to stay around the house in case he's needed, but lately he's just as happy to have him gone, because…" Gil's mouth turned down at the corners. "I don't think his mom has a lot of time left."

Kerry's eyes burned. "No wonder he's having a tough time at school."

"Anyway." Gil braced his elbows on the bar and leaned in. "How're you holding up? You barely had a chance to drink your coffee this morning, the store was so busy. You feeling all right?"

His concern touched her, and she fought a blush as she recalled the cozy, naughty sensation of waking in his bed.

Concern, disdain…what did he truly feel for her? Whatever the answer, she couldn't help the warm prickle in her belly that sparked into life whenever she thought of him. Couldn't stop from imagining him naked in her bed, his back against the headboard, hands behind his head, displaying biceps as defined as the abs she'd found been so gratifying to explore. The night they'd met he'd claimed to be out of shape, but that same night he'd proved himself to be more than fit, again and again.

Her thighs clenched tight as she imagined him telling her in a low-pitched voice that he'd never been this desperate for anyone. Slowly he'd take off his glasses and lean to the side to set them on the nightstand, muscles bunching, eyes never leaving her face...

"Kerry?"

There was no stopping the surge of heat this time. Not even her ears dodged the burn. She ducked her head and stared wistfully at the ice bin. "I'm fine, thanks," she managed.

"Good." He sounded doubtful. "I was hoping you and I would get a chance to talk tonight, but I have to go see Joe about Audrey's gift for Snoozy. Joe's the one who built Mitzi's pen in the first place, so I volunteered him to help install the tub. After that I have to drive to Buffalo to pick up a special order for a customer. If I get back before you close, could we talk then?"

She bobbed her head. "Sure."

He seemed to want to say more, but the door opened and a noisy group of young professionals tumbled in.

At least things were looking up, business-wise.

Gil left, and Kerry watched those khakis moving away until a thirsty customer blocked her view.

KERRY TOOK HER time closing the bar, but Gil never returned. She didn't know whether to be disappointed or relieved.

The route back to the apartment remained deserted, and as she parked in the lot beside the dress shop, her chest ached with a misery she had no reason to feel.

"Sorry, baby," she whispered into the shadowed quiet of the car. "This isn't about you. I'm just feeling a little blue." Whether from Dylan's situation, or wishing things could be different between her and Gil, she couldn't say.

She cut the headlights and sat, listening to the metronome-like ticking of the engine as it cooled. The sound wasn't as soothing as she'd hoped.

She lifted her gaze to the hardware store's second story. No lights. She squinted toward the alley, but couldn't detect any telltale glints of metal or glass. Gil wasn't home yet from picking up that special order. That explained why he hadn't shown back up at the bar for their talk. Still she couldn't help wondering if he was okay.

She could call. They were having a baby together—surely the protocol for that sort of thing would allow her a wellness check. She'd almost puked on him, for God's sake.

But she didn't want to intrude. Which meant that once she got inside her apartment, she'd sit in the kitchen in the dark until his truck rumbled into the alley.

She started up the metal staircase to her apartment, the clang of her footsteps echoing in the empty lot. A gentle night breeze brought her the scent of sunbaked rocks and seaweed and she leaned against the railing, closed her eyes and breathed in.

When something scraped the pavement behind her she popped open her eyes and took the stairs as fast as she could. No sense in looking over her shoulder—ten to one she wouldn't like what she'd see.

She was halfway to the top when Gil's truck pulled into the side lot, where she'd parked her car. He'd barely braked to a stop before he was out and peering up at her, face twisted with worry.

"What's going on?" he demanded.

She sagged against the railing, lungs working overtime. Like her imagination. "Just got a little spooked," she gasped.

He nodded, looking a bit winded himself. "Don't run up those stairs again, okay? It's not safe."

"I won't."

Slowly he climbed to meet her, each measured

step sending her pulse rate one notch higher. His gaze was shadowed, his mouth a determined line. He stopped one step below hers. She shivered, and his eyes softened.

"Hey," he said.

"Hey."

"I'm sorry I didn't make it back to the bar tonight. On the way back from Buffalo, I had some engine trouble. I should have called."

"I almost called you, but it smacked of stalking."

"You should feel free to call." He scrubbed his hair. "Anytime. We need to talk about that. And I want to apologize again, but at the moment all that I can think about is the last time we were on these stairs together, and how we ended up naked."

Her breath snagged in her throat. "Gil…" She didn't want to just fall into bed with him again. As much as she fantasized about it, she needed to know he wanted more from her than casual sex.

"You don't have to say it. I screwed things up." He motioned with his chin at the landing above them. "What's the word from Dylan?"

She frowned. "You know what, I never heard back from him. I asked him to text me when he got here and again when he left, but he never did. We got so busy at the bar, I forgot to follow up."

"Maybe he changed his mind. Maybe Liz sweet-talked him into babysitting and at this very moment he's asleep on her living room floor, coated in pureed peaches and cuddling a Winnie-the-Pooh blanket."

Kerry laughed, then went quiet as the breeze ruffled his hair. Her heartbeat slowed to a thick, syrupy throb, and behind Gil's glasses, his eyes flared.

Abruptly she turned and led the way up to the landing. She had to get her door between them. Now. She had to lock herself in and him out or she'd end up all over him like hot fudge sauce on an ice cream sundae.

She lifted the mat but didn't see her key. She flipped the mat entirely over. Still no key. Dylan had left it either in his pocket or inside the apartment. She straightened, and turned to find Gil right behind her.

"I think I'm going to need your key again," she said breathlessly.

"I don't think so." He was frowning at the door. "It's open."

She whirled, the anticipation in her belly turning to apprehension. "Well, that doesn't make me happy."

Gil nudged her out of the way. "He must have left in a hurry." He pushed at the door and took a single step inside, Kerry hovering at his back.

"Anyone here?" He switched on the light.

One look over his shoulder and Kerry wished he'd left the light off.

CHAPTER TWELVE

"OH, MY GOD," she gasped, and shoved past him. That's when the smell hit. With a choking cough, she pressed her nose to the crook of her elbow.

Swearing a blue streak, Gil moved carefully to the pair of windows facing the outside stairs. Debris crunched with every step he took. After shoving open the windows, he turned back to survey the ruined apartment.

"Must have been some party," he said grimly.

Jagged holes pockmarked the walls. Thick splashes of a viscous fluid—engine oil?—oozed down the white brick of the fireplace. Crackers and chips and M&M'S must have been tossed like confetti because they littered every available surface. A pile of broken lamps and kitchen appliances blocked the entrance to the bedroom, every electrical cord fashioned into a mocking bow.

Tears swelled in Kerry's eyes and scalded her throat.

At least the elegant teal sofa and love seat had been upended and shoved into a corner—they appeared unharmed. No one had bothered to roll up the once-white rug, though. It lay matted with stains of every hue, half buried under pizza boxes, paper plates, crumpled chip bags, empty beer bottles, soda cans and red plastic party cups.

Both hands pressed to her mouth, Kerry lurched forward. Gil reached for her, but she evaded him and turned the corner into the kitchen. The wreckage wasn't as bad there. Although every cabinet had been opened, the contents strewn across the floor, nothing structural appeared to have been ruined. The countertops were intact, the walls free of...whatever that was in the living room.

Kerry drew in a shuddering breath. The refrigerator door sagged open, and someone had thrown up in the middle of the table.

Hence the god-awful smell.

Gil followed her into the kitchen and did a slow three-sixty, pushing one hand through his hair. "Unbelievable," he gritted. "How many kids did he have in here?"

"It'll take days to clean this up," Kerry whispered. "Holy Hannah, what have I done?"

"You had nothing to do with this."

"Of course I did. I let Dylan in here. I gave him a key. Oh, my God, Eugenia's beautiful apartment. How am I going to tell her?"

"Over drinks. Somewhere else." He eased the refrigerator door shut and gave it a slap. "Get Dylan on the phone. I'm going to check out the bedroom."

"It's two in the morning."

"Call him, Kerry."

With shaking fingers, she pulled her cell from her pocket. Not surprisingly, Dylan didn't answer. After leaving a terse message, she went in search of Gil.

He was in the bathroom, shaking his head as he gazed down into a toilet bowl jammed with clothes. T-shirts, panties... Kerry swore. *Her* panties. And a cell phone. Dylan's?

Gil swung around, phone to his ear. "Hey, Clarissa. JD around?"

Sadness lay leaden in her chest. Of course he had to call the sheriff. A report had to be filed. An investigation had to be opened. Someone had to be held accountable.

But earnest, sweet-faced Dylan?

Water sloshed beneath Kerry's shoes as she peered into the bathtub, which was blessedly empty.

"Send him to the apartment above the dress shop, would you? There's been some property damage. We'll wait outside. Thanks, Clarissa." Gil disconnected. "He's out on a call but he'll be here soon."

"How bad is the bedroom?"

"Not as bad as the living room."

She sagged against the wall. "I can't believe Dylan would do something like this. This just seems so angry."

"He may not have done it. He may not have

done anything more than let the others in. But that doesn't let him off the hook. This is felony vandalism."

Kerry wrapped her arms around her waist. "I don't have renter's insurance, and how is it fair to expect Eugenia's policy to cover this? They'll raise her premium."

Gil didn't respond. He didn't have to.

"She'll be beside herself. She'll wish she'd never met me. And as for my father…" She pressed a hand to her throat, but it didn't ease the scratchiness. "I didn't get a chance to tell you that we finally talked. He said he'd forgiven me a long time ago. Even offered to let me move in with him. And now this. What if he changes his mind?"

"Stop it." Gil palmed her shoulders and squeezed. "You tried to do a good deed. It failed miserably. Once she gets over the shock, Eugenia will understand."

"Yes, because look how her good deed failed. And you just got her check for the baby fund." She massaged fingertips gone suddenly numb. "Should I call her?"

"Any way these assholes could have made their way downstairs?"

"No." Thank God. "Eugenia locks the door from the other side when she's done for the day. I already checked it. It's still locked."

"Then I don't think there's any need to drag

her out of bed. We can give the sheriff all the info he needs."

Slowly Kerry shook her head. "One step forward and two steps back. How could I not understand that throwing a conveniently empty apartment and a cupboard full of junk food into the path of an insecure teenage boy was a terrible idea?"

His hands flexed on her shoulders. "I think you need to stop looking for ways to punish yourself."

Kerry eased out of his grip. "You're saying I'm trying to be a martyr."

"I'm saying give yourself a frickin' break." He trailed her out to the living room. "You were thinking like a friend, not a parole officer."

He hadn't meant it as a dig, but the crack about the parole officer stung. Kerry wandered back out onto the metal landing and watched for the flashing blue lights of the sheriff's car. "Why do you have to be so logical?" she muttered.

Gil moved up behind her. "I'm glad your father forgave you. Now why don't you try forgiving yourself?"

She swung around. "You first."

"What?"

"It's been six years and you still haven't forgiven yourself for not reconciling with your father before he died. It's only been two years that I haven't been able to forgive myself. I know you can do the math."

He glowered down at her. "What are you talking about?"

"Six minus two is four. If I follow your example I have at least another four years of not having to forgive myself."

He grabbed a handful of railing on either side of her, crowding her into the corner. "You're trying to piss me off so I'll storm out of here and leave you to figure out on your own how to fix this crap fest."

She doubted he meant for the frustrated rasp of his voice to turn her on. She swallowed. "Did you just say 'crap fest?' *I* say 'crap fest.'"

"Lots of people do. Don't distract me when I'm ranting." He leaned in, pressed a kiss to her forehead and leaned back. "Kerry."

"What?"

"You are more than your mistakes. Stop underestimating yourself."

His words were half comfort, half rebuke. He followed them with the gentle drag of his fingers down the side of her neck. An effective distraction.

She swatted at his hand. "You keep giving me advice you need to take yourself."

He held up his hands. "This one's all you. You can't stay here tonight. After the sheriff takes our statements, you should come home with me. You can have the bed and I'll take the couch." When she hesitated, he let go of the railing and eased back a step. "Don't say you'd rather go to the motel. Joe's a new father. He needs his sleep. And you don't want to show up on your dad's doorstep tonight, do you?"

Kerry peered up into his Kahlúa-colored eyes, holding her breath. Her brain was still stuttering over the phrase *"come home with me."*

He was so sweet, and she was so tired of holding back. But it seemed wrong to want him so fiercely, to hope he wouldn't go anywhere near his couch tonight, when the disaster behind them would devastate Eugenia.

And the fault was as much Kerry's as it was Dylan's.

With his index finger, Gil stabbed at the bridge of his glasses. "After breakfast we'll come back and tell Eugenia what happened. Together."

When she remained mute, his brow wrinkled.

"Damn it, Kerry." He pushed the words through clenched teeth. "Now you're not talking to me?"

"I'm sorry, I just… I feel so guilty."

He sighed, and gathered her against him. "That's understandable. It's going to take a lot of work to restore this place. You know I'll help, right?"

"That's very generous. I appreciate that."

"Generous." He exhaled. "You may not realize it, especially after the things I said last night, but you're important to me."

"I'm having your baby."

"Kerry." He set her away from him and shook her once, gently. "You. Are important. To me."

Her heart tripped over itself and sparks scattered beneath her skin.

She opened her mouth to thank him, but lost track of the words when his mouth came down on hers.

The shock of warm, firm skin and the intimate brush of his breath started a fizzing in her feet that quickly bubbled up her legs and hot-flashed through her body.

Holy Hannah, this man could kiss.

And oh, how she'd missed it.

He gripped her biceps as his tongue swirled around hers. His lips worked hers like he had only seconds to discover their secret. She followed his lead because, dear Lord in heaven, she wanted him to have that secret. She wanted him to have everything. Know everything. Feel everything.

Then she could feel it, too.

Except…

Slowly she withdrew from their embrace. He relaxed his hold on her arms with reluctance, trailing his fingers from her biceps to her elbows, and finally letting his hands drop to his sides.

Kerry mourned the loss of connection as soon as it was broken. She reached out and pressed a palm to his heart.

"Even with everything that's happened here,

I want you so much I ache. Please tell me that doesn't make me a bad person."

He gave his head a shake. "That makes you a person after my own heart."

His voice wobbled on the last word and she was lost.

She stepped forward and arched into him. With a groan, he widened his stance and pulled her in tighter. They shared a shudder when their hips met and the softness between her legs cradled the hard heat of his erection.

She was trapped between Gil and the railing, and the cold, hard band across her back nudged her out of her sensual daze. He must have sensed her discomfort because his hands slid from her arms to her hips, then around to her butt where his caresses drove her mad with need. She thrust her hands into his hair. "God, Gil," she gasped against his mouth. He angled his head the other way and plunged in again. Their deep kisses sent ripples of bliss straight to her core. His groan nearly sent her over the edge.

She gripped his neck, his shoulder blades, his back. Clutched at his shirt, desperate to separate it from his jeans so she could touch bare skin. Their coming together was too much, too intense, too frantic to last, but she reveled in the feeling of being wanted, of having nothing else matter but the need between them.

When the pressure of his mouth eased, she

broke away and greedily pulled oxygen into her lungs. "You are so damned good at this."

He chuckled unsteadily, then went still. He lifted his head. "Do you hear that?"

All she heard was the desperate rasp of her own breathing. Gil stepped away, urging silence with an upraised hand. Then she did hear it. Banging. From inside the apartment.

"Wait here," he said, and disappeared.

She did, for as long as it took her to realize she didn't like being left outside in the near-dark. Cautiously she stepped through the door, stopping to listen when she heard Gil's voice. She broke into a jog when she realized who he was talking to.

She followed the voices to the bedroom, where a grim-faced Gil was helping Dylan out of the closet. The teen was red-faced and sweating, soaked head to toe in what smelled like beer and sporting a bloody nose.

"Oh, my God," she said, and pulled him into a hug. "Who did this to you?"

He stood rigid in her arms, head bent, the occasional choking noise making it clear he was fighting tears. Over Dylan's head, Kerry locked gazes with Gil, who was rhythmically clenching and unclenching his fists.

"It's okay," Kerry crooned softly. She kept her eyes on Gil as she rubbed Dylan's back. "It'll be okay."

Eventually she was able to coax Dylan to sit on the bed.

"Let me get a washcloth for your face," she said, but when she started to move away, Dylan reached for her.

"I'll do it." Gil squeezed the boy's shoulder as he passed.

Kerry settled next to Dylan on the bed, and placed a tentative hand on his knee. "Are you hurt anywhere else?"

He shook his head.

"Can you tell us what happened?"

"It was my fault," he said miserably. "I told them I was here. They showed up and made me let them in."

"The boys you've been having trouble with at school?"

He hesitated, then gave a reluctant nod.

Gil returned with the washcloth. Kerry reached for it, but he handed it to Dylan instead. Oh. Right. The poor kid was already embarrassed enough. The last thing he needed was to be treated like a toddler.

She shot Gil a grateful smile.

Dylan ran the washcloth over his face, then folded it tightly between his hands. "Do you have to call the police?"

Gil grabbed a chair from the corner, pulled it close and sat. "We already did."

Dylan's hands flexed on the washcloth. "They're going to ask for names."

"Somebody has to be held accountable," Gil said. He leaned forward, resting his forearms on his knees. "These boys who came over. They're classmates of yours?"

Dylan nodded.

"Do they live around here?"

A shrug this time.

Kerry watched Gil closely. What was he getting at?

Gil rubbed at an imaginary spot on his khakis. "If these boys are your classmates, they're too young to drive. So how did they get here?"

The dismay on Dylan's face was almost comical.

Gil reached out and patted the side of the teen's knee. "Dylan. You owe me a solid. You'd be doing Kerry one, too, by telling the truth about what happened here tonight."

Kerry gave her head a bemused shake. Oh, he was good. He was really, really good.

Dylan was shaking his head, too, but not in admiration. "Dad's going to hate me."

Gil frowned. "Why would you say that?"

"'Cause we need his paycheck."

"Whose paycheck?"

"How're we going to buy medicine if my brother's in jail?"

Kerry closed her eyes and swallowed against

MAKING IT RIGHT

a suddenly scratchy throat. This poor kid had the weight of the world on his shoulders.

"Why did your brother lock you in the closet?" she asked huskily.

"He said it would make it look more like those dicks from school did this."

Kerry and Gil shared a half appalled, half amused look.

"I'm sorry," Dylan croaked. "I asked my brother for a ride and he said he might hang for a while, you know, watch TV and stuff. Then he showed up with all his friends and they had beer and some of 'em were already drunk. When I kept yelling that they had to go, they took my phone and grabbed me and—" He broke off on a sob and buried his face in his elbow.

A sympathetic burn plagued the backs of Kerry's eyes as she rubbed slow, soothing circles along Dylan's spine.

"Hello?" Someone hollered from the front door. "Sheriff's Department."

With one last, violent shudder, Dylan dropped his arm, and inhaled. He thrust the washcloth at Kerry and got to his feet.

"I'll go talk to him," he said raggedly.

"Be right out," Gil called, then palmed Dylan's shoulder. "This isn't your fault. At all. But you and I both know you're going to end up paying for it somehow. Contributing more money to the household, or just being there for your dad because your brother can't… It isn't fair, but that's what happens when someone in the family screws up."

Dylan swiped at his cheeks. "I might have to quit school," he whispered.

"You can't," Gil said firmly. "You have to be sixteen. Even then, don't do it."

Slowly Kerry got to her feet. Her entire body sagged under the weight of the poor choices she'd made, including loaning Eugenia's key to Dylan. "You can't sacrifice your education."

Gil bent his knees so he and the teen were eye to eye. "Don't take this all on yourself. Quitting school would be following one bad decision with another. Of course you can help, but don't let it become your life. That's not your responsibility. Okay?"

"Okay."

"You can forgive your brother. It might take a while, but you can do it. It's better for you, better for your family. But that doesn't mean you have to forget what happened here tonight."

"Okay," Dylan repeated, more steadily this time.

"Good man." Gil held up his fist for a bump. "We can talk more later."

Kerry followed Dylan and Gil out of the room, wishing she'd had at twenty-five half the guts this kid had at fourteen.

GIL UNFASTENED AND refastened the top button of his shirt as he followed Kerry up the metal staircase, this time the one leading to his apartment. After working at the store all day and spending most of the evening on the road, then dealing with Kerry and Dylan and a grumpy sheriff afterward, Gil should be beat. He wasn't. Instead his entire body throbbed with an electric urgency he was doing his damnedest to hide. Because it felt wrong, after all they'd just been through, to hope he'd have Kerry in his bed for what was left of the night.

And though she'd said she wanted him, she could very well change her mind.

Even if she didn't, he should let her sleep. They were both shell-shocked. Neither had said anything since Sheriff Suazo had driven away with Dylan in the back of his cruiser.

They'd tried to convince JD to let them drive Dylan home themselves. Spare his father seeing one kid get out of the police car only to have the other escorted into it. But the sheriff had wanted more time with Dylan. How could they argue when the alternative was taking the kid down to the station?

As they reached the landing and Gil pushed the door open, Kerry stopped him with a hand on his arm.

"Those things you said to Dylan back there."

Gil grimaced. "I shouldn't have thrown all that at him. Not on top of everything else he was trying to process."

"You did a fine job, and it was very brave of you. Gil Cooper, you are full of surprises."

He stared down at her, at her wide, sincere eyes and earnest, moonlit face, and his fingers tightened painfully around his keys. "I missed the opportunity to be brave a long time ago." Somehow he managed to push the words past the cramping in his throat. "But thanks for being on my side."

"I thought we made a good team." She sighed. "I feel so bad for him."

"He'll be okay. We'll make sure of it."

She squeezed his arm tighter and she let her head drop to his shoulder. "I'm scared to death."

He knew exactly what she meant. "You know what scares me more than the prospect of being a father?" He wrapped his arms around her and spoke into her hair. "That you'll leave. Just as I'm looking forward to the baby. Just as I'm realizing I love you."

Her head came up. "Gil," she breathed.

"You said you were already halfway in love with me. Please tell me I didn't ruin that."

Her arms trembled as she wound them around his neck. "You didn't," she whispered. "But you can forget about the halfway part."

"Thank God." He closed his eyes against a surge of tears and rocked her gently. "I was sure I'd blown it."

"I love you, Gil. That's not going to change."

"That's good," he said gruffly. "Because a lot in our lives is about to."

"Maybe we should take this one day at a time." She kissed his chin. "It's when we get too far ahead of ourselves that things get complicated."

Disappointment flared, but she was right. There was nothing wrong with slow.

"Slow can be good," he said aloud.

Her smile was half bashful, half coy as she took his hand. "Remind me."

He'd never crossed his threshold so fast.

Inside, even before he could ask if she'd like something to drink, she pressed up against him. It didn't take him long to realize it wasn't in a good way.

She clutched his arm. "There's something in here with us."

His first thought was that Dylan's classmates had somehow found a way into his loft as a means of hiding out from the sheriff. Then he realized what Kerry was hearing and slowly willed his muscles to unlock.

It would help if he turned on the lights.

Instead of the floods, he turned on a lamp. "That's my clock-bot you're hearing. It's over by the kitchen."

Kerry zeroed in on the clock, which had started to beep as it butted heads with the wall.

Gil walked over, scooped it up and turned it off. "I must have programmed it wrong."

"Talk about surprises. So you have to chase it around in the mornings?"

He grinned. "It does like to play hard to get." He took her in, all tousled hair and teasing lips and luscious curves tapering into long, shapely legs, and his chest fluttered. "I like that in an alarm clock," he said gruffly.

Kerry laughed, a breathy, trembling sound. He set the clock on the nightstand and moved to the foot of the bed.

"Jitters?" he asked. "Or second thoughts? Because I can still take the couch."

"Don't even," she said. With fluid, leisurely motions, she tugged her shirt up and over her head.

She wore a purple bra with lacy cups seethrough enough to provide a hint of nipple. And a lot of smooth, creamy flesh.

"Damn," he said.

Gorgeous. That's the word he should use. *Stunning*, even.

She didn't seem to mind his lack of eloquence. She dropped her shirt and stepped toward him, and the bounce of her breasts turned the discomfort of his erection into full-on misery. He grabbed the back of his shirt with one hand and yanked it over his head, eager for the feel of her bare skin against his.

It had been too damned long.

When her foot got tangled in one corner of the

sheets and she stumbled forward, somehow saving herself at the last moment from a face-plant, heat scaled his cheeks. He cupped her elbows and pulled her close. "I'm sorry. I should change those, anyway."

"Don't bother. I know how comfortable they are." She leaned her head against his chest and ran her hands up his arms, leaving a rippling trail of pleasure behind. "I'm sorry I didn't help you change them before I went home last night."

"I wanted to keep them." He gave an awkward half shrug. "They smell like you."

She inhaled sharply, and lifted her head. He took advantage, kissing her roughly, possessively, as he'd learned she liked it.

"Crème brûleé," he murmured.

"Sorry?"

"That's what you taste like."

He felt the warmth of her delighted sigh against his neck. She slid her hands to his ribs and lowered her mouth to his nipple. His entire body jerked. A few strokes of her tongue and his hands were fumbling with the fastener on his jeans.

One last, swirling lick and she raised her head, her beautiful green eyes slumberous with need. "You know what you taste like?"

He shook his head, unable to form even the simplest of words.

"You taste like more," she said, and lowered

herself to her knees, taking his jeans and his boxers down with her.

He caught her by the arms before she could so much as breathe on him, and coaxed her back to her feet. "Can we come back to that?" He kissed her hard, and reached for the button on her hiphuggers. "I'm not done tasting you."

Her eyes flared and her body shook and oh, yeah, she wanted it, but not as much as he did.

"Let me get my boots," he said. "You get your jeans." He tipped his head at the bed. "Last one in gets her legs thrown over my shoulders."

With a breathless laugh she shed her jeans. When Gil groaned in appreciation and reached for her, his boots tumbling to the floor, she gave him a push. He landed on the bed on his back and worked hard to contain his grin.

With a part nervous, part naughty smile, Kerry shed her bra and panties and crawled up to hover over him on all fours. Jesus, she was built.

"You win," she said, and pretended to pout.

He took off his glasses and set them on the nightstand, then pulled Kerry down on top of him. "I'm thinking we both win." His hips lifted all on their own and when she ground against him, a savage tingling zapped the base of his spine. He groaned and rolled them both, kissed her hard and started working his way down her body.

A few hours later Kerry teased him awake, her mouth seeking, her hands urgent. She rode him hard and fast, so fast he couldn't hold back. He used his fingers to help her along and when hot, sharp pleasure shook his body, then receded into a dazed ache, her euphoric cries moments later allowed him to drift back into a contented sleep.

The next time he woke, the space next to him was empty, the loft quiet. He lay with his eyes closed, body tense, every muscle in listening mode.

Nothing.

He rolled onto his side and pulled her pillow to his chest. She'd be back. They weren't done. But that didn't stop the loneliness from dragging him down. And this despite expecting her return.

He brooded about how his father must have felt, when his girlfriend had left him for good and his wife and son had forsaken him.

With a pained grunt, Gil shoved the ill-timed thoughts away, and concentrated instead on his feelings for Kerry.

He'd never intended to consider forever, with anyone. How could he support a family when he was barely making ends meet? Still he'd sometimes wondered what it was like for Seth and Joe and Reid. Waking up to kids bouncing on the bed. Waking up to a wife you could pull close and plan your day with. Your life with.

The door at the top of the interior stairs opened and Kerry padded in, phone in hand, wearing nothing but socks and his Steelers T-shirt. The way her breasts moved under the cotton had him perking up, until he saw her face. His gut cramped at the sight of her red-rimmed eyes and folded lips.

The fact that she moved faster the closer she got to the bed told him he wasn't the problem, praise God.

He held up the covers and scooted over. She crawled in beside him and rested her head on his chest, her left leg across his thighs. One by one, his muscles unclenched.

When she sniffled, he pressed a kiss to the top of her head. Her hair smelled like raspberries. "Dylan?" he asked. "Or Eugenia?"

"Both. I went downstairs to call so I wouldn't wake you. Dylan is feeling sore and guilty, but grateful because his teacher's letting him postpone that test. Eugenia..." She sighed. "I think I broke her heart."

He worked his arm free and stroked her hip. "She'll be okay. Her apartment will be, too. Is she going to call the adjuster?" When Kerry nodded again, he found her hand and gave it a squeeze. "There's nothing more you can do right now."

"I can apologize to her in person."

"Want me to go with you? We can head over to the diner first, buy a cake or a pie or something so she'll let us in."

Kerry levered herself up on one elbow, blinking rapidly. Apparently his offer had loosened a few tears. "That's sweet," she said, her voice husky. She kissed him on the cheek. "But I need to do it on my own."

"I'm here if you need me," he said.

His stomach grumbled.

Kerry gave up a laugh. "Sounds like what you need is breakfast."

"You need it, too. The baby needs it more."

"I'll get something to eat as soon as I've seen Eugenia." She made a face. "Maybe if I go over there looking hungry enough, she'll feel so sorry for me she'll feed me *and* forgive me."

Gil cocked an eyebrow. "If I were you, I'd have a plan B."

"You're right." The smile she threw him was uneven, but at least he'd made her smile at all. She shoved at the covers. "A pie it is."

When he sat up and swung his legs over the side of the bed, she rose to her knees and hugged him from behind.

"There's something I need to say."

The gravity in her voice kicked his stomach into a spin. "Okay…"

"I did some research. There are grants for people with bachelor's degrees who want to become licensed to teach." He stiffened, but she squeezed him into submission. "Hear me out. You could take online courses and get your degree in eighteen months. You'd have to do some practicums, but I could run the store while you're doing all that, and once you start teaching, too. With the grant, you can afford to take the classes *and* pay an employee."

She kissed his ear. "What do you think?"

"I think—" The words barely made it past the cramping in his throat. He turned and framed her face with his hands. "—that you're amazing."

"Does that mean you'll consider it?"

"I will," he said gravely.

"Good. Now it's time for me to consider getting dressed." She kissed him again and slid off the bed. She bit her lip as she disappeared into the bathroom and he knew she was thinking about Eugenia again.

Slowly he reached for his boxers, and tried to imagine how it would feel to be getting ready to face a classroom of unenthusiastic ninth graders instead of a struggling hardware store.

EUGENIA WAS BEING petty and unreasonable but she couldn't help it. Something juvenile inside her refused to let her shake off the pout this time. She faced the backside of the bright spring display she'd so cheerfully arranged in the store's front window only the month before. April was too soon to be thinking of a summer scene, but she was no longer in the mood for glittery raindrops and colorful flowers.

She gazed through the large front window, at

the bustling Saturday morning street beyond, and sighed.

She was tired of being the calm one. The sensible one. She was so over playing mediator, biting her tongue, wrapping her dreams in tissue paper and storing them in an airtight container because a certain former marine refused to pull his head out of his ass.

And she was over the big-hearted but infuriating daughter who just couldn't bring herself to leave well enough alone.

My apartment. My lovely, cozy sanctuary. It had taken her months to achieve the perfect combination of style, comfort and ridiculousness, and in the course of one evening, it had all been ruined. *Desecrated* was a better word. She was anxious to start scrubbing, to remove every filthy trace of those jackass juvenile delinquents, but her insurance adjustor had advised her not to touch a thing until he'd had a chance to take photos.

Last summer her dress shop had flooded. Now this. She sighed again. What was it Harris liked to say? No good deed goes unpunished?

His daughter stood silently watching as Eugenia dismantled her front window display. Time to replace the white picket fence and tire-sized blooms with something less sentimental. And more realistic.

Kerry shifted her grip on the pie box in her hand and Eugenia couldn't help wondering what

she had in there. Apple? Blueberry crumb? Or—
God help her—Cal's mocha truffle brownies? She
sniffed the air, but couldn't detect anything except the lavender potpourri she kept by the cash
register.

"Can I help?" Kerry asked quietly.

Eugenia stacked the fence pieces against the
wall and grabbed the broom. "I think you've
done quite enough, thank you," she said, and instantly hated herself for it. She turned in time to
see Kerry flinch.

"I'm sorry," she began, but Kerry stopped her
with a violent shake of her head.

"*I'm* sorry. So deeply sorry. I made a terrible
mistake—"

"Yes, you did," Eugenia snapped. At the stark
regret on Kerry's face, she drew in a deep breath,
and relented. "I know you were just trying to help
someone out. It's not your fault it got out of hand,
but I wish you'd checked with me first before
handing out a key."

No one who knew Harris Briggs could deny
his daughter had inherited the stubborn set of his
chin. Kerry set aside the bakery box. "I'd like to
be part of the cleaning crew. Gil said he'd help,
too. Hopefully we'll save you some money that
way."

"You don't have to do that. I have insurance."

"I'd like to take care of your deductible. Snoozy's
paying me a full wage now, so I have two checks

coming in." Her eagerness wavered, but she met Eugenia's gaze head-on. "Though I was hoping you and I could work out a payment plan."

"Absolutely." Eugenia eyed the bakery box. Lemon bars? "You can stay in my guest room while the work's being done."

"I appreciate that. I can't tell you how much. But you have to realize that's the last thing I could bring myself to do."

Eugenia opened her mouth to protest, then nodded. Sometimes favors did more harm than good. She and Harris knew that better than anyone.

"Where will you stay, then?"

The door to the shop opened and Eugenia had a split second to regret that Saturday was her busiest morning when she realized her first customer of the day was not a customer at all but Harris himself. She stacked her hands on the end of the broom.

"Good morning," Eugenia said crisply.

"Mornin'." He pulled at the collar of his shirt. "I heard what happened and I just wanted to see if you were doin' all right."

"Thank you, Harris. I'm fine. Possessions can be replaced. It was time that apartment had an overhaul, anyway." Eugenia hid the urge to preen as she managed to sound like she actually meant it.

"How about you, Kerry girl?"

"I'm okay, Dad, thanks. The apartment is a terrible mess, but Gil and I both plan to help clean up. Dylan, too."

Wait, *what*?

Eugenia shoved the broom aside and slapped her hands onto her hips. "Am I imagining things, or are you two actually talking to each other?"

Kerry's smile held more than a little relief. "We had a good conversation the other day. I think we're going to be okay."

"What she means is, I finally pulled my head out of my ass and offered her an apology, and she had the grace to accept it."

Eugenia grabbed a felt coin purse out of a nearby bargain bin and heaved it at Harris. The little purse bounced off his elbow. "Why didn't you tell me?" she demanded.

He rubbed his elbow. "Why do you think I'm here?"

"To apologize to *me*."

He nodded solemnly. "I'm workin' on that." He stared at Eugenia a moment longer, then turned to his daughter. "Looks like you'll be needin' a place to stay. You movin' in with Cooper, or with me?"

Kerry blinked. "I don't think he'd appreciate that. He likes his privacy."

"That's settled, then. Monday, we'll get you moved in."

Kerry shared a sweet smile. "Thanks, Dad."

It took Eugenia a few seconds to find her voice. Yes, she was happy. She'd given up hope that these two would ever make peace with each other, let alone set up house together.

But she couldn't help feeling like an outsider. She glanced at Harris, and the tenderness on his face—tenderness aimed directly at Eugenia—both shamed and thrilled her.

"I'm happy for you both," she said mistily. She hugged Kerry and walked her to the door. "I know you need to get back to the hardware store." She ignored Kerry's knowing glance. "You go ahead. Your father can stay and help me with my display."

After Kerry left, Eugenia locked the door and swung around. "I'm proud of you."

"You are? What for?"

She took his hand and led him toward the office in the back. "For setting aside your pride for the sake of your relationship with your daughter."

"I know what you're thinking."

"You do?" She guided him toward the club chair in the corner of her office, backed him up and with a gentle push, encouraged him to sit. "And what's that?"

"'Took you long enough.'"

She gave a throaty laugh. "Yes, well, where you're concerned, that applies to more than one area of your life."

"I lost you from bein' a hardheaded SOB," he said, his voice full of gravelly regret. "Finally I realized I couldn't stand to lose her, too."

When Eugenia kicked off her shoes and started unbuttoning her blouse, he went still. "Uh, Genie? Whatcha doin'?" He grimaced. "We're not goin' to start cleaning upstairs, are we? I mean, I want to help, but right now I got stuff to do."

"You are so right." She peeled her blouse down her arms, revealing one of the very best bras she carried, a push-up style in black and light blue lace. She couldn't have planned this better if she'd tried. With what she hoped was a saucy smile, she reached for the zipper at the back of her skirt. "Have I ever told you what a turn-on it is when you get all self-reflective and your voice goes scratchy?"

His hands curled around the arms of the chair and his fingers went white. "Self-reflective, huh? I, uh…" He cleared his throat. "I know I can be bossy."

"Mmm-hmm." Slowly she lowered her zipper, and began to work the pencil skirt down her hips.

Harris flushed when he spotted the matching panties—what there was of them. Gaze riveted on her hips, he swallowed hard. "And I sure can hold on to a, uh, a grudge."

"No argument here." She stepped out of her skirt and threw it over her shoulder.

Harris scrubbed a hand over his mouth. "My coffee's too strong."

"Strong? Try lethal." Leisurely she ran her

hands over her breasts and down her sides, and hooked her thumbs in her panties.

He was leaning forward, an expression of pained anticipation on his face. "And," he growled, "I've never been able to turn down a piece."

Eugenia's head shot up.

"Of pecan pie," he finished smugly.

Dear Lord, did this man need to be taught a lesson. She inched down her panties. "Harris?"

"Uh-huh?"

"Do me a favor." She ditched the panties and reached around for the clasp of her bra, trying not to grimace at the pull of not-so-limber muscles. *Why* did she think she'd be able to undo the thing this way?

As gracefully as she could manage, she slipped her arms through the straps and twisted the bra so the clasp was in front. A flick of her wrists, and the girls were free.

Harris hissed in a slow breath.

"About that favor," Eugenia drawled.

"Anything," he choked. Bless his deprived libido, he hadn't seemed to notice her struggle. "Anything at all."

"Shut up."

"But I never got a chance to apolo—"

Eugenia pressed a hand to his mouth and eased herself down onto his lap. "Shut. Up."

His lips curved against her hand, but she wasn't in the mood for lighthearted. She spread her legs wider and snugged in tight, enjoying the upward thrust of his hips. The quiet, too. As much as she enjoyed the deep rasp of his voice, she enjoyed his silence more, because it usually meant he was concentrating on something. And at the moment, that something was the gentle sway of her breasts.

Her breathing quickened as she slid her hand from his mouth and went to urgent work on the buttons of his shirt.

Harris had nothing coherent to say for a solid thirty minutes.

Neither did she.

CHAPTER THIRTEEN

KERRY YAWNED AND guzzled the rest of her ice water. Almost done. Once she prepared the bank deposit, she could go home.

She was tempted to text Gil that she'd be coming by after all, but another crazy-busy Ladies' Night and too many early morning trips in and out of Gil's bed meant she was ready for some heavy-duty sleep. No doubt he was, too.

She'd miss him, though.

She tamped down the desire rising in her belly. Now was not the time.

Another yawn caught her by surprise as she retrieved the heavy zippered bag from the bottom drawer of Snoozy's desk. She sorted the contents. Checks, credit receipts, cash.

Wait. She frowned down at the stack of bills in her hand and checked the bag again. Where was the rest of the cash?

There was more. She knew there was more because twice during the evening, she'd thinned out the register.

It had to be here somewhere.

She checked the drawer again and explored

every item on top of the desk. Nothing. One by one she yanked out the remaining drawers, metal slamming against metal, contents thudding against each end of the drawer. Still nothing.

Oh, God, oh, God, oh, God.

She dropped to her knees and checked beneath the desk and chair. She scanned the kitchen, but there was no earthly reason she'd mistakenly store cash in the sink, or the oven, or the walk-in freezer. She couldn't remember the last time she'd *been* in the walk-in.

She checked just the same, then hurried out front. She searched the register, the floor, every shelf under the bar. Nothing.

Hand in her hair, she turned a slow, desperate circle. They'd been slammed. Twice she'd taken cash out of the register. She thought she'd stuffed it in the bank bag, but obviously she hadn't, so what had she done with it?

She shook out her fingers and checked it all again.

Half an hour later, she was sitting at Snoozy's desk with her head in her hands and her heart in her throat. She should call the police.

Dear God, the last thing she wanted to do was call the police.

Someone pounded on the front door. She squinted at the time on her phone. Two thirty. Had to be Gil.

Or maybe a customer who'd suddenly discovered an extra thousand dollars in her pocket?

She swiped her cheeks and scurried out front. When she opened the door, Gil crowded in, bringing with him a flood of night air that smelled like wet gravel.

"It's been raining," he said. He pulled her close and kissed her hard. "I went by Harris's. When I saw you hadn't come home yet, I thought I'd better check and see if you were okay."

"Gil," she gasped, and clutched at him.

He stiffened. "You're not okay." Without looking away from her, he shut and locked the door behind him. "What's wrong?" His gaze dropped to her stomach. "Is it the baby?"

"No, the baby's fine." She tangled her fingers together and brought them up to her chin. "I'm short."

He was a businessman. He knew exactly what that meant. With a grimace, he sagged back against the door. "How much?"

"Twelve hundred." Walking backward, she tugged him into the office. "I didn't make a mistake ringing something up and I didn't have any deliveries I paid cash for. I didn't stash the money somewhere safe and then forget it, and I didn't make anyone's day by accidentally giving them the wrong change. The money was here, and now it's gone. It's gone because someone took it."

He peeled off his jacket. "Let's look again."

"It won't do any good. I've looked everywhere." She dropped into the desk chair and wrapped her arms around her waist. "It's not here and I don't know what to do."

"Did you call the sheriff?"

Miserably, she shook her head. "That'll ruin everything. Snoozy trusted me. I promised him I'd be dependable. What am I supposed to tell him when he gets back next week?"

"Kerry, if someone stole the money, that's not your fault."

"Yes it is. It means I wasn't paying enough attention."

Gil exhaled and sat on the edge of the desk. "The best way to make up for that is to find the money. The best way to find the money is to call the sheriff."

"And who do you think will be at the top of his suspect list?"

Kerry shoved to her feet, sending the chair rolling. "There were only four people in the kitchen tonight. Ruthie, Dylan, Liz and me." She started to pace, each hand cupping the opposite elbow. "None of them would have taken that money, and even if someone had their doubts about Dylan, he was never in the kitchen alone. That leaves me."

"The longer you wait to report this, the more

suspicious it's going to look." He hesitated. "Is there a reason you don't want to call the sheriff?"

She jerked to a halt and stared at him, speechless.

"You've been under a lot of pressure, what with the baby and all. And let's face it." His jaw worked. "This wouldn't be the first time."

"You think I did this?" she whispered raggedly. "You seriously think I took the money and I'm pretending I didn't? You think I'm a thief *and* a liar?" A bolt of anger made her blood sizzle. "*That's* what you think of me?"

"Shit." He scrubbed a hand over his mouth. "I don't know what to think."

"I can't believe... I just...what are we doing? My God." She stumbled to the sink and braced her hands on the cold metal lip. "You know what? I can't deal with that right now. I can't deal with you. I have to deal with the fact that I'm missing twelve hundred dollars."

"Kerry—"

"No. Stop." If she gave any more thought to his words and what they meant, she'd end up a howling, fist-pounding mess on the tile floor. *Later*. Later she could run home, mash her face into a pillow and bawl her eyes out.

One crisis at a time. That's all she could manage.

Kerry turned her back to the sink. Stacked her

hands on top of her head and aimed her gaze at
Gil's Timberlands.

"What if I didn't tell anyone? What if I used
my own money to make up the difference? If I
tell anyone they'll all believe I took it, just like
you." She lifted her gaze. "But if I used my own
money then Snoozy wouldn't be out the evening's
take and I wouldn't be out of a job."

Slowly Gil got to his feet. He looked as sick as
she felt. "You want to cover this up?"

"I don't have anywhere near enough money
saved yet, but...how much do we have in the baby's fund?"

He ran a hand through his hair and held it there
as he turned and paced away. With a disbelieving
grunt he let go and swung back.

"Please tell me you're kidding. Please tell me
you don't want to take money away from your
own baby—*our* baby—just to avoid telling
Snoozy the truth."

"What's the alternative? I'd have to move to
Erie to find another full-time position." She held
on tighter to her elbows to disguise the spasms in
her fingers. "Of course I'll replace every dollar."

"Jesus Christ."

"I can't lose this job, Gil. I'll pay it all back, I
promise."

He dropped his head and rubbed the back of his
neck. When he looked up again, the revulsion on
his face sent her stumbling back a step.

"Is that what you told the people you swindled?" he demanded.

"That's not fair. I'm not swindling anyone."

"No, you're trying to hide a crime to save your ass, and isn't that one of the reasons you ended up a felon?"

She shuddered as she stared at him, cold, bone-jarring spasms that wracked her from head to toe. She gripped the edges of the sink behind her and swallowed against the nausea surging into her throat.

"You're right," she whispered. "I just… I over-reacted. I don't know what I was thinking. I'm sorry." She launched herself toward the desk. "I'll call the sheriff now."

"It's too late, Kerry."

She shook her head. "No. I'll explain. Sheriff Suazo knows my history. He'll understand why I waited."

"I mean it's too late for you and me."

She froze, then turned slowly to face him. "I didn't take the money. Why won't you believe me?"

He tugged off his glasses and pressed the heel of his hand to his right eye. He heard the echo of his brother's words. *"I said I was clean. Why won't you believe me?"*

Gil opened his eyes, put his glasses back on and grabbed his jacket.

"Your dad was right," he said. "You're not interested in changing. Things don't go the way you expect and your first instinct is to cover them up so you don't have to deal. The thought of facing responsibility scares the hell out of you. What am I supposed to do with that?" His gaze hardened. "I can't control the kinds of lessons you teach our kid, but I sure as hell don't have to legitimize them. And that's exactly what I'd be doing if I stayed with you."

Her throat itched with the urge to bark a defense, but lashing out wouldn't get her anywhere. "I made a mistake," she said evenly. "I panicked." Kind of like she was doing now. She swallowed hard. "I've worked so hard to prove I deserve another chance and suddenly it looked like I was going to lose all that. You can't blame me for reacting the way I did."

He shoved his arms into his jacket. "And if I weren't here to talk you out of it?"

"I would have talked myself out of it."

The slow shake of his head cut through her like one of Ruthie's kitchen knives. "I wish I could believe you," he said hoarsely.

"I wish you could, too." Her stomach roiled. "Is this really about the missing money? Or is this about punishing me for getting pregnant? For making you give up your dream of becoming a teacher?"

His stunned expression shamed her. "I can't believe you would think that."

"Exactly how I feel."

He started to speak, had to stop and clear his throat. "Whether or not you stay in Castle Creek, I need you to keep in touch. About the baby. I want to be involved."

She responded with a jerky nod, and somehow pushed past her pride to whisper, "I thought you loved me."

His jaw clenched as he zipped up his jacket with one abrupt motion. "I loved the new Kerry. The old Kerry isn't someone I want to know."

They're both me, she wanted to shout. But he was already gone, the kitchen doors swinging gently in his wake.

KERRY SAT IN the passenger seat of her car, engine running, heat turned to full blast. Still, she was freezing. Arms wrapped around her knees, she rocked back and forth as her mind floundered, struggling to make sense of her situation.

She should be inside, where it was warm. Straightening the mess she'd made of Snoozy's desk. Combing the first floor of the bar again for the missing cash.

Fixing herself a big-ass margarita.

Then again, she wouldn't be able to drink it.

Once she'd finally accepted she wasn't going to find the money, she'd wandered the bar feeling like she no longer belonged there. Like she was trespassing. She'd been having a hard time breathing, as if Mitzi had escaped her pen and decided to play ring around the rosy.

Now Kerry lurched forward and turned up the heat. Dropped her head to her knees and inhaled, fighting the urge to throw up.

Twelve hundred dollars, gone. Despite what she'd said to Gil, she couldn't afford to replace it. Oh, if only she could. No one would think her careless or irresponsible. Or guilty. No one would have a reason to say, to Snoozy or to Gil, "I told you so."

But Gil was right. She was reckless, and irresponsible, and had become much too intimate with denial.

With a damp, quivering sigh she sat up, retrieved her phone from her purse and dialed the sheriff's department.

By the time she spotted the blue lights, she'd stopped shivering. The sight of the brown and gold cruiser with the big five-point star on the side should have started her up all over again, but she didn't have the energy.

Slowly, Kerry pushed out of her car and moved over to the bar's front entrance. She crossed her arms and waited, blinking against the glare of the headlights, regretting that her sweater didn't provide better protection against the early morning chill.

Sheriff JD Suazo emerged from his cruiser and settled his hat on his head. He was lean, maybe half a dozen years older than she was, with olive skin, sharp, dark eyes and a face that could transform from dangerous to jovial with one twitch of the lips. His gaze flicked over her as he stepped up onto the sidewalk beside her, his hand resting on the weapon at his hip. "Are you all right?"

She nodded, teeth steadily chattering. "Just a little, um…" She choked on a sob. *Good grief, chickie, pull yourself together.* "I'm s-sorry."

"Don't be. You have a right to be upset." He rocked back on his heels and his shoes creaked. "You're having one hell of a week, aren't you?"

The clicking of her teeth was louder than her "yes."

He frowned. "There's no need to talk out here in the cold. How about we take this inside?"

"I'd rather not." His arrival had roused a very strong need for fresh air, the colder the better. How guilty would she look if she stepped inside the bar and promptly vomited?

His frown deepened. "Hold tight a minute." He returned to the cruiser and grabbed something from the trunk. Seconds later he settled a wool blanket, smelling of motor oil and pine, over her shoulders.

"Now." He added a little take-charge to his tone. "Why don't you tell me what happened."

It didn't take long to explain how she'd discovered she was missing almost an entire day's worth of cash profits. She followed that up with an extended explanation of why she wasn't the one who'd taken the money.

Kerry knew she was implicating—and embarrassing—herself, but she couldn't seem to stop. It was as if the sheriff was a stand-in for Gil.

The lawman offered an occasional nod, and made the occasional note in a pad he'd pulled from his equipment belt, but he didn't interrupt her. When she finally ran out of things to say, he closed his notebook and tucked it away.

"I'm going to need you to take me inside," he said. "Walk me through what happened."

She pushed away an overwhelming yearning for her bed. "Is there any reason we can't open tomorrow?"

"I'm thinking that's up to Snoozy."

Oh. Right. Her stomach twisted.

"Somebody has to call him," he continued. "Would you like me to do it?"

"No. No, I'll do it."

"Why'd you wait for me out here?"

The change in tone from mild to brusque caught her off-guard. She gathered the blanket more tightly around her.

"Guilt," she admitted. "It felt worse to stand around in there. Because I didn't keep a closer eye on things."

Sheriff Suazo remained silent, but the angle of his head broadcasted his opinion of her answer.

The suspicion stung. Good thing she was used to it.

"Plus I'm still not thrilled about being alone with Mitzi," she confessed.

He looked away, but not in time to hide the twitch of his lips. She didn't know whether to be relieved or offended.

Then he looked back, and his lips had thinned again. "I'll need to search your car. Your person as well. Our female dispatcher will pat you down at the station."

Kerry swallowed a protest that wouldn't do anyone any good. "I understand."

"And I'll need you to come in tomorrow and provide a statement. You're not planning on taking any trips, are you?"

Her heart spiraled downward as she shook her head. Oh, God, she was in trouble here. The kind of trouble she'd vowed never to find herself in again.

"No, Sheriff," she said, and winced at the shredded quality of her voice. "No plans to leave town."

No plans at all, now that she'd dug herself an even deeper hole.

So deep she couldn't detect one single glimmer of light.

THE RICH SMELL of beef and onion greeted Kerry as she opened the oven door and checked the meatloaf. Yep. Done. She pulled out the heavy loaf pan and set it on the stove. Meanwhile the potatoes started to burble. She tipped the lid so they wouldn't boil over, and shut off the stove.

Once her father got home from work, all she had to do was make the mashed potatoes, heat up the carrots and the rolls and Project Distract Yourself by Overfeeding Your Father would be complete. More than complete, since she had a pecan pie thawing on the counter and a half gallon of vanilla ice cream waiting in the freezer.

She'd better get used to this cooking thing. She'd be doing a lot more of it.

"I can do this," she said out loud.

Still wearing her oven mitts, she pressed her hands to her belly. Imagined Gil's hands there instead. Or his mouth, as he traced the growing curve of her stomach. Then she pictured shopping for a crib on her own, running into him at the grocery store and struggling to make polite conversation with the stranger whose baby was growing inside her.

Gil.

A hot swell of grief nearly pushed her to her knees and she sagged against the counter. Her lungs felt like bricks walling up her chest and she panted like she was already practicing for the birth.

I can't do this.

He'd said he'd join her for all of her doctor's

visits, but how would she even be able to handle that? Seeing him, standing next to him, sharing this miracle with him while knowing that if she hadn't screwed up so badly, if she hadn't indulged in that idiotic relapse, they could touch and kiss and wonder together instead of sitting on opposite sides of the room, wearing identical wooden expressions?

She slid down the cabinet onto her butt and pulled her knees in. Rested her forehead on the bright red mitts and fought the need to sob. Once she started, she might not be able to stop.

Breathe in. Breathe out. Breathe in. Breathe out.

The loud metallic dance of the lid on the potatoes brought her head up. She swiped the mitts across her cheeks and slowly got to her feet. Her dad would be home any moment now, and finding her like this would not be the optimal start to an evening of comfort food.

She was draining the potatoes when the front door opened and closed. Her father strode into the kitchen, stopped and surveyed the table she'd arranged with tablecloth and linen napkins. All plaid, of course.

"This is quite a welcome," he said. "If I'd known you were doin' all this, I'd have come home earlier. You know, to supervise." He winked, and kissed her on the cheek. "What's the occasion?"

Kerry set aside the pot, eyeing him closely. "You tell me."

"What do you mean?"

"You seem awfully pleased with yourself."

He hooked his thumbs behind the straps of his overalls. "Of course I'm pleased with myself. I'm a handsome hunk of man. Genie told me so."

Kerry snorted. "Then it must be true." It did her heart good to see her dad looking so happy. It did wonders for her conscience, too. "Dinner in ten minutes."

He moved to the sink and washed his hands. "Anything I can do to help?"

The prickling behind her breastbone intensified. "Yes. I am hereby declaring a moratorium on discussing Snoozy's, money or Gil Cooper." It had been over a week since the money had gone missing, and still no one had any clue what had happened. She hadn't seen or talked to Gil in all that time, so the past several days had felt more like a month. She pointed at the glasses on the counter, then quickly curled her index finger when she saw that it was shaking. "Also, you could get us something to drink."

He opened the refrigerator and took out the pitcher of tea. Moved back to the counter and hesitated before pouring. "How did things go at the bar last night?"

"Dad." Kerry turned, both hands tightening

around the pepper mill. "What did I just say about what we won't be discussing?"

Harris set down the pitcher. "Snoozy knows damned well you didn't take that money. He didn't fire you, did he? If he did so help me God—"

"He didn't fire me." Not yet, anyway. "He called this morning to let me know he's scheduled an employee meeting." So much for relaxing on her day off. She hadn't even managed her Monday morning sleep-in. "It's at two tomorrow. We'll all find out then what he has in mind."

Hence the comfort meal. Maybe a food coma would help her sleep tonight.

Of course she knew better. Thoughts of Gil would keep her up. Too often they were thoughts of how delighted she used to be when Gil kept her up.

Her breath hitched and she fumbled with the pepper mill, then placed it on the counter behind her.

Harris held open his arms, and with a grunt of gratitude, she took him up on his offer. She laid her head on his shoulder and he held her for a long while, patting her back.

"I'm sorry about you and Gil," he said.

She couldn't help a tiny laugh. "Three for three, Dad. You succeeded in bringing up every subject I wanted to avoid."

When he pulled away and stomped toward the

kitchen door, Kerry shoved the hair out of her eyes. "Wait, where are you going?"

"By the time I get through with that softheaded, hard-hearted, tool trafficking bastard, he'll have to purchase a fuel line from himself so he'll have something to use to suck up his lunch."

"Dad!" Holy Hannah. Kerry curled her finger through a loop on his overalls. "Leave Gil alone. Besides, I thought you said no more flying off the handle?"

"I never said that."

"Maybe you should have, because this is not a good example to set for the baby."

He stopped, and blew out a breath. "You're right. Anyways, I'd rather stay here and dig into that meatloaf."

"Good idea." Kerry released him, and moved back to the stove. When he sidled up next to her and reached for the salt shaker, she smacked his knuckles. "So. Are you going to tell me now, or after we finish eating?"

The tips of his ears turned instantly red. "Tell you what?"

"You were practically bursting with good news when you came in. Anything I should know?"

He stopped fighting the grin that had to hurt, it was so expansive. "Genie and I are gettin' married."

"You are? Dad, that's wonderful! Congratulations!" She set aside the spoon and clapped her hands. "Holy Hannah. *Engaged.*" Stepping closer, she wrapped her arms around his neck and hugged him tight, reveling in the fact that she felt comfortable enough *to* hug him. And that he felt comfortable enough to accept it.

He untangled himself and beamed. "I think we finally got it figured out this time."

"I'm so glad. She should be here. We should celebrate. You deserve a celebration." *Easy, chickie.* She was starting to ramble. She couldn't have been more thrilled for the two of them, and yet it felt like every motion she made was underwater.

"Though after all you two have been through," she added, "you deserve a party that involves something fancier than meatloaf."

Maybe even a different hostess. Though Eugenia was clearly relieved that Harris and Kerry had patched things up, she still acted a tad frosty around Kerry. She really had loved that apartment. Luckily a lot of progress had been made getting it cleaned up. Allison's husband, Joe, had sprung for a Dumpster. Kerry did what hauling and cleaning she could in the morning before work, while Gil, Seth and Joe pitched in renovation labor whenever they found the time. And every day without fail, Dylan showed up after school. Chastened, but determined.

"Genie's workin' on some kind of shindig," her father said. "We'll let you know." His expression dimmed. "I'm sorry to be springin' this on you when you and Gil—"

"Don't even," she said, and something jagged moved in her chest as she realized she'd borrowed one of Gil's favorite phrases.

The doorbell rang and Kerry turned down the burner. "Is that her? If it is, we should have a toast. Wine for you, and I'm sure there's some juice in the fridge for me. I'll look."

Scratching his head, her father ambled out of the kitchen. "Hold that thought. I didn't think she was coming over tonight."

As Kerry rummaged through the fridge, finally unearthing a bottle of apple juice, she heard voices in the living room. Masculine voices.

Gil?

She popped upright and held her breath, deliberately leaving the fridge open to battle the sudden swelter of apprehension.

Her father appeared in the doorway, face pale, expression grave. "Kerry girl? The sheriff's here. He wants to see you."

GIL RESTARTED HIS truck and dialed up the heater. His fingers had stiffened, and the tips of his ears stung. But the pre-dawn April chill didn't bother him anywhere near as much as the time.

Three in the morning and Kerry still wasn't home from her shift at Snoozy's. What the hell was she doing out so late? She needed her sleep.

The baby needed her sleep. His sleep. Something light and bouncing unfurled in Gil's chest. He'd been fantasizing for days about how it would feel to hold his child in his arms, but the imaginings had his heart pulsing with as much grief as jubilation, because he'd screwed up royally with Kerry.

She'd proved her determination to make things right, again and again, yet when she'd needed his trust the most, he'd let her down.

Now it was his turn to make things right. He had to find a way to undo the damage he'd done because life frickin' sucked without her. It wouldn't be easy to convince her to give him another chance. She refused to return his calls, and she hadn't come by the hardware store like he'd asked via Harris. He'd stayed away from the bar because he didn't want to upset her at work, but he'd finally realized that wasn't the right way to handle things.

It had been over two weeks since he'd made the biggest mistake of his life and it was way past time to rectify it.

She needed to know how much he loved her. She needed to see he'd go to any lengths to win her back.

Hence the fifty-degree vigil outside Harris's place. He'd sit out here naked if he thought it would make a difference.

He turned off the engine, and in the sudden

stillness heard the whinny-like call of a screech owl. Then he heard the sound he'd been waiting for—the oncoming rumble of Kerry's car. The swing of her headlights as she turned in to Harris's driveway fell just short of Gil's pickup.

He rubbed his palms on his jeans and scraped a hand through his hair, then got out of his truck. She was halfway up the walk when he slammed his door shut and she spun at the sound, hand on her chest.

He half expected her to make a run for it, but she stood her ground. He found out why when he stopped in front of her and she whacked him with her purse, a la Audrey Tweedy.

"You scared the hell out of me."

"I'm sorry," he said gravely. "But these are desperate times." The lights on either side of Harris's front door cast an amber glow that emphasized the shadows under Kerry's eyes and made her wavy hair glimmer. He reached out to stroke her cheek. When she flinched, he dropped his hand.

"You're not returning my calls."

"I'm not cutting you out. I'm taking time to adjust." Her words were clipped, her eyes bleak. Her fingers were rolled into snug fists.

"Are you planning to stay in Castle Creek?" he asked, and held his breath.

She pulled her sweater, a dark baggy thing that reached to her knees, tighter around her waist. "I know you expect me to take off in a huff. But I have someone else in my life to consider now, and taking this baby away from his or her family is not the right thing to do."

He remembered what she'd said about alternating pronouns, and the sweetness of it pierced his heart. Then she shuddered and made him feel like even more of an ass.

"You're cold," he said. "Can we go inside and talk? Maybe make a pot of coffee?"

Her glance told him not only no, but hell, no.

He rubbed his hands over his face. "Listen, I'm sorry I reacted the way I did the other night. I have no excuse. I was an out-and-out son of a bitch and I deserve a thorough ass-kicking. But please, Kerry." He reached for her hands, and this time she didn't shy away. He pressed her chilled skin between his palms and raised them to his heart. "I know you panicked. I know you wouldn't have followed through on any of those things you said. Can't you understand that I panicked, too? Please give me another chance."

"What's ironic is that I can't trust you," she whispered. "I can't trust that this is about me and not the baby. Or some misguided need to make amends with your family. With your father."

"You are my family." When she didn't respond he squeezed her hands tighter. "I blew up at you the other night because I'm tired of being conned." When she tugged on her hands, he held fast. "The thing is, I ended up conning myself. I convinced myself I couldn't overlook your mistakes. But that's exactly what I'm prepared to do as a parent. It's what I told Dylan he needed to do. Forgive and move on. I'm as bad as Harris. I moved beyond your past a long time ago but was too chicken to admit it because the thought of not having you in my life hurts like hell."

She tugged on her hands again, and this time he let go. Down the street a dog started to bark and someone shouted a protest.

"You heard about the money," she said. It wasn't a question.

He nodded grimly. "That's not why I'm here."

"Did you know the sheriff came by to tell me? That up until the moment he said Burke Yancey's name, even I was wondering if I'd done it?" She choked out a poor excuse for a laugh. "But Snoozy believed in me. We had a staff meeting after he got back from his honeymoon, before we found out about Burke. I tried to apologize, but Snoozy wouldn't let me. He offered me a permanent position at the bar. Apparently Audrey wants to travel."

"Congratulations."

"Thank you."

"Kerry…"

The look on her face made it clear she wasn't up for another apology. He swore under his breath.

"Did you find out why Burke did it?"

"I'm the why. Apparently Ruthie resented me

for getting the manager's position instead of Liz. Burke figured he'd impress Ruthie by making me look bad and it didn't take much—he's always hanging around the kitchen, anyway. When he finally told her what he'd done, she drove him and the cash to the sheriff's office." Kerry was moving now, shifting side to side to stay warm. "And here you have the other reason I won't consider a relationship. I loved my husband and I did things for him…" She shook her head. "I won't put myself in that position again."

"That's bullshit. You're saying you don't trust either one of us and I don't buy it."

"You were right about me. Everything you said about how I can't face up to responsibility. The reason I took that deal that landed me with home detention? It wasn't what the police assumed, that I wanted to get back at Trent for cheating on me. It wasn't even because I was anxious to get started on making amends. It was because I wanted to hurry up and hide. I couldn't face what I'd done."

"We both know that's in the past."

"What does that even matter?" She rubbed the cold-reddened tip of her nose. "You already said you couldn't trust me."

"I was wrong." He turned his head to stare up the quiet road, flanked by dew-damp grass that glinted in the moonlight. "No, I wasn't wrong. I lied. I lied because sometimes the thought of being responsible for you and the baby scares the ever-loving hell out of me." He threw out his arms. "You were right. I'm stuck. Ferrell, too. We're stuck in these roles we've played for years and years and meanwhile our parents moved on. Not necessarily to better things, obviously, but at least they got out of the rut. But my brother and me? Too chickenshit to fight the status quo."

"That's not true. You made the decision to switch to teaching. The baby and I forced you to set that aside."

He turned back and stared into her gorgeous green eyes, currently misted with defeat. "I did resent that," he admitted. "But only at first. It wasn't long before I realized that nothing was more important than making sure our baby feels loved."

Kerry sucked in a quavering breath. But she didn't speak, and she didn't touch him.

"I put the store up for sale," he blurted.

"Y-you did?"

"Yeah. I finally realized that turning Cooper's into a shrine was not the best way to honor my parents."

"Holy Hannah." She stepped in for an awkward hug, pulling away almost before their chests could make contact. "Good for you."

Except he felt like he was toting a load ten times heavier than the beer-soaked wing chair he'd carried out of Eugenia's apartment and dropped into the Dumpster.

"You're what's good for me," he said savagely.

"I'd never have made the decision to sell without you."

"You've known all along what you wanted to do."

"I need you, Kerry. You and the baby. I love you. I don't want to do this without you."

"Do what?"

"Any of it."

She palmed his cheek. "Like you once told me, give yourself a frickin' break. You don't need me. You just need to continue proving to yourself what you're capable of. I need to do the same."

"You're saying we can't do that if we're together."

She pulled her hand away and backed toward the porch steps. "You deserve someone you'll never doubt. And I deserve someone who'll never doubt me."

He shoved his hands into his pockets to keep himself from holding her prisoner on that bottom step. She was going to back right into the house, and shut and lock the door between them, and God knew when he'd see her again.

"I didn't mean what I said. Please. Give me another chance."

"I can't," she whispered, and moved up to the bottom step. "It's selfish of you to ask. It's a mistake to try to force this. When it doesn't work out, the person who will suffer most is our child."

"We don't know it won't work out," he snapped.

"God*damn*it." He swung away, paced to the lamp-post at the end of the walkway and slapped it. Held his hand there, despite the acid bite of the cold metal, and hung his head.

"I do trust you." He pushed upright. "Want to know how I know? Eight days ago I got the results back from the paternity test. I haven't opened the letter. I don't need to. You said I'm the father. That makes it true."

"And you said you'd be there with me every step of the way. All we're doing is taking turns breaking each other's trust."

"No," Gil said stubbornly. "We're building more than we're breaking. I called my mother, you reconciled with your father—"

"Wait, you called your mother?"

"Yeah." He made a gesture with his hand, and it looked more helpless than dismissive. "I needed to remind her not to enable Ferrell. I'm not sure she'll pay any attention to that, but we ended up having a nice conversation."

"I'm glad for you."

When she started to turn away, a bolt of anger shot through him. He hollered at her to stop. "So that's it?"

"That's it," she said, not quite steadily. "Good night, Gil."

He watched her slip inside and realized he'd better start searching for a place to live. Once Valerie Flick managed to sell the store, he wouldn't be going house-hunting with Kerry after all.

TWO WEEKS AFTER Harris bragged that he and Eugenia were getting married, they did. They decided on a small courthouse wedding—like, four people small—because after all they'd been through, neither wanted to put their union off any longer.

Kerry stood behind them, watching as her father stumbled over his vows and he and Eugenia laughed together. Moments later Eugenia choked up and Kerry's father used his hankie to stroke the tears from her cheeks. All the while a tight-throated Kerry thought back to all the ups and downs the couple had shared, all the arguments and reconciliations and adaptations they'd made in their struggle to create a life together. They'd changed, and their love had changed, too. Strengthened. Deepened.

She was so happy for them. And so ashamed of herself for the envy poking at her heart.

After the ceremony, Eugenia and Kerry walked arm in arm to Eugenia's Volvo. The plan was to gather at Eugenia's house—now the official residence of Mr. and Mrs. Harris Briggs—for cake and champagne.

"You're a lovely bride," Kerry said tearfully. And the new Mrs. Briggs was, in her elegant lavender suit and headband of fresh white roses, her skin flushed with happiness.

"Thank you." Eugenia beamed. Her expression sobered, and she patted Kerry's arm. "That must have been hard for you, having to listen to all that sentiment without Gil at your side."

Kerry shrugged, but it was an effort to lift her shoulders. "I'm hoping we can stick to the plan to be friends, for the baby's sake." Though she was desperate for more. So much more. Everything, even.

"Enough of that," she said determinedly. "It was a lovely ceremony and I can't wait to celebrate with you two." She winked. "But I won't be in your way for long."

Eugenia laughed. "We appreciate that. Oh, here comes Harris." She smoothed her skirt and touched her hair. Caught Kerry watching and blushed.

"You two are so sweet together," Kerry said.

Eugenia smiled, and nudged the festive waves of Kerry's hair behind her shoulder. "Have I told you how proud I am to be your stepmother?"

They hugged, and choked out a matching set of self-conscious laughs. As Eugenia stepped away and dabbed a tissue to her eyes, Kerry felt a giddy swell of thankfulness that they'd finally managed to recover their old footing. The successful restoration of the apartment had helped. A lot. Once Gil, Seth and Joe had finished their repairs and reconstruction, Eugenia had hired a decorator who shared an equally obsessive appreciation of the color white.

One more reason Kerry was glad to be settled in her father's house—that plaid-covered furniture of his could hide a stain better than a piña colada could hide the taste of alcohol.

Only, Harris would be living with Eugenia from here on out. The quiet had already shrouded his little home.

Now that Gil was going to be selling the store, she wondered where he'd be living.

Don't do that to yourself. Not today.

Harris ambled up to them, looking even more radiant than his bride. He made a rude noise as he opened the passenger door of the Volvo for Eugenia. "Maybe now that we're married, I can convince you to drive somethin' with a little more style."

"Like a pickup truck?" Eugenia blew a raspberry. "I love you, Harris Briggs, but there are things even I would never do for you. You may as well get used to that, old man. No pickup trucks, no hemming your overalls, and no chewing gum." She winked at Kerry. "Don't worry, I'll make you a list."

After getting Eugenia settled in her seat, Harris opened the door behind her. "Ready to go, Kerry girl?"

She managed a nod, though her head felt way too heavy for her neck.

"...there are things even I would never do for you."

Why had she worried she'd lose herself trying to make Gil happy? She'd changed. Grown. And as he'd so convincingly—so *logically*—explained, they trusted each other. They'd be there for each other.

She would never do for Gil what Burke had done for Ruthie, and he'd never expect or want her to. And she would never do for Gil—for anyone, ever again—what she'd done for her ex-husband. What she'd done for herself. *To* herself.

Because she wasn't that Kerry anymore.

And she was actually starting to believe it.

But a big part of that new Kerry was Gil, and how he made her want to be a better person. And she'd shoved him away with everything she had.

She got in the car and buckled her seat belt, and pressed both hands to her stomach.

"You are more than your mistakes," Gil had once told her. Fingers crossed he still felt the same way, because it was her turn to beg for another chance.

A COUPLE OF HOURS LATER, Kerry finally managed to break away from the newlyweds. She considered running home to change, then decided her plum-colored dress and high heels might very well give her an advantage. And she could use all the help she could get.

Cooper's Hardware closed at six, but when she parked out front at ten minutes past, the Open side of the sign still faced the street.

She pulled open the door, frowning over the crack in the glass. If things didn't go well here today, her heart was going to look an awful lot like this. Once inside the store, she turned the sign around. The cowbell, of course, had announced her presence.

"We're closed" came Gil's impatient voice from the office. "Come back tomorrow."

"I won't be wearing this dress tomorrow," she called. Instantly sweat sprouted on her palms, and she caught the inside of her cheek between her teeth.

Gil slowly emerged from the back, clothes rumpled, hair every which way, gaze wary. "Hey."

"Hey."

He hesitated, eyeing her neckline, then gestured with his pencil. Given the state of his hair, and the slowly fading preoccupation on his face, she must have interrupted his calculations.

"That is a nice dress," he said.

At least he hadn't totally lost interest in her. "Thank you."

"Wedding go well?" As soon as he asked it, he winced. A mighty blow to her hope that he might still want a commitment.

"It did. I officially have a stepmother."

"Congratulations."

She clasped her hands behind her back, taking the opportunity to wipe the clammy from her palms. She moved farther into the store, her heels click-clacking on the old wood floor.

Gil stuck out his hand and leaned against a circular rack of batteries to his left. She was impressed he didn't knock the thing over.

He lowered his gaze to her belly. "How are you?"

"Good, thanks. The morning sickness is kicking in, but it hasn't been too bad so far."

"I'm glad." With his free hand he pushed at his glasses. "Your hair looks nice."

She swallowed a sigh. All this "nice" talk wasn't exactly encouraging.

"What do you need, Kerry?"

It seemed a little too soon to say "you."

"I need to apologize."

His expression shuttered. "For what?"

"For everything. For not being trusting. For pushing you away. For letting my stubbornness get in the way of you and me."

"That's a lot of apology."

"It comes with a lot of honest regret. The only thing I don't regret is not telling you who I was when we met. I apologized for that, but I didn't mean it. If I'd been straight with you, I would never have found the love of my life."

He cocked his head, but the iron grip of his jaw made it clear no words would be escaping anytime soon.

"Gil, I'm sorry," she said huskily. "I'm sorry for calling you selfish. You're the least selfish person I know, and you've done so much for—"

"Screw that," he ground out. He strode forward, no longer the wounded lover but an infuriated, stone-faced man. "It doesn't matter what I did for you. What matters is why. I love you. I told you I love you and you didn't believe me."

Her palms itched with the need to touch him, but she and Gil needed to hear each other out. And she wasn't entirely sure he wouldn't reject her, anyway.

"I didn't think you loved me enough," she said. "I'm clued in now, so if you want to rant and rave and say hurtful things, you go right ahead, because I love you enough to take it."

His eyes narrowed, and his chest rose as he pulled in a breath. Then he moved forward again, crowding her against the checkout counter, his hands on her hips. "You're not going anywhere, right?" The rumble of his voice traveled straight to her core.

She closed her eyes, hoping it wouldn't be the last time she felt his touch. "Not while you're holding me here."

Instantly he was gone. She lifted her head and watched him step back, hands held up as if in surrender. His chest rose and fell with ragged breaths. "I'm not holding you," he said.

"Yes." She pressed her palms to her flushed cheeks, and felt the tremble all the way through to her teeth. "Yes, you are."

His face lit, and his throat worked as he swallowed. "I love you."

Her heart punched once at her ribs, as if to say yes. "I love you, too," she said. "And I'm not going anywhere."

"Thank God." He gathered her close again and tipped up her face. "I missed you so much. Both of you."

She squeezed her eyes shut against a sudden surge of tears. "Please kiss me."

"Damn it," he growled.

She opened her eyes to see Gil staring in the direction of the front windows.

His jaw pulsed. "Did you call in reinforcements?"

"What?" She turned to look. Hazel, June and Audrey stood in a row outside the window, peering in through cupped hands. June gave an excited wave, her entire body shaking with the force of it. Her hand connected with Audrey's earring, sending a plastic cheeseburger the size of a golf ball swinging wildly. Audrey elbowed June, who tipped into Hazel, who braced both hands against the glass as she turned her head and gave the others what-for.

"I just cleaned those windows," Gil said with a sigh.

Kerry winced. "Actually, the ladies are with me, though they weren't supposed to show up quite so soon. Well, Hazel and June are here for me. Audrey came along to see if you'd decided to mark down your garden hoses yet."

"So you're not done punishing me," he said wryly.

"A small part of me did want to see you suffer. I'm not proud of that."

Someone thumped on the window and they both jumped. Hazel and June continued to peek through the glass, their brightly painted lips stretched wide with approving grins. Hazel gave them two thumbs-up while a scowling Audrey stood with one hand on her hip and the other rounded into a fist, poised to bang on the window again.

"Ten percent discount?" Gil asked.

"Make it fifteen. She's the only one of the three who doesn't stop me in the grocery store and talk baby-talk to my belly."

Bang, bang, bang.

Gil groaned. "Do we have to let them in?"

"They'll keep banging until we do." With an apologetic smile, Kerry moved away and opened the door the ladies hadn't realized wasn't locked. They scurried in and formed a line in front of

Gil, who was back to looking wary. Kerry, meanwhile, pressed a hand to her fluttering belly.

Hazel stepped forward. One hand faced up, the other down as she clasped her fingers in front of her waist, looking like a member of the von Trapp family.

She cleared her throat. "As we are all well aware, building a clubhouse on the lake for community use was the former mayor's pet project. If he hadn't forged the property deed, we might actually have a clubhouse by now."

June stepped up beside Hazel, her hands in prayer position.

Kerry shot a glance at Audrey, almost expecting her to have her hands over her eyes. Instead they were rummaging through her purse, no doubt in search of a processed meat snack.

"We've been fund-raising for years for a Castle Creek community center," June said. "The former mayor tabled that whole effort so he could concentrate on his clubhouse. As nice as a lakeside facility would be, as co-mayors, Hazel and I believe a centrally located community center would better serve the county."

Audrey rolled her eyes at Gil. "They want to buy your store."

Hazel reached across June and smacked Audrey on the arm. "Blabbermouth."

"Audrey's right. We'd like to make you an offer." June bounced up and down on her toes.

"This is a perfect location, and the store is practically a landmark. We wouldn't have to hear everyone complain about how a brand-new facility would spoil Castle Creek's charm."

Gil scratched his head. "But don't you already own property, over by the motel?"

June gave her head a mournful shake. "Dear heart, the mortgage on that land is heavier than a truckload of blue jeans caught in a rainstorm."

"Still, we do have some equity," Hazel said, and ruined her businesslike tone with the excited clap of her hands. "So we'll sell it. Use the proceeds to do whatever improvements are necessary here. As little as possible, of course."

"We'll need a separate meeting room," June said.

"A bigger kitchen," Hazel added.

"And a game room." Audrey folded her thick arms over her chest. "With a foosball table."

"So what do you say?" Kerry asked breathlessly.

Gil pushed a hand through his hair. "This can't be up to me."

"The town council will have to vote on it, but we can't have a vote without a signed intent to sell." June sidestepped over to the basket on the counter and helped herself to an apple.

With a gasp, Hazel rounded on her. "We forgot the best part."

"We did forget the best part." June polished the apple on her sailboat sweater.

Gil's eyes narrowed. "What's the best part?"

"The tenderloin," Audrey said. "Or it would be, if we were talking beef cattle."

"Oh, for heaven's sake, Audrey." Hazel clicked her tongue on the roof of her mouth.

"It's not her fault," June said. "We skipped dinner to come here."

"Fine," Hazel snapped. "Burgers at Cal's after this, on me." She turned to Kerry and gave her shoulder a pat. "Kerry, hon? You want to tell him the best part?"

Kerry drew in a breath and cursed the sudden swelling in her throat. "The community center," she said huskily. "Since it will be here, where your family ran their store for so long, they want to name it after your father."

"The Edgar F. Cooper Community Center," Hazel announced, with more than a little satisfaction. "What do you think of that?"

June bounced some more, this time with a bite of apple in her mouth. "Isn't it wonderful?"

Gil shook his head, not seeming to know where to look. "That's...wow. That would be amazing," he said.

"We thought so, too," Audrey said gently.

Gil blew out his breath and faced Kerry. "You did this." With his thumb and index finger, squeezed the bridge of his nose. When he dropped his hand, his eyes were wet. "All of it. Saving the building, naming it after Dad…this was your idea."

"Teaching is your passion. Solving obscure math problems…that's your passion, too. You were getting lost here, every day moving farther and farther away from ever being found. Selling was absolutely the right decision. But this store represents a legacy, a part of you I didn't want you to have to surrender. Not completely."

He reached for her. "What did I ever do to deserve you?"

Her eyes filled, and she gave herself time to blink the tears away by dropping her head to his shoulder. "You say the sweetest things."

He bounced his shoulder to bring her head back up. "You make it easy." When he licked his lips her skin went hot, her breath tight. He squeezed her hips as he bent toward her. The instant before his mouth touched hers, he paused.

"I thought you ladies were going to the diner?"

Kerry's fingers curled insistently into his shirt and his gaze smoldered with promise.

"Not me." Audrey sniffed loudly. "I'm going home to my husband."

"Guess it's just you and me, sis," Hazel said. She waited a beat, then another, finally huffed a resigned sigh and fell quiet. A moment later, the cowbell applauded their departure.

Gil's hands tightened on Kerry's hips. "I'm suddenly a big fan of purple," he said gruffly. "And heels. Please tell me you get to keep those heels."

Kerry laughed. "I get to keep the heels." She wriggled closer, enjoying the needy rasp of Gil's breathing. "Are you going to kiss me now?"

"Now, and all the way up the stairs." He flashed his dimples. "Only maybe this time you should walk. I have the feeling I'd better conserve my energy."

EPILOGUE

KERRY HUMMED AS she bent over the row of geraniums, separating the brown leaves from the ruffled scarlet blooms. She dropped the offending leaves in the pail at her feet and moved farther down the bench, enjoying the slight breeze from the fans overhead, and the mingled scents of soil, sun-warmed plastic and nutmeg.

When she reached the end of the bench, she straightened, placed her hands at the base of her spine and stretched. "Oh, that feels good."

She turned toward the entrance to the Quonset hut, and admired the lush rows of rainbow-colored blooms between her and the door. Luckily, they were rows she'd already inspected. Once she finished in here, she'd be helping her father load up one of the trucks. Pansies and petunias, headed for a high-end grocery store, where her dad always treated her to a mocha latte. After that, she'd finish her day in the potting shed Parker used as an office, updating the database system she'd created to track pretty much every aspect of the Macfarlands' business.

No day was the same, and Kerry enjoyed the

unpredictability of that. She enjoyed even more the opportunity to work with her dad, who continually impressed her with how much he knew about things like vegetative propagation and castings and perlite.

But most of all, she enjoyed the fact that she spent the majority of every day with the sun no farther away than a quick lift of her chin.

And all because of that cup of coffee she'd finally shared with Liz. The more they talked, the more they'd realized they would both be much happier if they simply traded jobs. Now Kerry worked full-time for Castle Creek Growers, and Liz and Ruthie both worked for Snoozy, alternating shifts so neither was stuck closing the bar every night.

She bent to pick up her bucket of castoffs and heard the scrape of boots on concrete behind her. "Coming, Dad," she said, but when she turned, it was Gil walking toward her, their six-month-old baby girl tucked upright against his chest.

"There's Mommy," he said. "Say 'Hi, Mommy. How are you, Mommy?'"

"Ga," said Chloe, and shook the caterpillar teething toy her grandfather had given her.

Kerry shared an eye roll with Gil. Figured their kid would try to say "Grandpa" before "Mommy" or "Daddy." With Eugenia's wholehearted support, Harris was spoiling Chloe rotten.

Kerry, too. Her father had insisted on giving

her and Gil his little brick house. More precious than that, he and Eugenia had both eagerly given their blessing when Kerry had expressed her desire to name her baby after Kerry's mother.

"Hello, sweetie." Kerry covered her daughter's face with kisses, then lifted her mouth for an adult kiss from Gil. His lips lingered on hers, and as much as she loved her job, she suddenly couldn't wait to be back home, sandwiched on the couch between Chloe and Gil.

"This is a nice surprise," she said huskily.

He grinned. "We thought we'd join you for lunch. Chloe insisted on dressing up for you."

"I can see that." Kerry eyed the orange and yellow striped sundress that sported a large green stain. "You do remember what a bib is, right?"

"Hey, if I hadn't been wearing it at the time, we'd both be advertising strained peas."

"Very funny."

He went into bounce mode when Chloe started to fuss. "Okay if I take her to the poker game tomorrow night? The guys say it's been too long since they've seen her."

Kerry turned Gil around and guided her family toward the door. She was getting hungry. "You mean my dad twisted your arm."

"Not your dad. Seth."

"*Uncle* Seth. He hears you leaving off the 'uncle,' he'll make you ride Hubbard Ridge twice. In the rain. Blindfolded."

"True." Gil pulled a cloth from his pocket and wiped the drool off his daughter's chin. "Dylan's going to be there, too."

"At Hubbard Ridge?"

"At your dad's."

"Dylan plays poker?"

Gil shook his head. "He has a trig test Wednesday. Wants me to give him extra problems to work out. I get to check his answers between hands."

Kerry adjusted Chloe's hat before they stepped out of the hut and into the summer sun. They headed for the picnic table under a massive oak tree, where Kerry and Harris usually ate lunch.

"Dylan is determined, you have to give him that," Kerry said. "Has he mentioned anything about his situation at home?"

"He doesn't talk about it much. But it has to be hard. With his brother moved out and his father spending his evenings staring at the TV, it's quieter than ever." Cooing to Chloe softly, he shifted her to his other arm. "I talked to Mom today. She's definitely coming up next month for the community center dedication."

"I'm so glad she can make it. What about Ferrell?"

"I talked to him, too."

Kerry watched Gil closely as she settled on the bench, her back to the table. "He actually took your call?"

Gil handed the baby to Kerry and settled on

the bench beside them. Chloe became instantly enamored with the buttons on her mother's shirt.

"What did he say?" Kerry asked.

"He told me I had no right to put any conditions on his share from the sale of the store."

"And you said?"

"That he'd already spent his inheritance and to consider what I promised him a bonus for staying sober."

Chloe started to wiggle. Kerry picked her up and bounced her, lifting her higher every time her toes touched Kerry's knees. The sputtering giggles made it clear Chloe was liking this game.

"Think Ferrell can do it?"

Gil shrugged. "We'll find out in a year."

"I think he can do it."

Slowly, one of Gil's dimples appeared. "That's why I love you."

"There she is. There's my Chloe girl." Harris ambled toward them, his smile as wide as his head was bald. He held out his hands as he approached, and Chloe's bouncing took on a whole new level of manic.

"Good to see you, son," Harris said to Gil, but he never looked away from Chloe.

"Dad." Kerry surrendered her daughter. "Aren't you forgetting something?"

"Like what?" He danced Chloe away, and both giggled like loons when he turned in a circle.

Gil shook his head. "He keeps that up and he's going to earn his own green stain."

"Lunch, Dad." Kerry's stomach grumbled. "It's your turn to bring lunch."

"Oh. Right." Harris shot Gil a look. "I left it in Parker's fridge. There's enough for all of us. I'll go get it. You two wait here."

Kerry leaned to the side and rested her head on Gil's shoulder. "If he's not back in five minutes, I'm going after him. I bet you ten bucks he's going to fall asleep with her in Reid's recliner." She blinked, soothed by the mild heat of the sun and the gentle drone of a nearby insect. Maybe a nap wasn't such a bad idea.

Gil kissed her hair. "You know, you and I, we have a pretty perfect life. A gorgeous daughter, good friends, our families are healing, our jobs are satisfying."

"In six months, anyway, when you get your teaching license."

"I don't know. It's been pretty satisfying, helping to turn the hardware store into a community center. Cathartic, you know?"

Kerry nodded lazily. "Don't forget we have a lake view from the house."

"Right on."

"And furniture that might be secondhand but at least isn't plaid."

"Sing it."

"And we do happen to be crazy about each other."

"QED."

Kerry sat up and scrunched her nose. "What does that mean?"

"Quod Erat Demonstrandum." Gil brushed the hair out of her face. "'That which was to be demonstrated.' It's used to mark the end of a mathematical proof."

She laughed. "You are such a nerd."

"And you are beautiful." He picked up her hand and kissed it. "You're also creative and smart and giving, and I don't know what I'd do without you."

Tears sprang into her eyes as she interlaced her fingers with his. "That's not fair of you to go all serious on me. But thank you." With a sniffle, she tipped her head. "I suppose you'd like me to return the favor."

"If it's not too much trouble."

She stared into his gorgeous brown eyes. Eyes their daughter had inherited, along with Kerry's thick hair and plump cheeks. "Gil Cooper, you've been watching out for me since the moment we met. You're sexy and funny and brilliant, and I don't deserve you, but I'm looking forward to spending the rest of my life trying."

"I'd correct you on that *don't deserve you* thing, but I like the sound of all that trying you plan to do."

Their mouths met, and just as Kerry leaned in to take the kiss deeper, her stomach growled. She shot upright and frowned toward the house.

"I should go in there," she said.

"Hey." Gil shook their joined hands. "There's something I... Kerry. Kerry?"

"What do you think he's doing in there?"

"Pay attention," Gil demanded.

Slowly she turned and gave him an *oh, no, you didn't* look. "You know what, you already sound like a teacher."

"You mentioned the rest of our lives."

"Which won't be very long if we don't eat soon."

He gazed at her sternly. "Kerry Mae."

"I'm sorry. I'm listening. The rest of our lives. You were saying?"

"That I'd like to spend them married. To you," he hastened to add.

"Gil," she breathed. She clutched the edge of the bench.

"We talked about it once," he said, his deep voice serrated with nerves. "I know you said you wanted to wait until things settled down, but I don't think things are going to get any more settled than they are now." He fished in the front pocket of his jeans and with a triumphant grin held up an emerald solitaire ring. "Seth was convinced I'd lose it."

He shifted off the bench and onto his left knee. "Kerry Mae Endicott, I'll be the happiest man in Castle Creek if you'll do me the honor of becoming my wife. Will you please marry me?"

"Gilbert Wayne Cooper, you are full of surprises." She laughed and cried and hiccupped, and dropped down onto the ground in front of him. "And the honor will be all mine."

He slid the ring onto her finger, then wrapped his arms around her and pulled her tight to his chest.

Above them the maple leaves fluttered in gentle applause. The steady thump of Gil's heart against hers and the joyful trill of Chloe's giggles in the distance filled Kerry's soul with a healing bliss she'd never take for granted.

"Thank you for believing in me," she whispered into his neck.

"Thank *you*," he said. "For showing me how."

* * * * *

Get 2 Free Books,
Plus 2 Free Gifts—
just for trying the Reader Service!

Get 2 Free Books,

Plus 2 Free Gifts—

just for trying the Reader Service!

HARLEQUIN®

SPECIAL EDITION

READERSERVICE.COM

Manage your account online!

- Review your order history
- Manage your payments
- Update your address

> *We've designed the Reader Service website just for you.*

Enjoy all the features!

- Discover new series available to you, and read excerpts from any series.
- Respond to mailings and special monthly offers.
- Browse the Bonus Bucks catalog and online-only exculsives.
- Share your feedback.

Visit us at:
ReaderService.com